"Long end........................out how Compassionate Systems will transform the delivery of medical care to the peninsula…and to scan the society column where you'd hoped to find at least your name, if not a picture of you hobnobbing with the Port Hamilton elite at the Elk's Club ball."

He laughed. "I'm so damn disappointed. I thought reindeer antlers glued to my scrub cap would guarantee a spot on the front page. What the hell do I have to do?"

"Dunno." Sarah was laughing, too. "Be more elklike."

They sat there for a minute or so just grinning at each other until Sarah broke off a piece of his tortilla and scooped up some rice. "I've been thinking. It's not every day I apologize, but I'm about to do it, so don't make it more difficult. The words are practically choking me already."

"On the other hand, it could be the tortilla."

"I did kind of get on my soapbox, and I'm—" she swallowed "—sor-sorry."

"I heard it." He glanced around the cafeteria. "Where's the media when you need them?"

She looked up at him, her expression unreadable. "Okay, so now's where you tell me you've thought things over and you're ready to join forces with me."

Dear Reader,

How many of us still remember our first "love"? Was it the freckled boy who teased you unmercifully in third grade? A high-school crush? The guy you met in your college sophomore year? Chances are that even if you remember exactly who he was, he was not the man you eventually married. People change, and the special someone who made your heart race in your teens probably wouldn't even raise a flutter today. On the other hand, maybe he would. Sarah, the heroine of *The Baby Doctors,* never forgot her first love, Matthew. Marriages to other people and years apart never quite succeeded in dimming her love.

I hope you enjoy *The Baby Doctors,* and I would love to hear your stories of that guy you never quite forgot. Drop me a line at Janice Macdonald, PMB 101, 136 E. 8th Street, Port Angeles, WA, 98362, or e-mail me at janicemacdonald.com. You might also check out my new Web site, travelingromancewriter.com, for details on my books and chronicles from recent travels.

Best wishes,

Janice Macdonald

THE BABY DOCTORS
Janice Macdonald

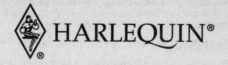

TORONTO • NEW YORK • LONDON
AMSTERDAM • PARIS • SYDNEY • HAMBURG
STOCKHOLM • ATHENS • TOKYO • MILAN • MADRID
PRAGUE • WARSAW • BUDAPEST • AUCKLAND

ISBN-13: 978-0-373-71450-6
ISBN-10:   0-373-71450-5

THE BABY DOCTORS

This edition published by arrangement with Harlequin Books S.A.

® and TM are trademarks of the publisher. Trademarks indicated with
® are registered in the United States Patent and Trademark Office, the
Canadian Trade Marks Office and in other countries.

www.eHarlequin.com

Printed in U.S.A.

ABOUT THE AUTHOR

When she's not traveling—which she does whenever she can—Janice Macdonald lives in Port Angeles, Washington.

Books by Janice Macdonald

HARLEQUIN SUPERROMANCE

1060—THE DOCTOR DELIVERS
1077—THE MAN ON THE CLIFF
1132—KEEPING FAITH
1157—SUSPICION
1201—RETURN TO LITTLE HILLS
1244—ALONG CAME ZOE
1378—OUT OF CONTROL

To Barbara and Lee for their inspiration, and to the Fishers for their hospitality and turkey burgers!

CHAPTER ONE

THE GUY SELLING medicinal herbs at the Port Hamilton farmer's market had shoulder-length hair, a small stud in his nostril and the palest blue eyes Sarah had ever seen. The lack of color disconcerted her. Something about the way the light hit them made it difficult to tell whether he was looking directly at her or at something over her shoulder.

His T-shirt read Stop The War On Drugs, but when he noticed her trying to read the small print, he stopped in the middle of a discourse on the health-giving properties of the dandelions leaves he was holding to launch into another on the kind of drugs he was trying to stop.

"Big Brother pharmaceutical companies," he said, his English accent becoming more pronounced as he spoke. "If you're popping pills you've bought from the drugstore, you're not really in touch with nature, and my goal, simply put, is to reconnect people's consciousness with the environment." He waved his hand at the row of baskets brimming with plants. "Nature's pharmacy," he said. "Echinacea, Saint-John's-wort, calendula. *Atropa belladonna*—"

"Commonly known as deadly nightshade," Sarah said.

He smiled. "Ah, a gardening enthusiast."

"A medical doctor, actually," Sarah's mother, Rose, said, materializing at Sarah's side. "She's been practicing in Central America for the past fifteen years. And, let me tell you, she knows a thing or two about woo-woo medicine."

Sarah shot Rose a glance. "A focus on prevention and well-being rather than disease is not woo-woo medicine." She turned back to the guy, whose spare, almost emaciated frame suggested nature's pharmacy probably did double duty as his pantry. "My mother's a doctor, too." She jerked her head at Rose. "Runs in the family. Except my mother's the conventional kind."

"I'd hardly say that," Rose replied.

"I was referring to your profession. She's a dermatologist," Sarah said, mostly to mollify Rose, who disliked being thought of as conventional in any way, except perhaps in her approach to medicine.

"Right." He stuck out his hand and directed his pale eyes at Sarah. "Curt Hudelson."

"Sarah Benedict." She shook his hand. "And my mother, Rose Benedict. I'm really interested in what you're doing. It ties in with the sort of thing I'm planning, an integrated approach that combines both conventional and alternative medicine."

He nodded approvingly. "Right, well, we definitely need more of your type here on the peninsula before big medicine kills everyone off." As he talked, a young woman who had been waiting on customers came over to stand beside him and he put his arm around her shoulders. "My girlfriend, Debbi. We farm a piece of land on the west end. These two ladies are doctors," he said. "Tell them how we cleared up your asthma with natural stuff."

Debbi smiled. "I used to get these really bad attacks, I was always at the E.R. getting treatments so I could breathe and I never went anywhere without my inhaler. Then I met Curt. I haven't had a bad attack since." She reached into a small tin box on the wooden counter, withdrew a card and handed it to Sarah. "I also make cosmetics. Natural."

"Curly Q House of Hair," Sarah read.

"Well, that's where I work right now," Debbi said. "But I'm probably going to quit pretty soon. It's too far to drive. Plus, Curt needs help on the farm. His business is really growing."

"Literally." Curt turned to Debbi. "Tell Sarah about Alli."

Debbi's smile faded. "Well, that's kind of different."

"No, it isn't." He addressed Sarah, "Our daughter was having intestinal problems, which, naturally, Dr. Big Medicine diagnosed as kidney failure and, left to his own devices, would have had her hooked up to a dialysis machine. And how was she this morning, Debbi?"

"Fine, but—"

"Exactly."

Rose cleared her throat. "Ready, Sarah?"

"Come out and see my gardens sometime," Curt said. "Debbi and I had intended to organize them according to the various systems of the body, but then it got a wee bit too complicated, so now we have them grouped into historic herbal remedies, folk medicine, homoeopathic medicinals and plants that are currently under investigation by drug companies."

"Crackpot," Rose muttered after Sarah had taken down his address and she and Rose were weaving their way back through the crowd toward the car. "Perfect example of how a little medical knowledge can be a dangerous thing."

Sarah shrugged. "I'd be interested in seeing what they're doing."

"Probably growing marijuana," Rose said.

"Nothing like an open mind."

They walked along in silence for a while. "I thought you might have changed, being away all this time," Rose said finally. "Maturity, and so forth but you're still like just like your father."

"Idealistic and humanistic?"

"Impractical and naive, not that there isn't room for some of this hippy-dippy stuff," she amended as they reached her ancient Volvo, parked behind the courthouse, "but it does seem to attract the fringe element."

"In the same way that conventional medicine seems to attract those with an unhealthy interest in making money?"

"Get in the car," Rose snapped.

"I ANSWERED A PAGE for you, Dr. Cameron," one of the nurses said, opening the door to the O.R. where Matthew had just finished surgery.

"Who was it?"

"Administration. Mr. Heidenreich said he had you down on his calendar at ten. I told him you had an emergency surgery."

"Thanks." Matthew removed his blue cotton cap, pulled on a white lab coat over his scrubs and started down the corridor. He glanced at his watch—twenty after. Emergency surgery was an acceptable excuse for arriving late, but these days he was late for everything.

"Coffee?" Jim Heidenreich asked as Matthew walked into the inner sanctum. "Georgia just made a fresh pot."

"No thanks." Matt dropped into a chair opposite. A small, dapper man with sparse white hair, Jim had aged visibly in the six months since Compassionate Medical Systems had initiated efforts to buy out Peninsular Memorial.

"One of the nurses said there was someone outside SuperShop yesterday getting signatures," Matthew told his boss, then instantly regretted the remark. Jim didn't need anyone confirming what he already knew: That some anonymous conglomerate from Seattle taking over the hospital where just about everyone here had been born, was about as welcome as learning that Port Hamilton High's football team had lost to Olympia. No one wanted outsiders taking over the hospital.

"Take a look at this." Jim reached into his desk and

brought out a glossy press kit. "Compassionate Medical went into a one-hundred-twenty-five-bed hospital in Oregon—same size as ours and in the same financial hole. They were welcomed with open arms. Happy to have CMS come in…like a guardian angel when you think about it. They provide the capital, recruit physicians. They've got the managed care expertise, the experience running rural facilities…"

Matt shrugged. "On the other hand, I know a guy in Virginia—we were in medical school together. His local hospital was gobbled up by—" he gestured at the press kit "—one of these conglomerates. He's frustrated as hell by it all. Endless paperwork, restrictions on where he refers patients. Diagnostic workups according to cost."

"What's the alternative?"

Matt shook his head. He'd pulled together a group of physicians with the idea that among them, they would raise enough capital to counter CMS's offer. Still, it would be difficult to pull off. Peninsula was drowning in red ink and none of the medical staff were exactly rolling in money. You practiced medicine on the peninsula because you loved the natural beauty and small-town lifestyle, not because you expected to make money. He tried to imagine his ex-wife's reaction if he approached her about selling the home she and Lucy lived in. The home he still made payments on.

"I had a meeting with human resources this morning," Jim said. "Their concern was lost jobs. Naturally. And the rumor mill is running full-time. I managed to convince them that for the first two years no jobs would be cut. CMS guaranteed it."

"And after that?"

"Two years is a long time.

"The physicians will walk," Matt said. "I've heard that from almost everyone. They'll move off the peninsula if they have to."

"Not if you come around."

Matthew blinked. "If I—"

"Matt, if you get behind this takeover, the other physicians will fall in step. You know that."

"I can't, Jim. *You* know that."

The administrator shifted some papers around on his desk. "Where were you last weekend?" He looked directly at Matthew. "Your daughter's birthday, wasn't it? Thirteenth?"

"Fourteenth. Your point?"

"My point is that you were in Seattle performing surgery. Sure, you could have referred the kid like any other physician would have done, but not you. The kid's your patient and you're going to see it all the way through. Your patient, your responsibility."

"So?"

"So your daughter spent her birthday without her father. She's your responsibility, too, Matt."

"Sorry." Matthew folded his arms. "You're losing me."

"If we'd had the setup, the sophisticated equipment, you could have done the surgery here. If we'd had the surgical support staff, you could have done the surgery here. If—"

"But we don't."

"I'm not finished. That's last weekend we were talking about. What about last night?"

Matthew rubbed his neck.

"I'll tell you. You were right here, three floors below doing an emergency appendectomy. And today, same thing." He got up and walked to the window. "You're one surgeon, Matt. A terrific one, but you're not Superman. You need a day off every once in a while. And that's never going to happen the way things are right now. Compassionate Medical Systems is not only going to save this hospital from going under, it might save you from burning yourself out before you reach fifty."

"It's not the answer, Jim."

"Well, when you figure out what the answer is, you let me know. But I won't hold my breath. You need to take a cold hard look at the way things are right now. Wanting things to work as they always have isn't enough."

An hour later, scrubbing up for surgery, Matthew was still hearing Heidenreich's words.

CHAPTER TWO

❖

UNTIL ROSE BROKE with tradition by relocating three generations of Benedicts had been practicing medicine in Port Hamilton from the same red barn of a house on Georgianna Street, one block from the waterfront. Sarah's father had been a general practitioner, seeing patients until the day he dropped dead of a heart attack while Sarah was still in high school.

But all that was changing, Sarah thought, as she took an early-morning walk through town on her way to see Matthew at the hospital. Empty storefronts now dotted Port Hamilton's once thriving business district. In the years since she'd been away, businesses had come and gone. What was once Betty's Bakery was now Mombasa Coffee with three-dollar cappuccinos and biscotti in jars on the glass-topped counter.

The Curly Q House of Hair where Debbi worked had once been the old Wharf house. Seeing it now, Sarah tried to recall how old she'd been when she found out that it was going to be demolished to make way for a row of stores. Twelve? Thirteen? She'd tried to enlist Matthew in her cause.

"Can't they see it's part of the history of Port Hamilton?" she'd wanted to know. And he'd pointed out the light shining through the warped and rotted boards and the evidence of termites everywhere.

Undeterred, she'd gone from door to door with a petition protesting the destruction.

Maybe Rose was right; maybe she was a dreamer. She'd always had tons of ideas for how things could be better. And not just in Port Hamilton. Deep inside, she had always had this quest for the answer to what would really make her life meaningful. She'd read it in a book, find inspiration in an incredible poem or experience something profound that would totally change everything. Or she'd get on a self-improvement kick about this or that. Yoga, fasting. Whatever. Age imparted some wisdom and she'd learned to keep most of these "answers" to herself. As a kid she'd had no such constraints. Her friend Elizabeth's mom had called her cute and said she wished Elizabeth cared about such things. Rose had called her overly idealistic.

"Life's the way it is," Rose would say. "Things change. Nothing's perfect. Accept it and move on." Rose now practiced from an office in an ugly, mustard-colored cement-slab complex on the road out of town. Sarah thought wistfully of the big airy waiting room in the old house, the mismatched chairs lined up around the walls, a table in the middle stacked with kids' books, most of them her discards. The battered trunk of toys she'd sometimes sneak down to play with after the offices were closed for the day.

According to Rose the house had been inefficient. More practical to have a separate office.

"But I have good memories of that consulting room," Sarah had said. "Daddy coming up to the kitchen for lunch—"

"His damn seafood chowders." Rose had rolled her eyes. "The consulting rooms reeked of squid."

"What *I* remember," Sarah had countered, "was how much more personal it seemed. You and Daddy were part of the community, not sterile strangers in white coats. I think it had something to do with being in the house."

But Rose had been adamant. "Medicine isn't the same as it was when your father and I practiced together. It's much more sophisticated. Diagnostic tests have to be done right away…no room for sentiment these days."

Sarah pictured Rose, long gray hair curled into an untidy bun, her chunky sweaters, tweed skirts and gray flannel trousers. The thought occurred to her that one day she would probably look just like Rose. She made a mental note to drop by Curly Q, maybe see what Debbi could do. Debbi and her pale-eyed medicinal gardener boyfriend. Somewhere between Rose the traditionalist and Curt, nature's pharmacist, there had to be a middle ground that would be just right.

Which was exactly the case she intended to present to Matthew, she thought as she reached the hospital.

The receptionist in the administrative suite looked young enough that Sarah wondered whether she might have babysat her at one time. Behind her were three doors, all closed, with frosted-glass windows. Matthew's name was on the middle door, underneath the title Medical Director.

"I'm here to see Dr. Cameron," Sarah said.

"Do you have an appointment?"

Sarah smiled. Her palms were sweating. She knew that if she dodged into a restroom to check her teeth for lipstick or her eyelids for rivulets of the Tender Taupe shadow she'd bought on sale at Gottschalks along with the tube of Black Velvet mascara, she would find damp patches at the armpits of the beige Ann Taylor blazer, also bought in the same sale. All purchased on an impulsive and, she realized now, misguided thought that if she looked businesslike as she presented her plan it would seem less like one of the old Sarah's wild-eyed schemes and more worthy of Matthew's professional consideration.

"Matthew and I are old friends," she told the receptionist. She'd considered calling for an appointment, but…come on, she'd known Matthew since they played in the nursery-school sandbox together. When he was forever trying to pour sand down her top. "Could you just let him know I'm here? Sarah. Benedict." She cleared her throat. "Dr. Benedict, that would be."

The receptionist smiled. "Unfortunately, Dr. Cameron is doing an emergency surgery. I'm not sure how long he'll be. Can I leave him a message?"

"I'll just give him a call," she said. "No, wait…" She delved into her purse, found a grocery receipt and scribbled a message on the back. Not very elegant, but it put the ball in his court, which she preferred. "If you could just stick this on his desk."

Outside, walking down the corridor again, she listened to the click of her heels on the linoleum. Two nurses in blue scrubs walked by. One of them, tall and blond with boobs like a shelf, smiled uncertainly as though Sarah was someone she might know. Port Hamilton was small enough and isolated enough, sitting at the tip of the Olympic Peninsula, that pretty much everyone knew everyone. But this Sarah with her makeup and power suit was not the bohemian Birkenstock Sarah who had skulked off to Central America after being scorned by her—

"Sarah." The nurse stopped in her tracks. "Wow. When did you get back?"

"Betsy." Her archenemy in high school. She was a good fifty pounds heavier than Sarah remembered. "Hi."

Betsy's smile faded. "I'm sorry about your husband. I read about it in the paper, and then I saw your mother and she told me. What a tragedy, huh?"

"Thanks." Frozen, feeling awkward by the sympathy she saw in Betsy's eyes, Sarah struggled for the right thing to say. "Anyway, I'm… I have to go so—"

"Well, hey, it's great to see you again." She hugged Sarah, then pulled back to look at her. "Listen, I know it's got to be tough. If you ever need to talk to someone, call me. I'm in the phone book. My last name's Becker now. I married Vinny. Remember him?"

She would be okay, Sarah thought as she continued on. Once she was working again, seeing patients, getting back into the swing of things. She would find a place to live, no matter how much Rose begged her to move back home. She would feel strong and whole again, discover a place where the sympathy and pity, no matter how well intended, would no longer make her want to crawl into a hole and hide.

MATTHEW WAS BACK in his office when his secretary put a call through from his daughter reminding him that the school play was at seven and if he didn't want her to hate him for the rest of her life, he'd better be there.

One elbow on the desk, chin propped in his hand, Matthew studied the framed picture of her—one of many that filled his office—and grinned. Lucy was fourteen, a budding actress and, although she was always listing ways in which he wasn't the perfect father she felt entitled to, he loved her as much as any father possibly could. The prospect of having more free time to spend with her was one of the more compelling reasons to join CMS.

"I'm supposed to have tarot cards," Lucy said. "Mom said she'd pick some up, but she forgot. Could you get some for me? Please?" she added in her wheedling voice. "I really, really need them."

Remembering she was a Gypsy in the play, he asked, "Something to do with fortune-telling?"

"They tell you stuff that happened and what's going

to happen in the future. You spread them out in a cross and then you read them. Listen, I've got to go. Don't forget them, okay?"

"I won't," Matthew said. After he hung up, the receptionist—she was very new, very young, and he could never remember her name—stuck her head around the door.

"This lady came in to see you. She left a note, but—" she gestured to his desk, piled high with papers and journals and more than a few empty coffee cups "—I thought you might miss it. It's on the back of that Safeway receipt right there."

"Thanks." Matthew picked up the receipt and glanced at the back.

He saw the familiar scrawl and laughed.

The note read: "So where the hell were you at four o'clock this afternoon anyway?"

No signature. It wasn't necessary.

Sarah.

BY THE TIME she left the hospital and walked back into town, it was not quite eleven, too early for lunch. With nothing more pressing to do, Sarah decided to stop by Curly Q. Maybe work up the nerve to get her hair all lopped off and learn a little more about Debbi and Curt's magical medicinal garden.

The blonde who checked her in wore heart-shaped earrings and a diamond in her left nostril. The entire shop was awash in red paper hearts. Up the walls, around mirrors and across the top of the reception desk, where they competed with a massive arrangement of red balloons bobbing amidst pink carnations.

"Must be Saint Patrick's Day," Sarah joked.

The girl gave her a long look. "It's Valentine's Day."

Sarah smiled. "I wondered if Debbi is available."

The blonde regarded Sarah doubtfully. "Are you a client of hers?"

"Not yet."

Moments later she was escorted to a chair at the far end of the room and seated before a mirror. A towel was draped around her shoulders. Debbi would be with her in a few minutes, she was told. A blond stylist to Sarah's left, in red jeans and a fluffy white sweater, was telling a customer that Valentine's Day was the sole reason more babies were born in November than in any other month. To her right, the topic was those clueless types who walk into restaurants on Valentine's Day without reservations expecting to get a table. "That's my husband," someone said. "We're going to end up eating pizza tonight, just like we did last year."

Sarah had the strange sensation that she'd landed from some distant planet. Was an aversion to beauty shops genetic or learned, she wondered. Maybe both. Her mother had once calculated the time and money saved over a ten-year span by wearing her own long, untrimmed hair in a knot at the nape of her neck and allowing it to turn iron-gray

Debbi smiled when she saw Sarah. "I didn't think you'd really come by. I thought you were just being polite." In the mirror, her face above Sarah's was round and doll-like, smooth pink skin framed by a dark shiny bob. Her own face looked angular, Sarah thought, her skin tanned but on the verge of leathery. She felt a tug of guilt for neglecting it. Maybe Debbi had something for rejuvenating forty-two-year-old faces.

"Wow, how long did this take to grow?" Debbi asked, lifting the heavy braid.

"Forever. I keep thinking I want to do something different, but I don't like messing around with it. "

Debbi's lip jutted thoughtfully as she unbraided Sarah's hair. "I could cut some layers into it. Maybe put in some highlights to give it body." She made a few exploratory moves with the comb. "And you've got some gray."

"Cut it all off and dye it…fuchsia," Sarah said, only half joking, then lost her nerve. "You know what? Just trim the ends."

"You don't want me to cut a little more? Shoulder length would look good on you."

"A trim's fine for now." After Debbi had finished shampooing and escorted her back to the chair, Sarah spotted the row of pictures in Lucite frames on the narrow shelf beneath the mirror. Most were of a dark-eyed toddler with a mass of black curls. "Your little girl?"

"Yeah." Debbi smiled as she went to work with the scissors. "Alli. She's two. The terrible twos they say."

"How is she?" Sarah asked, recalling Curt's comment about an intestinal problem.

"Pretty good. She gets a lot of tummy aches, but Curt said it's because I feed her too much processed food. He's so smart. He wanted to be a doctor, but he doesn't have the patience to sit in a classroom all day. Plus he's totally turned off to the way most doctors think."

"I got that impression," Sarah said wryly.

"He's a really good dad. I mean, he loves Alli to death. But he's got this idea that he can treat anything that comes up and sometimes it kind of worries me. It's his way or the highway." Debbi snipped the ends, then, brandishing a purple hair dryer, directed a blast of hot air at Sarah's scalp. "There's no in-between."

"That's what I want to do," Sarah said. "Provide the in-between. Conventional medicine doesn't have all the answers, but alternative medicine can't do everything, either. I want to have a practice that uses both approaches."

"Cool." Debbi smiled. "When can I sign up?"

"I've still got some things to work out. There's another doctor, a pediatrician who's a good friend of mine. We grew up together. He'd be perfect."

"What's his name?"

Sarah hesitated. "Well, I haven't discussed it with him yet. We used to talk about this kind of thing years ago, but—"

"There aren't that many pediatricians in Port Hamilton anymore," Debbie said. "It's got to either be Dr. Cameron—"

"Yep."

"He's fantastic. I used to take Alli to see him. Until I met Curt."

Sarah felt a vague sense of misgiving.

She watched Debbi try to turn a lock of wiry, recalcitrant hair into something resembling a curl and wanted suddenly to be somewhere else. "Hey, listen, that's fine. Really."

Debbi looked doubtful. "You're sure? Want me to spray it?"

"No." Sarah stood. Her shoulders felt damp. She followed Debbi to the front of the shop. What did a haircut cost these days? She had no idea. She dug three twenties out of her purse, set them on the counter....

"You need some good conditioner." Debbi took two of the twenties to the cash register, and returned a ten and a five to Sarah. "The next time you come in, I'll do a hot-oil treatment."

"Probably a good idea." Sarah left the twenty and the five on the counter. "Good luck with your daughter," she said.

CHAPTER THREE

"CHOCOLATE CHIPS." Lucy snapped her fingers, a surgeon demanding an instrument. "Butter. Two sticks."

"Coming up." Matthew held out a bag of chips, semisweet, as she'd requested when she made the shopping list for him. He watched as she carefully measured flour into a bowl. Her long dark hair, pulled back into a ponytail, was dusted with flour. More flour had fallen like snow around her feet; a dusting of white covered the granite counter tiles.

He couldn't have been happier.

"Want some music?" he asked.

"Your kind or mine?"

"Since I don't think of that stuff you listen to as music, it would have to be mine. And if you'd really listen to the words, you'd realize the Eagles—"

"Oh, Dad, no. Please. Not the Eagles."

He grinned and wrapped his arm around her shoulders in a quick hug. "Do you know how much I like having you here?"

"No, but hum a few bars," she said.

"Old, old joke."

"I learned it from you."

"I guess that makes me an old, old guy then." He pulled out one of the bentwood dining chairs, sat on it backward, his chin propped on the curved wood. "If I decide to go with the Seattle company that's moving onto the peninsula," he told her, "you could spend every Saturday with me."

"Do it," she said.

"Would you like that?"

She beamed.

He grinned back at her. Ultimately, it might not take much more persuasion than his daughter's approval. "I'm thinking about it. It's just…" The phone rang. "Hold on," he told Lucy.

"Pleeese, pleeeese, don't let it be a boring old patient," she muttered.

He picked up the phone from its hook on the wall. "Hello."

"I have no pride," a female voice said. "I leave you messages—"

He burst out laughing. "Sarah!" No salutation, no polite preliminary chitchat. No acknowledgment that it had been fifteen years since they last spoke. "My God. You haven't changed."

"Yeah, well, there's nothing I can do about that," she said. "By forty the character's pretty well established. So anyway, I stopped by to see you—"

"I know. Well, I was pretty sure it was you. I'd heard you were back. But the receptionist said a *lady* came by to see me and the *lady* part threw me."

Sarah laughed. Same old raucous laugh, somewhere between an engine starting and a gaggle of geese.

"I ran into your mother in the cafeteria last week," he said. "Almost literally. You know Rose, a hundred miles a minute. She said you were coming back. She seemed surprised that I didn't know, but I reminded her that keeping in touch was never one of your priorities."

"Yeah, well…you know."

"Listen, before anything else, I'm so sorry about— Ted…"

"Thanks. Me, too."

Something in her voice warned him to move on. "I want to see you," he said. "Soon. *Now*. Damn it, I can't…when are you available? What are your plans?" He could see Lucy in his peripheral vision; the wooden spoon in one hand had gone very still. "My daughter's here with me," he said. "Lucy. Fourteen going on thirty and about to set the theater world on fire." Lucy flashed him a look over her shoulder and he winked at her. "And you didn't hear this from me," he stage-whispered, "but she's a dead ringer for a young Elizabeth Taylor."

"She looks like her mother then," Sarah said.

An almost imperceptible change in her voice reminded him of the last time they'd exchanged anything more than polite formalities and he found himself at a loss for words. "Very much."

"Don't you owe me a Frugal burger?" Sarah asked.

"Frugals." Smiling now, he leaned back against the wall. "Haven't eaten one of those in years. I'm of the age where I have to think about cholesterol."

"We both are," Sarah said. "But you still owe me a Frugals."

"Hold on." He glanced at the calendar above the phone. "How about…tonight?"

"Dress rehearsal, Daddy," Lucy said. "Remember? You promised."

"Okay, tonight won't work." He scratched the back of his head. "I'm on call tomorrow night, but if we keep our fingers crossed that no one gets creamed on the 101 or mistakes their significant other for a shooting range, I could pay off my debt to you."

"Great," Sarah said. "What time?"

"Around six? I'll pick you up." He thought for a minute. "Guess I need to know where you're staying. Your mother's?"

"Actually, I just rented an apartment," Sarah said. "Yesterday. At the foot of Peabody, just above Front Street. The Seavu. I was walking back to my mother's, saw the For Rent sign, called the landlord and moved right in. I'm still bringing boxes over from my mother's."

He mentally located the place, a rambling multistory wooden building with fire escapes running up the sides and seagull droppings on the front steps.

"You don't mean the old hospital?"

"Yep. I always wanted to live there. Especially after it became a place for shady ladies. Kind of appeals to the outcast in me."

He was still laughing when he hung up the phone.

"That wasn't very nice of you, Daddy," Lucy said, her back to him.

"What wasn't very nice?"

"What you said about people getting into accidents and getting shot at."

"Oh, honey," he said, still thinking about Sarah, "it was just a joke."

"People dying is just a joke?"

"Give me a break, Lulu," he said. "How're the cookies coming?"

"They're not." She carried the pan to the sink. "Who was that, anyway?"

"I CAN'T BELIEVE that out of all the places in Port Hamilton, you actually chose this," Rose said when she dropped by to see the apartment. She stood in the middle of the tiny living room, gazing out through the window. "Nice view, though."

"Isn't it?" Sarah stood beside her mother. Windows on this side looked out over the Straits of Juan de Fuca to the distant coast of British Columbia. From the bedroom, she could see the soaring Olympic Mountains, still covered with snow as they would be for much of the year. "Last night I watched the ferry until it disappeared out of sight." She glanced at Rose. "Want some coffee?"

"Sounds good," Rose said. "I'm going to check out the rest of the place."

"Actually you could do it from where you're standing," Sarah said. "But go ahead."

She filled the coffeepot with water, took a package of muffins from a basket on top of the refrigerator, and stuck two of them in the toaster oven. On the battered three-burner stove was a blue enamel kettle. Above it, on a shelf she'd tacked up that morning, she'd filled a yellow jug with wooden spoons and whisks, a couple of candles and a wicker basket. Just looking at the arrangement pleased her. Amazing how much better she felt than this time yesterday. Hearing from Matthew was another part of it.

She'd felt so terrific after talking to him that she'd thrown caution to the wind and gone on a shopping trip of sorts. At the Goodwill store, she'd found the coffee-maker, some floor pillows, a couple of rugs. Tomorrow, she would bring over the last boxes from Rose's base-ment. Home. I'm home again, she thought. I *have* a home, she amended.

"I see you've erected your tent," Rose called from the bedroom. A moment later, she was back in the tiny kitchen. "I remember you making tents in your room when you were a child. You'd crawl inside, close the flaps and shut out the cruel, nasty world."

Sarah grinned. Her purchases had also included yards of pale gauzy fabric that she'd pinned on the walls and ceiling around her bed. It did feel rather tentlike, very cozy. Lying in bed last night, covered with quilts, she'd felt completely at peace.

"Long-term lease?" Rose regarded Sarah over the top of her wire-rimmed glasses, strands of steel-gray hair already escaping from the knot at the back of her neck.

"Just six months. I'd like it to have been longer, but

apparently the building is up for sale. Actually, I'd like to buy it."

"Why not just enjoy it while you have it," Rose said. "Enjoy it for what it is. A place to stay for now."

"Because I want…" To feel secure, she thought. She poured coffee into two mugs and spread the muffins with butter. In the fridge, she found the marmalade and blackberry jam she'd picked up from the farmer's market.

"I still don't understand paying rent for a place when I'm rattling around in a house that's far too big for me." Rose spooned sugar into her coffee.

Sarah said nothing. It was pointless to argue with Rose, cruel to voice what they both knew: living together would drive Sarah nuts because Rose was an exacting, demanding perfectionist given to dark, morose moods when things didn't go her way. Sarah reluctantly conceded she'd inherited the trait herself and, so, found it doubly irritating to deal with in her mother. Ted had once suggested that everything she did was an attempt to prove she wasn't like Rose. She'd fought him on that, told him he didn't really know Rose. Later, she wondered if he really knew her.

"Have you spoken to Matthew yet?" Rose asked.

"He was in surgery. But I called him. Actually," she tried for a casual tone, "we're going out for a Frugals tonight."

Rose smiled.

"What?"

"Nothing." She drank some coffee, set her mug

down. "You should look at your face. You look like Queen of the Hop."

Sarah laughed. "You need to update your termi-noogy, Mom." Through the window behind Rose, she watched a flock of seagulls circle, their cries faintly audible above the sound of traffic going down Front Street. "It was funny talking to him. All these years and it was as if we'd just seen each other the day before."

JUST AFTER MIDNIGHT, Matthew woke to the sound of his beeper. Fumbling in the dark, he picked up the phone from the bedside table. "I'm not the one on call tonight," he told the page operator. "I changed with Dr. Adams. You need to call him."

"Then there's been some kind of mix-up," the oper-ator said. "I have you down, Dr. Cameron."

"Call Dr. Adams," Matthew said. "I'll come in if I have to, but try him first." He hung up the phone, rolled over and closed his eyes. Just as he drifted off, the phone rang again. Adams couldn't be reached. He sat up, switched on the light. The operator put him through to the E.R. The patient was a child with intestinal prob-lems.

"Give me ten minutes," Matthew said. He dressed then, shoes in hand, padded silently across the hall.

From his room, he heard his pager go again. He sprinted downstairs, scribbled a note to Lucy and went out in the dark cool night.

Something had to give, he thought, as he drove through the deserted streets. As stubborn as he knew himself to be—and as Elizabeth was always quick to confirm—he understood the mess the system was in. If it was a business other than Compassionate Medical Systems coming to the rescue, he could go along with it, but Olympic Memorial, like a desperate spinster, attracted few suitors.

Sure, he could rhapsodize about the joys of a small-town practice, the majesty of the Olympic Mountains, the achingly beautiful coastal trails. But none of the major players he'd hoped would offer their hand had shown much interest in what was also a debt-ridden, rural, blue-collar town with an aging population.

The truth was, you had to know Port Hamilton to love it. He did. And Sarah did. Sarah. Who he used to think he knew better than anyone in the world and then realized he didn't really know her at all. Still, it made him feel good to think of Sarah being back. If you were lucky, you had one, maybe two friendships that lasted a lifetime. Like a plant. A few leaves might fall off through lack of nurturing, but the roots never died. That was how it was with Sarah.

He pulled into the parking lot and switched off the ignition. Through the glass doors of the E.R., he watched a nurse in blue scrubs. His beeper went off again.

"Hey, Debbi." The mother looked young enough to have been the patient. "What's up with Alli tonight?"

"She's been throwing up and pooping all day." Her face pale in the harsh overhead lighting, Debbi soothed the child lying on the examining table.

"Well, let's take a look at her." The toddler, listless and pale, eyed Matthew as he examined her but didn't make a sound: That didn't reassure him. Healthier children tended not to submit so easily to being poked and prodded. "Haven't seen you around for a while."

She bit her lip. "We moved out to the end of the peninsula. I met this guy and we bought some property together. He's into a naturopathy, which worked pretty good on my asthma. Really good, in fact. But nothing was working with Alli and I got scared. He went to Olympia to some workshop and I decided I'd bring her in, just in case."

Matthew said nothing. Mainstream medicine clearly didn't have all the answers, but there was an almost evangelical zeal about some so-called natural medicine proponents that he found alarming. He'd suspected kidney disease the last time he saw the child and suggested testing. He hadn't seen her since.

Now he reminded her again. "If it is kidney disease, it can be controlled with medication or even cured. But if it isn't treated, it'll just get worse until she ends up needing dialysis or a transplant."

Debbi's face clouded. "How much would that cost?"

He looked at the child. He didn't know exactly what Debbi's financial situation was, but he had an idea she was one of a number of patients in the practice who paid on a sliding scale according to what they could afford, which in almost all cases wasn't very much.

"We'll work something out," he said. "The important

thing is that you shouldn't delay it. Call my office to-morrow, okay, and set up an appointment."

But as he scribbled a couple of prescriptions and handed them to her, he doubted that she would follow through.

CHAPTER FOUR

ELIZABETH WANTED to scream. Walking through Safeway with her mother and her daughter was more irritation than anyone should have to tolerate. Lucy was acting like the princess she thought she was. And Pearl, her mother, was the snoopy old Queen Mother.

Which would make her, Elizabeth, the queen, except that no one ever treated her like one. She set a bottle of champagne in the cart.

"I thought you weren't drinking anymore," Pearl said. "You fallen off the wagon?"

"Champagne doesn't count."

"Booze is booze," Pearl pronounced.

Lucy, who had gone off in her own direction as soon as they walked through the door, reappeared with a six-pack of socks. "Can I buy these?"

"Do you mean, can *I* buy them?" Elizabeth asked.

"If you can afford champagne," Pearl said mildly, "I would think you could afford socks."

"That's not the point." Elizabeth said, but no one was listening.

"Thank you, Grandma," Lucy said.

"You're welcome."

There were days Elizabeth reflected, when every-thing Pearl said seemed like some sort of attack. Matt always said she was overly sensitive when it came to her mother. But Matt had always idealized Pearl. Once she'd asked him, only half joking, if Pearl was the real reason they got married. Pearl was the mother he'd never had. Pearl wasn't weird and eccentric like Sarah's mother. Pearl was sweet and kind and baked cookies. Right. Sweet and kind to everyone but me. Pearl would have preferred a daughter like Sarah. Pearl would have loved to talk about her daughter the doctor.

"Who's Sarah?" Lucy asked as though she'd just read Elizabeth's mind.

"Sarah who?" Elizabeth picked up a heart-shaped box of candy and stuck it in the cart for George, the guy she'd been seeing lately. Giving was as good as receiv-ing. Kind of.

"Those will all be on sale next week," Pearl said. "Fifty percent off."

"Next week's too late for Valentine's," Elizabeth said. George treated her like a queen. The way Matt used to. Before they were married.

"Dad was talking on the phone to some woman called Sarah," Lucy said. "Who is she?"

"Lucy, I don't know every woman your father talks to. Maybe it was a patient."

"He said she was an old friend."

Elizabeth looked at her daughter. "Sarah Benedict?"

"How would I know?" Lucy said irritably. "They were talking for ages. And Dad was laughing."

"Sarah Benedict's back," Pearl said. "I had to see her mother for this little thing on my nose." She turned her face to Elizabeth. "See? That little rough patch. Precancerous legion."

"Lesion," Lucy said.

Pearl beamed. "How did I get to have such a smart granddaughter?"

"I take after my dad," Lucy said.

Elizabeth eyed the champagne. Typical of Sarah to breeze into town and not call. "Sarah and your dad grew up together," she told Lucy. "Then she went off to medical school and married this doctor and they traveled all over the place. Then he got killed."

"Your mother broke them up," Pearl told Lucy. "Your dad and Sarah."

"I did not." Elizabeth glared at Pearl. "What kind of thing is that to say to your granddaughter?"

"I'm not a child," Lucy said.

"I'm just stating the truth," Pearl said. "Your dad and Sarah were joined at the hip."

"Gee, thanks, Mom." She followed Pearl, wearing a snappy red pantsuit and a heart-shaped broach, down the paper-goods aisle, waited while her mother debated between Angel Soft and Dream Puff. "Lucy, go pick up some milk and let's get out of here."

"He's taking her out for a Frugals," Lucy said.

"Good for him," Elizabeth said, although the idea of Matt and Sarah being a twosome again made her feel weird. Still, maybe it would be good for Matt to get a life instead of working all the time. He looked like hell these days. Like he hadn't seen sunshine for ten years or something.

When she told George that her ex-husband was a doctor, George figured she must have all kinds of money. A doctor's wife, he kept saying. And then she had to explain Matt didn't make a whole bunch of money, not that he *couldn't,* just that he chose to work at the ends of the earth. What she hadn't told George was that Matt also drove a truck. An old truck that didn't even have a decent stereo system.

They continued their procession down the aisles. Next stop: jams and jellies. Lucy had disappeared again and Pearl was holding a jar in each hand and studying them as though she was about to take a test. Elizabeth couldn't help resenting how Pearl always took Lucy's side and Lucy always took Matthew's side and Matthew acted as though she, Elizabeth, never had an important thought in her life. That was the good thing about George. He made her feel interesting. And smart.

Unlike Pearl, who was now yammering on about Sarah Benedict and how smart she'd always been and what was she doing back in Port Hamilton when she could live anywhere in the world and wasn't it rude of Elizabeth not to even give her a call to welcome her home?

Elizabeth ignored her. Sarah didn't need a welcome-home party. She had Matt. Sarah had always had Matt. One night after they'd been making out down at the spit, steaming up the windows of Matt's old truck, she'd asked him about Sarah.

"You're not two-timing with her, or anything?" And he'd laughed. "Oh, Sarah's my friend," he'd said. "We tell each other everything."

"So you'll tell her about us?" she'd asked.

"Of course," he'd said.

And maybe he had. But you certainly couldn't tell from the way Sarah acted. Still, she and Sarah had never been close. Sarah always made her feel dumb. And it felt uncomfortable being around Matt and Sarah, the way they were always laughing and joking, finishing each other's sentences. It was like they had their own secret world and nobody else knew their special language.

Overhead the music turned into a Rod Stewart song. Suddenly tears started flowing down Elizabeth's face. *That's what I want. That's all I've ever wanted.*

As SARAH WALKED OUT of Ming Dynasty with a container of mu shu pork, she ran into Curt Hudelson.

"Loaded with chemicals." Curt tapped his finger against the take-out carton and slowly shook his head. "You need to toss it."

"No way," Sarah said. "My philosophy allows me a few guilty pleasures."

"Sorry if I annoyed your mother the other day," he said. "Medical establishment and all that. It's rather like trying to move a dinosaur."

"I wouldn't call Rose a dinosaur," Sarah said, slightly

offended on her mother's behalf. "Set in her ways about some things, but then she hasn't had much exposure to alternative forms of practice."

Curt smiled. "Yes, well, I encounter that resistance all the time. Even with my own family. Debbi knows quite well what works, yet if I'm not constantly reinforcing it, she'll slip right back into going to the doctor for every little thing. Her asthma is a case in point. She knows how to control it but insists on carrying that bloody inhaler."

"Well, I'm against taking unnecessary drugs," Sarah said, "but asthma can be dangerous if it spins out of control."

"Exactly. Which is why I teach her self-hypnosis."

Sarah said nothing. Maybe it was the eyes, but there was something about him that made her vaguely uneasy. It was that whole balance thing, not swinging too far in either direction. She made a mental note to see if Matthew knew him.

FORTUNATELY, Curt Hudelson's disapproval of her mu shu pork didn't interfere with her enjoyment of it. Later, sitting on the living-room floor, cushions piled up around her, the take-out carton in easy reach and John Coltrane on the stereo, she started unpacking the boxes she'd brought over from her mother's house. The first one contained half-a-dozen photograph albums documenting the first sixteen years or so of her life. The earlier photos were on black paper, stuck into tiny gilt paper corners that she used to buy in small plastic bags from the Bay Variety store on Lincoln. They predated the sticky white boards with plastic sheets that she'd discovered by the time she was twelve. Taking on the role of family archivist had been an act of desperation. After a stack of the shoe boxes Rose always dumped pictures in fell from the closet shelf, spilling all over the floor. Sarah had decided to impose order.

She speared a piece of pork with her chopstick and savored the taste.

A storm had blown in during the night and stuck around. Wind rattled the windows, and rain lashed against the glass. Northwest weather. She hadn't realized how much she'd missed it. Missed everything from her past. Ted, who had left his native England as a child, seemed to have spent much of his adult life looking for a sense of place. She set the chopsticks back in the carton and carried it into the kitchen.

"I want to feel that kind of connection," Ted used to say when she would talk about growing up in Port Hamilton, about the generations of Benedicts who had practiced medicine there. "I want to know, deep inside me, that this is where I belong. I want to feel a part of the community, of the land. I want to know the people, I want them to matter to me personally. I want the kind of life you had."

As an adult, she had a less rose-tinted view of what that had been, but until she was fifteen, she really had thought everything about her life was perfect. The big red barnlike house on the bluffs above the Strait of Juan de Fuca. Her attic bedroom, with the window seat where she'd watch the *Olympic Princess* carry passengers and their vehicles back and forth between Port Hamilton and Victoria, British Columbia. Curling up under blankets at night, gazing at the lights across the water, imagining a Canadian girl just like her staring at the lights from Port Hamilton.

Rose would label it nostalgic yearning, but she had always felt so safe back then. Happy. Long golden summer days, perfumed by the red and pink roses that filled the backyard. Fourth of July parades and picnics on the beach. Time in endless supply, it had seemed. At Christmas, bundled up in coats and scarves, she would hold her parents' hands as they walked into town for the Christmas-tree lighting on Main Street. Snowshoeing and skiing in the winter, bonfires on the beach in the summer and fireworks to light the dark sky.

Best of all, there was Matthew, the boy down the street. Matthew the star of her childhood memories. Racing their bikes along the jetty that protected Port Hamilton's deep harbor from the choppy waters of the straits, screeching and whooping, the wind in their faces. Walking home from the beach together, wet hair and sandy feet.

On her thirteenth birthday, she'd scrambled over huge boulders to the rocky beach, Matt right behind her. With their backs against a rock, they'd watched the shorebirds and he'd told her the Latin name of the Black-bellied Plover.

"Pluvialis squatarola," he'd said, and she'd burst out laughing because she thought he was making it up. She'd looked it up later, of course, and he'd been right.

If there was a time when Sarah hadn't been in love with Matthew Cameron, she couldn't remember it. It wasn't puppy love or a crush or anything like that. She'd never carved their initials into tree trunks or scribbled intertwined hearts on her schoolbooks. They'd never talked about it, this bond between them, never even held hands. She could hardly even explain it to herself, the deep, certain knowledge she'd had that she loved Matthew with every fiber of her being and that they would always be together.

At least, she'd felt that way until Elizabeth moved into the house next door. Elizabeth, with her almond-shaped eyes and naturally rosy lips. Elizabeth, who knew how to talk and laugh with boys but still act like a girl. Her family was from Los Angeles and she wasn't happy about moving to Port Hamilton, which she considered a hick town that she intended to leave as soon as she could. Elizabeth was always talking about how things were in Los Angeles: the way the girls dressed, the cool places kids hung out, the movie stars all over the place. And when Elizabeth talked, everyone listened, boys *and* girls.

Before Elizabeth, Sarah had never given a moment's thought to her appearance, but Elizabeth's long silky hair made her painfully self-conscious about her own unruly curls, about the freckles that spattered her cheeks and nose and her skinny, boyish frame. More than that, Elizabeth forced her to acknowledge there really was a difference between the way boys and girls behaved.

It was also while watching Elizabeth that Sarah first realized she lacked the ability to do what others girls seemed to do naturally. Elizabeth danced with her head at just the right angle to look up into a boy's eyes. Elizabeth could walk into the Parrot Cage, where the kids hung out after school, and all the boys crowded round her, falling over themselves to get her attention. Matthew included.

Before Sarah realized what was happening, it was no longer just Matthew and Sarah, the way it had always been. It was Matthew, Sarah and Elizabeth. And then Matthew and Elizabeth. One night he'd started telling her about Elizabeth. "She's sweet and pretty and..." He'd shaken his head as though words alone weren't adequate to sum up Elizabeth.

"Wow," Sarah had said, "sounds serious. Like you're in love with her."

"I think I might be."

And Sarah had forced herself to smile.

"The thing is, I can't talk to her the way I talk to you," he'd gone on to tell her. "She doesn't get my jokes."

"Yeah, but she's pretty."

And then, safe in her own room, Sarah had cried herself to sleep.

By the time Matthew went off to premed in Seattle, he and Elizabeth were officially a couple. Sarah had immersed herself in her own studies and, for the first time in her life, days and weeks, then months went by when she didn't think about Matthew. But never, ever, did she stop loving him.

The night he married Elizabeth, Sarah had wandered away from the reception out to the small patch of beach just past the hotel. Matthew had found her sitting on a piece of driftwood, staring out at the water. Allergies, she'd said when he'd asked about her red eyes. And then she'd hugged him. "I hope you and Elizabeth will be very happy."

The following year, she'd gone off to medical school herself and met Ted, a fellow student. Ted, a gentle dreamer who wanted only to help. His death still haunted her dreams.

CHAPTER FIVE

LUCY CALLED just as Matthew was leaving the house to pick up Sarah.

"Daddy." A pause. "Can I come with you to Frugals?"

"I didn't think you liked it," Matthew said. "You never want to go when I suggest it."

"But I do this time."

"How about tomorrow?"

"Daddy." Her tone turned wheedling. "I'm hungry now."

He laughed. "Well, I'm sure you can find something in the house to eat." He glanced at his watch. "Listen, Lulu, I'm running late."

"To see Sarah?"

"Right."

"Why can't I go?"

He frowned. "Lucy, what's this about?"

"Nothing. I just want to go with you."

"Not this time." He could almost feel the sullenness of the silence on her end and, although she'd never shown any interest in the women he occasionally introduced her to, he sensed something different. "But I do want you to meet Sarah. You're going to like her a lot."

"Yeah, right."

"Lucy?"

"What?"

"Come on, honey."

"I gotta go," she said.

He heard the disconnect, debated whether to call back, then decided against it. No real reason she couldn't come along, but it had been years since he'd seen Sarah and, he reasoned, Lucy would be bored listening to them play catch-up.

THE TEST OF A TRUE FRIENDSHIP, he later decided was how easily you could slip back into a natural rhythm. Sarah looked like a slightly older version of the Sarah he'd always known. Skinny bordering on scrawny, the small triangular face and shrewd gray eyes that seemed to bore right through any kind of dissembling. Hair always dated people, but Sarah wore her reddish brown hair just as she always had, in a thick, heavy braid that came halfway down her back. The row of small silver hoops in her ears were new, as were a few lines around the eyes. He could imagine her squinting into the bright sunlight. No sunglasses for Sarah. He'd teased her about the sprinkle of gray and she'd done the same to him.

After they picked up the burgers, they'd driven out to the end of Forbe's Hook, found a spot on the rocks and watched the sun dissolve into the water.

"So what are your plans now?" he asked as the sky

turned to shades of pink and red. "Are you going to stick around for a while?"

Head down, Sarah picked at the threadbare knee of her jeans. "Actually, I am."

He waited a moment. "And?"

"I have a plan."

Matthew grinned. "You've always had a plan."

"This is different. This is a grown-up plan. A huge plan. And it involves you."

As Matthew dug around in the paper sack for more fries, he felt the shift in her mood. Whatever Sarah's huge plan turned out to be, he wasn't in the right frame of mind to hear it. Her presence had been a welcome distraction from the looming Compassionate Medical Systems crisis, and he felt a reluctance to be drawn into more serious discussion. He also knew that Sarah in full-steam-ahead mode could be nigh on impossible to stop.

She shot him a glance. "You want to hear it?"

"Do I have a choice?"

"You sound tired, Matthew."

"I am."

"Work?"

"Essentially." In the gathering darkness, he saw the glimmer of a smile flicker across Sarah's face. "Don't tell me, your plan is the solution."

"It could be."

He gave in to the inevitable. "Tell me."

"Okay." She drew in a breath. "Remember when you first started medical school, you used to talk about the kind of medical practice you wanted to have? Not just treating disease and patients who were already sick, but patient-centered care that promoted wellness with traditional healing arts, home mind-body therapy—"

Matthew groaned.

"What?"

"Tell me I was never that hopelessly naive."

Sarah turned to face him. Eyes gleaming, body tensed, she seemed a cat poised to pounce. He braced himself.

"Matthew," she said, "listen to me. There's nothing naive about that. It's exactly what I want to do. What I want us both to do. An integrated approach that doesn't abandon mainstream medicine. I mean, kids are still going to break bones or need surgery…"

Presumably where he came in, he thought, as he listened to her describe the practice they would set up together along with herbalists, hypnotherpists and an assortment of other practitioners.

"Ted used to talk about establishing that kind of practice," she said. "And when he died, I thought that his dream died with him, but then—" her voice softened "—it was the strangest thing. I was going through a box of old letters that you had sent me when you were in med school and I found this one that almost spelled out word for word the same thing Ted and I were planning to do. That's when I knew I had to come back."

Matthew looked out at the water. The ferry from Victoria appeared on the horizon, its lights punctuating the darkness. "Sarah, I don't know how to say this—"

"Please don't tell me it won't work, because—"

"I wasn't going to say it won't work. I think it could. I appreciate the fact that medicine is changing. I don't believe one school of thought offers all the answers. It's just not going to work for me."

Sarah took a deep breath. "Why not?"

"For one thing, your timing couldn't be worse. I've spent most of the day in meetings, listening to reasons why Compassionate Medical Systems is the only answer."

"You don't believe that."

"I don't not believe it. CMS has an excellent reputation," he said, hearing the hollowness in his voice. "And, frankly, the peninsula needs an infusion of cash. We need more doctors, a new hospital, new equipment. That's never going to happen the way things are now."

Sarah began picking at the knees of her jeans again. Moments passed. "You're not thinking of selling out yourself, are you?"

"It's not selling out, Sarah," he said, his voice sharper than he intended. "The bottom line is providing quality care. Olympic can't do that under the existing structure. The money isn't there."

"Wait." She cupped her hand to her ear. "That sounded suspiciously like an affirmative."

"I haven't decided yet." In Sarah's world, he was remembering now, there were no shades of gray. Black or white. Good or bad. Right or wrong. Fair or unfair. Remembering too the impossibly high standards she expected, from others as much as from herself. There was Sarah's way of doing things and there was the wrong way. "Just once," he remembered shouting, after they'd argued about some high-school project they were working on together, "I want to hear you say that something is good enough, that it doesn't need fine-tuning."

"I know something about Compassionate Medical Systems," Sarah said. "When I first left the peninsula, I made the mistake of going to work in one of their hospitals in Seattle. Ted had a similar experience. We both realized it would never work for us. That's when we decided to go to Central America. I mean, these companies answer to stockholders. I won't work in an environment where the real focus is money, not patients. Bottom line, money's going to dictate which doctor you see, how many tests can be run, what medicine you should take. Patients wait months for appointments that used to take days—"

"I can't decide whether it's the Frugal burger or this discussion," Matthew said, "but I'm getting a headache."

"Sorry." She stretched her legs out, wriggled her toes in her beat-up sneakers. "I get up on my soapbox and there's no stopping me."

"I noticed."

"Well—" she wrapped her arms around herself "—it's getting cold. I should probably get going."

But neither of them moved. Out on the horizon a few stripes of pink cut through the indigo sky. "Things change, Sarah," he finally said. "Sometimes that's a good thing, sometimes it's not so good. But it's reality. The way things are now, I go to work. Get home, sometimes not till one in the morning. Sleep the night, if I'm lucky. If not, I get a call from the E.R. because they can't locate the doctor who's supposed to be on call. I end up spending time on call that I'd rather spend with my daughter—"

"But I don't understand. You're chief of staff. Why would they page you?"

He laughed. "We have a chronic physician shortage. No new people coming in, old ones dying off. Right after you left, the mill closed, so one huge source of employment shut down and, well, you know the peninsula. There weren't that many jobs to begin with. A good percentage of my patients who'd worked at the mill lost their insurance, but I still see them. They'd pay if they had the money, but there are no jobs. All of that makes it harder to attract new physicians." He picked up a pebble and tossed it into the dark water. "So if it seems like selling out to you, I'm sorry. Idealism is fine, but I also have to make a living."

After that, they fell into silence again. Sarah, hunched into her windbreaker, her hair hiding her face. The mood had shifted, and he didn't know what to do about it.

"Aw, come on," he said, "it's not that bad." The sun had dissolved, turning the sky shades of pink and vermillion against the navy sea. "You don't get views like this everywhere."

THE FOLLOWING DAY, Rose stopped by the apartment and, as they were having coffee, announced she was selling the practice. "I was waiting for the right moment, but I didn't want you to hear about it from someone else."

Sarah stared at her. "You're not serious."

"Yes, I am."

"You're retiring?"

"Compassionate Medical Systems is buying me out. For a very good price, I might add. And take that horrified look off your face."

"I'm shocked."

Rose took a deep breath. "Welcome to the real world. The handwriting is on the wall. Sure, I can hold on for a few more years, but it's like those mom-and-pop stores—like McGregor's. I remember when I used to do most of my grocery shopping there and I still drop in to pick up milk or something I've run out of, but that's mostly out of loyalty. When I need a lot of groceries I go to Albertsons or Safeway. Everyone does, it's a fact of life."

Her hands suddenly icy, Sarah wrapped them around her coffee mug. Rose was going on about managed care being the wave of the future and encouraging her to apply to Compassionate Medical Systems. Sarah flashed back to the time as a kid when she'd saved her allowance to buy her mom a Norman Rockwell print: a country doctor's office, the small boy baring his bum for the kindly old doctor's injection.

She could still see Rose's bemused expression as she unwrapped the gift. Years later, she'd understood. Too sentimental. Generations of Benedicts might have practiced medicine out of the same family home, but they'd never been a Norman Rockwell family. And now that the money was right, Rose was casually parting with tradition. Selling out.

"Sarah, I know this is a disappointment," Rose said, apparently reading her expression, "but it's honestly the only way to go. It's getting harder and harder to make a living this way. More uninsured patients."

"Someone has to take care of them."

"Someone also has to make a living," Rose said. "And if you think I'm being hard-hearted, talk to Matthew—"

"I already have."

"Uh-oh." Rose's mouth twisted. "And?"

"Take a wild guess."

"Didn't I try to tell you?"

After Rose left, Sarah stood in the kitchen, staring out at the gulls and the tankers on the water and the wind-tossed trees. Things did not look promising.

On the wall of her clinic in Central America, she'd tacked up a pain-assessment chart with six cartoonlike faces whose expressions ranged from happy and smiling to great discomfort and unbearable pain. Small kids couldn't read the captions underneath—annoying, nagging, miserable, horrible, excruciating and so forth—but they knew that a furrowed brow, down-turned mouth and falling tears weren't good things.

She'd stuck the chart on the refrigerator. Right now, she was definitely among the scowls and grimaces group. Coming back to Port Hamilton was supposed to be like completing a circle. A return to the place where she'd been the happiest, an opportunity to practice medicine with a doctor she admired for his ideals and who was also her best friend.

So much for that.

She made more coffee, carried her mug into the living room, back to the window. Tempted to just go to bed, pull the covers over her head and shut out the world, she was stopped by Rose's voice in her head mocking her for doing that very thing. She pulled on her sweats and running shoes and jogged down to Francis Street Park, her favorite place in Port Hamilton.

The park was steeply banked with tangles of blackberries on either side and steps running down to the water. Even before she reached the steps, she could see the dark hull of a tanker at anchor, hear the seagulls screech. She felt an almost holiness, like walking into a church.

She took deep, slow breaths, tried to clear her mind. Minutes passed and, slowly, the turbulent thoughts began to subside. She would be all right. Things would work out. She would come up with a new plan. Maybe Matthew wouldn't have fit into the picture anyway.

They hadn't always seen eye to eye. Last night was a reminder of that.

In the silence that had fallen between them on the drive back to her apartment, she'd gone through all the things he would never actually say to her about why sharing a practice would never work anyway. He would never say them, because he loved her. Not the way she'd always wanted him to love her, but as a friend whose feelings he wouldn't want to hurt. You're too idealistic, Sarah. Too unpredictable. Too…much.

The wind picked up and blew in cold gusts that reached like bony fingers through the fabric of her sweats. She started to run. And this was the memory she wanted to run from now—she'd *preached* at him. Accused him of abandoning his ideals. Just thinking about it now made her run faster. His expression as he tried to explain was burned on her brain.

Her sneakers slapping the pavement, she continued down the trail. When she reached the ferry terminal, she stood for a moment trying to decide whether to run on to Lopez Hook or head back to the apartment and…what? Send out résumés? Return to Central America? She decided to continue for another ten minutes or so.

"THERE YOU GO." Elizabeth set a platter of bacon and eggs down in front of the guy at the table by the window. "Can I get you anything else?"

He smiled up at her. "Maybe just a refill."

She brought the coffeepot over and filled up his mug. If he hadn't been reading the newspaper, she might have got him talking. She liked to do that, hear people's stories. Chitchat about the weather. No big heavy stuff, just people being nice to each other.

Back in the kitchen, she stood with her arms folded, watching the gulls in the empty parking lot fight over a scrap of something. No one believed it when she'd taken the job as a waitress at the coffee shop down by the ferry landing. The ex-wife of a doctor, pocketing tips and getting paid minimum wage. But it wasn't the money—Matt was good about making sure she and Lucy had enough. It was being appreciated. People smiled when she brought their food, they thanked her like they really meant it.

Trouble was, business had slowed down to practically nothing. Now she was the sole employee. Cook, waitress and cleanup crew and she still had time to stand staring out of the window. Time to start feeling sorry for herself, Pearl would say. She looked around for something to do, but the kitchen and all the tables were spotless, so she called home to talk to Lucy. The phone rang five times before the girl picked it up.

"Hi, honey." Elizabeth smiled into the phone. "Watcha doing?"

"Sleeping," Lucy said.

"Hon, it's nearly noon." As soon as she said it, Elizabeth wanted to take the words back. Everything she said these days made Lucy mad. Being around her was like walking on eggshells. "Why don't you get dressed and come down here and I'll make you lunch."

"Can I come down without getting dressed?"

"Huh? No, I—"

"*Joking*, Mom," Lucy said, as if Elizabeth was a child. "I think I would have figured out that I needed to get dressed first."

Elizabeth felt tears prickle in her nose. Lucy would never talk to Matt like that. Lucy respected Matt, that was the truth of it. And she didn't respect her mother. She blew her nose. "Okay, suit yourself."

Through the row of spider plants in macramé hangers that separated the kitchen from the dining room, she could see the guy had finished his breakfast and was looking around the way people did when they wanted to pay their bills.

"I gotta go," she told Lucy.

"You here visiting?" Elizabeth asked the man as she filled his cup again. He wasn't one of the regulars, no one she'd seen around town.

"Just for a couple of days."

"Vacation?"

"I'm a reporter for the *Seattle Times*. Doing an article on the goings-on at your hospital. Compassionate Medical Systems coming in, shaking things up." He took a sip of his coffee. "How do you feel about it?"

"I'm all for it." Elizabeth leaned against the edge of the booth. "My ex is a doctor at the hospital and he's working himself to death the way things are now. I hear if Compassionate Medical Systems comes in, they'll bring in more doctors. There's even talk about building a new hospital, which, God knows, we could use. I was born in that place and I don't think it's been remodeled since."

"Your husband is a doctor there?"

"Ex."

"What does he think about it?"

"Oh…" She shrugged. "He's one of those idealistic types. He'd rather work himself to death than bend. But if enough people want it, I don't think he'll have much choice."

She set the check on the table in front of him, and

after he left, she went back to the kitchen for a rag and wiped down the already clean tables. Then the door opened on a gust of cold air and a woman came in. Navy sweat suit and baseball cap. No jacket, which meant she was a tourist not used to the local weather. The woman looked at her and then they both did a double take.

"Sarah?"

"Elizabeth! I didn't know you worked here."

And then there was an awkward moment when she could see Sarah didn't know whether to hug her or not, or maybe it was her feeling that way about Sarah who she'd never exactly been on hugging terms with, mostly because Sarah wasn't the hugging type. But then they both moved forward at the same time and wrapped their arms around each other like long-lost friends.

"I feel bad we haven't got together since you've been back," Elizabeth said, which wasn't exactly true, but what the hell. "Every day, I think, okay, I've got to call Sarah, but you know how it is." She plucked at the arm of Sarah's sweats. "You look frozen to death. How come you're not wearing a jacket? This is Washington, not… wherever you were. Where was it? Matt told me once, but I forget. Wait, wait, don't tell me. Panama."

Sarah smiled. "Nicaragua."

"But weren't you in Panama? I remember Matt saying something about the canal."

"I flew into Panama City." Sarah pulled off the baseball cap, blew into her hands. "And then I went to Nicaragua." She glanced around. "I had no idea you worked here," she repeated. "This was my favorite place as a kid. It was a big treat to come here for breakfast before we caught the ferry."

Elizabeth smiled. Sarah hadn't changed a whole lot. Same reddish hair that always looked like someone had taken an electric mixer to it, fuzzy and flyaway. Maybe a few wrinkles, but who didn't have those? And she didn't look like she weighed any more than she had in high school, which was more than she could say about herself.

"So, you going to have breakfast?"

Sarah seemed to be thinking it over, then she smiled and sat down in one of the booths by the window. "Sure. Why not?"

The phone by the cash register rang.

"The Landing," Elizabeth answered.

"I'm sorry for being mean," Lucy said.

"Aw, honey." Elizabeth set down the menu she'd picked up for Sarah. "Are you crying?"

"Yeah. I feel sad."

"Oh, Lulu." Elizabeth wiped her own eyes. "How come?"

"I don't know, I just do." A pause. "Dad called. He was supposed to take me to the mall to get fabric for my costume and now he can't go."

"Well, I can take you. As soon as I get off work. We'll go to the mall and go to the Olive Garden afterward. Mmm, that artichoke dip you like. And lots of bread sticks? How does that sound?"

"Okay," Lucy said in a small voice. "But I kind of wanted Dad to take me."

Elizabeth took a deep breath. "How come he can't?"

"I don't know. Something at the hospital."

"I'll talk to him, sweetie—okay?" Elizabeth signaled to Sarah that she'd be right there. "Cheer up."

She hung up the phone, grabbed a menu and set it down in front of Sarah. She poured coffee without asking because she remembered Sarah had always been a coffee fiend and she was pretty sure that hadn't changed. "The omelets are good." She watched Sarah scan the menu. "So are the scrambles. Especially the shrimp and crab."

Sarah looked up at her and smiled. "Sounds good to me."

"I'm running the show," Elizabeth said. "Meaning, I'm the cook, too. Come back and talk to me while I fix your food. Bring your coffee. I think I'll have some, too."

She poured herself a cup, got eggs and two stainless steel containers of vegetables she'd chopped earlier and set them down by the stove. "So how were your cheeseburgers last night?" she said as she scrambled the eggs.

"Cheeseburgers?" Arms folded across her chest, Sarah stood off to one side watching. "Oh, Matthew told you—"

"Matthew never tells me anything," Elizabeth said. "Lucy told me. My daughter," she added. "Well, Matt's daughter, too. She's definitely a daddy's girl. Twists him around her little finger like he's made of putty. He probably talked your ear off about her, right?"

"We started talking shop," Sarah said, "and that pretty

much took up the evening." She drank some coffee, set the mug down. "So anyway, how old is your daughter?"

"Fourteen," Elizabeth said. "And…" She stared hard at the chopped pieces of red bell pepper and onions in the frying pan and then, just like in the Safeway, felt the tears start up. "Sorry. Ignore me. I don't know what's wrong with me…."

"Sounds about the same way I'm feeling right now," Sarah said.

Elizabeth glanced at her, but it had always been difficult to tell what was really going on with Sarah. She slid a spatula under the eggs. "You want cheese, right?" Then, without waiting for an answer, she grabbed the container of grated mozzarella from the refrigerator. "You got any ideas why a girl who is loved to distraction by both her parents would rather have a root canal than spend time with her mother, but thinks her father can do no wrong and goes to pieces when she can't be with him?"

CHAPTER SIX

"NOT HAVING KIDS MYSELF," Sarah said as she sprinkled cheese onto the eggs Elizabeth had scrambled, "I'm probably not the best person to ask. But since you did, I remember at fourteen, I preferred my father to my mother. He was just less…I don't know, judgmental. Actually, Rose and I have always had a sort of prickly relationship."

"With Lucy," Elizabeth's voice trembled, "she knows she takes after me, but she looks at me these days and it kills her to think she might end up like me."

"Or she could just be a typical fourteen-year-old girl," Sarah said. "And it's just a stage you have to live through." She glanced around the kitchen, wondering about silverware. Somehow, without realizing it, they'd changed places and now Elizabeth, seated on a stool by the stove, was watching as Sarah finished cooking the breakfast.

"How did this happen?" Elizabeth blew her nose. "You're the customer. Oh, well, no charge." She managed a watery smile. "You must think I'm some kind of nutcase. We haven't seen each for years and you're here five minutes and I fall apart."

"I tend to have that effect on people," Sarah said. In fact, she'd barely recognized Elizabeth and might not have if Elizabeth hadn't said her name first. A glimmer of the old Elizabeth lingered in the husky screen-siren voice and the creamy complexion, but the flashing dimples and almond eyes were lost in soft folds of flesh. The lithe cheerleader shape was now pillowy breasts and hips sausaged into black stretch pants. She divided the food between the two plates Elizabeth had set on the chrome serving shelf. "I'm working on it though."

"Let's eat back here." Elizabeth pulled her stool up to the counter and sat down again. "I can see if anyone comes in."

Sarah dug her fork into the eggs. "Not bad. If I do say so myself."

"Remember home ec?" Elizabeth asked. "One time we were supposed to be making…what was it, some kind of cake together. And you drove me crazy because everything had to be carefully measured." She set down her fork. "You insisted on running a knife over the top of a cupful of flour to make sure it was exactly one cup."

Sarah smiled. "I remember that. You drove *me* crazy. You kept adding things that weren't in the recipe."

"But Matt liked my cake best," Elizabeth said.

"Yep." Sarah nodded, remembering. "Matthew liked everything best about you." Suddenly embarrassed at what she'd said and at the power still remaining in those memories, she made a production of getting more coffee for both of them. At the moment, Matthew didn't feel like a safe subject.

"Have you been working here long?" she asked.

"Six weeks."

"Must be interesting meeting new people…lots of tourists, huh?"

"It's a job," Elizabeth said. "Nothing like what you or Matt do."

"At the moment, it's *more* than I do," Sarah said. "I thought I'd come back here and—" She stopped herself. "Compassionate Medical Systems seems to have taken over. I gave Matthew a hard time about it. I accused him of selling out."

Elizabeth shook her head.

"I know, I feel bad."

"No, I don't mean that. It's just…the two of you. He's been agonizing about whether or not to join."

"He has?"

"God, yes. I tell him he needs to come down from his ivory tower once in a while, pay a visit to us real people. Everyone knows it would be the best thing that ever happened to Port Hamilton. I mean, how long has that hospital been there? It's a dump. They'd tear that down, build something modern. And right now, the way Matt is always on call, they'd get more doctors and they'd all be making more money, which, for sure, would be good for everyone. Matt needs to throw his support to CMC, Sarah. If he doesn't, he's going to kill himself."

Her appetite gone, Sarah pushed her plate away. "Now I really feel bad."

"Don't." Elizabeth looked at her for a minute. "It's funny, some people just kind of tiptoe through life, never putting their feet down too hard and then there's…"

"Me," Sarah said. "Sarah the trampler."

"*I* didn't say that."

"You didn't have to."

Elizabeth folded her arms. "Can I give you a piece of advice? I mean, it seems weird advising you, but—"

"Why would that be weird?"

"Well, it's always…you know, Sarah's so smart. Elizabeth's pretty, but Sarah's smart. But okay, here's the thing. So you said something that maybe you shouldn't have and maybe it bothered Matt. Well, so what? He's a big boy, he'll get over it. That's the way life is. I make you mad. You make me mad. The world keeps turning, right? Quit beating yourself up. Go see him, say hi and act like nothing ever happened."

Sarah considered. If nothing else it might help mend the personal rift. Plus there was always the chance that after thinking things over, he'd have a change of heart about her proposal. Maybe she'd give him a day or two though. Sarah finally nodded. "I might do that."

"Good." Elizabeth smiled. "You know what? I feel a whole lot better just talking to you."

"That makes two of us," Sarah said.

"Hey, Sarah." Elizabeth's smile grew less uncertain. "I should have said something before. I meant to, but I'm bad at this. Listen, I'm really sorry about your husband. That must have been tough."

"Yeah." Sarah looked beyond Elizabeth's shoulder. "Well, I guess I should get going."

As HE WALKED through the mall, Lucy on one side, his former mother-in-law, Pearl, on the other, Matthew was thinking about Sarah. His plan had been to call her, suggest another Frugals trip, this time without drifting into the murky waters of professional ethics. That it still irked him to be accused of selling out was, he realized, because he shared her opinion.

"Elizabeth's drinking," Pearl said. "I worry about her."

"She told me she was going to counseling," Matthew said.

"Huh." Pearl grunted and they both walked along in silence for a while. Lucy, who he was well aware had manipulated him into coming to the mall—a place he detested—was walking on ahead. Drawing, and enjoying, not so subtle glances from pimply faced adolescent louts who Matthew was ready to take on if they so much as laid a finger on her.

"I'll have another talk with Elizabeth," Matthew said.

"You were the best thing that ever happened to her. And she threw it all away for what? A long-haired hippy musician who lasted all of five minutes."

"Yeah, well, who could compete with me?" Impulsively, he put his arm around Pearl's shoulders and hugged her close, swept by a sudden surge of affection for the sprightly little woman walking along beside him in her natty red jacket and black pants.

Whenever he questioned why he'd married Elizabeth in the first place, he knew one of the answers was her mother. His own had fled the scene shortly after he was born, leaving him to be raised by his father who had never hidden the fact that he resented the burden. Matthew spent his childhood auditioning potential mother replacements. Given the amount of time he'd hung around Sarah's house, Rose had been an obvious choice. But Rose, cool and cerebral and slightly scatty, was not the kind of mother who would sit a child down with milk and cookies or dish out hugs and words of comfort. Pearl was. Pearl had always made him feel like the best, most brilliant specimen of the male gender.

Elizabeth seemed, at least until they were married, to have inherited that ability. The contrast between Elizabeth and Sarah couldn't have been more dramatic. If Elizabeth was a warm embrace, a source of uncritical affection, being around Sarah was often like navigating a minefield. And, he had to admit it, every male over the age of twelve had lusted after Elizabeth. How could he not feel flattered that she'd chosen him?

"…and of course, I liked it when the two of you were married," Pearl was saying. "My son-in-law the doctor. I could find a way to drop it into any conversation."

Matthew laughed.

"You two ever talk about getting back together again?"

"Not even for you, Pearl."

"It would make Lucy happy."

"Lucy's happy enough," he said.

"She'd be happier with two parents in the same house."

"Let's talk about something else," Matthew said. "I saw Sarah Benedict last night."

"And?"

He laughed. "And nothing. We had cheeseburgers. I told her I'll probably end up joining Compassionate Medical Systems. And she lectured me on selling out."

Pearl paused to glance at a window display of sandals. "Sarah was always a high-minded girl."

"Still is."

"Do you think you're selling out?"

"I don't know," he replied truthfully.

Two DAYS LATER, Matthew was sitting in the hospital cafeteria eating enchiladas and rice and reading the *Peninsula Daily News* when he looked up to see Sarah sitting across from him, clearly suppressing a grin. Strands of hair escaped from her braid curling in tendrils around her face, and she wore a dark green sweater that seemed to change the color of her eyes from gray to gray-green.

"How long have you been there?" he asked.

"Long enough for you to finish the article about how CMS will transform the delivery of medical care to the peninsula…and to scan the society column where you'd hoped to find at least your name, if not a picture of you hobnobbing with the Port Hamilton elite at the Elks Club ball."

Matthew laughed. His spirits had just taken a dramatic upturn. "I'm so damn disappointed. I thought attending the ball with reindeer antlers glued to my scrub cap would guarantee a spot on the front page. What the hell do I have to do to be included in the society column?"

"Dunno." Sarah was laughing, too. "Be more elk-like."

"Bigger horns maybe."

"Couldn't hurt."

They sat there for a minute or so, just grinning at each other.

"I've been thinking." Sarah broke off a piece of his tortilla and scooped up some rice. "I know, take two aspirins and call you in the morning."

"Works for me," Matthew said.

"Just shut up and listen, will you? It's not every day I apologize, but I'm about to do it so don't make it more difficult. The words are practically choking me already."

"On the other hand, it could be the tortilla," Matthew suggested.

"I've been told by, oh, one or two people…maybe three, that I'm argumentative and idealistic and kind of difficult sometimes. All lies of course, but I started thinking about how I gave you a hard time the other night and, okay, this isn't a concession or anything—"

"Of course not."

"I came here to say I'm sorry for accusing you of…abandoning your principles," she said solemnly. "Especially—"

"Considering I don't have any," Matthew said, beating her to the punch line. Laughing, he watched Sarah struggle to keep a straight face. "Give it up, Sarah. It's me, Matthew. You don't have to apologize for anything you say to me. You were simply expressing your opinion. Which is what I'd expect of you."

"You don't think I have a career in diplomacy? Or public relations?"

Matthew shook his head. "Sorry."

"But, I did kind of get on my soapbox and I'm—" she swallowed "—sor-sorry."

"I heard it." He glanced around the cafeteria. "Damn it. Where's the media when you need them? She apologized. Sarah Benedict apol—"

Sarah leaned over to slap her hand across his mouth. "I take it back. That word never left my mouth."

"Hey." He grabbed her wrist, brought it down to the table. Her sweater looked as if someone, not Sarah though, had knitted it. Her skin above the cuff was tanned, her wrist bony in his grasp. She looked up at him, her expression unreadable and then he released her and she withdrew her hand.

"Okay, so now's the part where you tell me you've thought things over and you're ready to join forces with me. Let's see, Doctors Benedict and Cameron, An Integrated Approach to Medical… Or are you going to insist that your name goes first?"

"Sarah." He sat back. "Look, I'm glad you came by. I felt bad the way we left things, but what I said before still holds. Maybe if I didn't have a daughter and… other responsibilities, I could entertain your idea. But I do."

"And I don't. Have kids and responsibilities, I mean. Which gives me the luxury of being able to entertain these foolish fancies. Is that what you're saying?"

"Damn it, Sarah." Two techs in blue scrubs passed the booth. One held a plate of enchiladas glistening with red sauce. Matthew took a breath. "I thought I'd already explained my posi—"

"You did." She looked directly at him. "And I apologize. Again. I guess I'd fantasized so much about how this whole thing would come about that I'd already made it into reality. Before I'd talked to you. I'm sorry. Truly. It's kind of taking a while for all the changes around here to sink in. My mom announced that she was selling her practice to CMS."

Matthew nodded.

She shot him a sideways look. "You knew that?"

"The hospital rumor mill is pretty efficient."

"I'm still struggling with that. My grandfather, my father, all these generations…and now she's just selling out to some anonymous conglomerate. I'm—"

"Speechless?" Her sudden flash of anger had abated, and he made a mental note to steer clear of professional issues. As he cast around for something to say, she grinned.

"Wanna do something?" she said, suddenly sounding like the ten-year-old Sarah he'd once known. "Go for a hike, ride bikes down Lopez Hook? Look for fossils?"

He tried to remember his schedule for the coming week. He was on call at least one day. And he'd promised Lucy something he could no longer recall until he checked his calendar. "Ah, let—"

"That's okay," Sarah said, her voice artificially bright. "You're busy, I know." She smiled. "Unlike me, unemployed and footloose—"

"Sarah, shut up. I'd love to do something, I'm just trying to remember what I have going. Let me check my schedule and talk to Lucy."

"I was thinking of driving out to Agate Beach," Sarah said. "There's this little girl in Nicaragua she was…probably about twelve. I used to tell her about the fossils. I promised I'd take some pictures for her. "

"She was one of your patients?"

"One of the girls in an orphanage. They were all my patients. Pepita was special though."

"I never asked you why you left."

"Difference of opinion with the people who ran the place. More and more bureaucracy. As much as I loved the girls, I could just see the way things were going. It was time for me to leave, to do something else. But I miss the children."

"You stay in contact with Pepita?"

Sarah nodded, her expression faraway. "Ted and I even discussed adopting her, but her birth mother fought it. The mother had fallen on hard times, which is why Pepita was in the orphanage, but the mother had first rights."

Matthew thought of a dozen things he wanted to ask her, but she'd retreated to that secret place again where questions felt like intrusions. And then as though a curtain had parted, Sarah was back again. "Remember when we got trapped by the tide at Agate Beach?"

"I know, I was just thinking about that. And that time you split your head open—"

"Trying to get away from you," Sarah said. "You were trying to make me eat seaweed."

"Why don't we all go to Agate Beach?" he suggested. "Checkout the tide pools. I think Lucy would enjoy that." But even as he spoke the words, he was imagining Lucy's reaction. As though he'd proposed a root canal sans anesthesia. "It would be educational for her," he said. "Left to her own devices, she'd spend all her time at the mall."

NOTHING WAS RESOLVED of course, but walking through the hospital lobby after seeing Matthew, Sarah couldn't stop smiling. She smiled at an old woman in a brown raincoat, smiled at a young mother holding the hands of a curly-haired toddler, smiled at the janitor. This feeling of happiness could get addictive, she thought as she walked out to her car. Just spilling her guts to Elizabeth, that surprised her no end, then actually confronting Matthew instead of just hiding out—which she would have done if Elizabeth hadn't suggested talking to him. It was like lancing a boil or something, letting all the poisonous feelings out. Maybe one of these days, she would tell him about Ted.

In the car, she dug out her cell phone and called Elizabeth at the restaurant. "If this is a bad time, I can call back," she said when Elizabeth answered, sounding distracted. "I just wanted to say thanks for the suggestion. About talking to Matthew, I mean. I did and I feel a whole lot better."

Elizabeth laughed. "Yeah, well, I can't always say I feel better after I've talked to him. Mostly he makes me feel like throwing a brick through the wall, but, hey, glad to be of help."

"I thought maybe I could buy you lunch?"

"Can't get away," Elizabeth said. "I *serve* lunch, remember? But call me, okay?"

ON THE WAY back to her apartment, Sarah stopped at her mother's house to pick up the rest of the boxes still stored in the basement. As she let herself in, an enormously fat tabby met her in the hallway and hissed at her. Since Rose had always professed to be allergic to cats, the cat was something of a surprise. It seemed to take an instant dislike to Sarah, hissing again as she moved past it.

"Listen, buddy," she told it, "I lived here before you did."

Undeterred, the cat followed her down the stairs but then largely ignored her for the next half hour as she sorted through the stack of boxes piled against one wall. She'd just opened one that contained some of the tools she'd collected during the year or so when she was deciding whether to go against family tradition and become a geologist instead of a physician when she heard Rose on the stairs. The cat rose from its noisy slumber to greet her.

"Where did he come from?" Sarah nodded in the cat's direction.

"He was down on the ferry dock, spitting at the

tourists. Fred at the chamber of commerce picked him up. They were going to take him to the pound. But—" she picked up the cat "—he has a sort of rascally charm, don't you think?"

"No." She eyed Rose, who was cradling the cat like a baby. "What's his name?"

"Deanna."

"Deanna?"

"I know, I know." Rose buried her face in the cat's fur. "But before him, I had this sweet kitten that I just adored and her name was Deanna. Unfortunately, she proved to be rather a slut. Ran off with the ginger tom that lived next door. Never saw either of them again. When this one came along, it seemed easier to give him the same name. When he misbehaves though, I just call him Cat."

"I never thought of you as a cat person." Sarah hauled a box down from the shelf and sat on the floor to open it.

"What are you looking for?" Rose asked.

"Collecting things for a fossil-hunting expedition." She looked under an old ski sweater she vaguely remembered from her childhood. "Eureka. A rock hammer!" She held it up to show Rose. "Remember that?" She dug into the box again. "And here's my ice pick and sledgehammer."

"Lovely," Rose said. "Shall I pack you some freeze-dried meals? Maybe a little caribou jerky."

"Would you?" Sarah stood and wiped her hands down the sides of her jeans. "I'm sure it would go down well with Matthew's daughter."

"Spoiled child, that one," Rose said tartly. "Elizabeth brought her in for acne treatment. "Quite the little princess."

Sarah absorbed that piece of information, wondered whether Matthew contributed to the spoiling. What had Elizabeth said about her being a daddy's girl? A vague unease settled in, clouding the prospect of the outing. Maybe she wasn't ready for Matthew, the doting daddy. Matthew and Elizabeth's daughter, flesh-and-blood proof that ultimately Matthew had chosen Elizabeth. Even if it hadn't worked out.

"I said," Rose's voice filled the basement, "what about Matthew's daughter?"

"Oh." Sarah shook her head, clearing her thoughts. "Well, we're all going to Agate Beach."

"Why?"

"Because they're there." As she grabbed the sledgehammer, she knocked over of an adjacent box. The silver sandals she'd worn when she married Ted fell out. "Damn it." She picked up the left one, threw it back in the box, tossed the other one in, sealed the box and hauled it back onto the shelf. "Why do you keep all this stuff anyway?"

"Why did you send it back, anyway?" Rose mimicked her tone. "I'd assumed it had some significance to you." She rubbed her hands together. "Well, I'm starving and it's freezing down here." She started up the stairs, Sarah following her. In the kitchen, she watched as Rose opened a can and dumped the contents into a bowl, which she then put in the microwave.

Sara picked up the empty can. "SpaghettiOs? You didn't tell me you were having a dinner party."

"Deanna enjoys them," Rose said. "And so do I."

"Yeah, why slave over a hot stove?" Sarah crossed her eyes at Deanna and the cat darted under the table.

"So." Rose pulled out a chair and sat down. "Matthew won't play. Now what?"

Sarah leaned against the sink. "Could you please not use that tone of voice? I am not ten and Matthew and I are not talking about building camps in the woods. To answer what I think was your question, Matthew isn't interested in joining me, which means I have to look at other options."

"You could make things a lot easier for yourself if you just called CMS tomorrow. Probably start work Monday."

"No, thanks. I'd rather flip burgers."

Rose shrugged. "Want to stay for dinner? I picked up some pad thai."

"Antibiotics should clear it right up."

Rose shook her head. "God, you're like your father."

"Actually, I meant to go to the library." Sarah grabbed an envelope from the table, which was littered with newspapers, napkins with notes scrawled over them, grocery receipts and medical journals. Although Matthew had only mentioned tide pools, Agate Beach was also a great fossil-hunting area. Maybe Lucy would enjoy that. On the back of the envelope, she made a list of other things they'd need: crowbar, chisels, ice pick, a camera, tape measure. Notebooks, of course.

Glimpsing at the list, Rose inquired, "You'll be gone for one month, or two?"

"Have you ever been fossil hunting?" Sarah asked.

"God, no."

"Then don't mock what you don't understand." She made a mental note to discuss rags, paper towels and newspapers to wrap the fossils in when she called Matthew later. "D'you think the library's still open? I'd like to pick up a couple of books. Maps, too."

"Why are *you* making such a production of this?" Rose asked. "She's a kid. Take her to the beach, let her run around and call it a day."

"This will be educational, as well as fun."

"Maybe the girl would rather *just* have fun," Rose said mildly. "By the way, I was also going through some of those old boxes." She reached for something on top of the refrigerator, then handed Sarah a notebook. Across the front, carefully printed in neat black lettering, it read: Sarah Benedict's Book of Ideal Qualities.

"Look at page one," Rose directed her.

Sarah felt her face color. Under the heading Ideal Qualities of The Perfect Man it listed the qualities he should possess. *Handsome, Friendly, Loyal and Trustworthy.* She'd underlined *trustworthy.* In the back of the book, something Rose probably hadn't discovered, was a small envelope glued to the last page. Inside was a picture of Matthew.

She looked up to find Rose watching her.

"By the way, chapter two lists the Ideal Qualities

of a Perfect Mother," Rose said. "Didn't recognize myself anywhere."

Sarah pushed her hair behind her ears. "Did you think you were perfect?"

"No," Rose said. "In most families, there's only room for one perfect individual. You'd clearly assumed that title, I decided not to fight it."

CHAPTER SEVEN

ELIZABETH SIPPED her margarita. She loved margaritas. George had taken her to Fidel's, Port Hamilton's only Mexican restaurant. The food wasn't as good as the Mexican food she remembered from her childhood in L.A., but for Port Hamilton it was okay. Plus, after serving up food all day, it was nice having someone wait on her. And she really liked George. Enough that she'd started waiting for the phone to ring, obsessing about the weekends. He was a musician, too. She had this thing for musicians.

Where's your daughter tonight?" he asked.

Elizabeth eyed him over the top of her glass. He had a goatee, which made him look slightly devilish. She liked devilish. "Sleeping at her best friend's house. Then tomorrow, my ex is picking her up."

George grinned. Under the table, she felt his foot touch hers. She smiled back even though the idea of taking her clothes off in front of him freaked her out. She'd turn off the lights, she decided. Light candles. Wear this long silky robe she'd picked up at Gottschalks. Get him drunk on champagne.

"So—" he was still smiling "—how'd your day go?"

"Pretty good. This friend, well, she isn't really a friend…but we grew up together and then she went off to Central America. She's a doctor." She saw George's eyes widen slightly, just like they had when they first met and she'd told him Matt was a doctor. "Anyway, she came into the restaurant. She didn't know I worked there and…it was kind of nice. We had this long talk."

George leaned back in his chair. Candlelight flickered on his face. "Yeah?"

"I was all bummed out about Lucy and…" She laughed. "It's strange, I can't even remember what Sarah said, but after she left, I felt a whole lot better."

"Huh," he said. "Interesting."

"It was," Elizabeth said, disappointed. People usually said *interesting* when they meant just the opposite. "Sarah's… I mean, she's not like me. She's very smart."

"You don't think you're smart?"

"Well." She bit her lip. "I don't think I'm *not* smart. It's a different kind of smart, I guess." She licked some of the salt off the rim of her glass. "She and my ex used to be good friends."

"They're both doctors," George said. "They would be."

"Even before that," Elizabeth said. "It was as if they had this secret world together. They thought the same way, laughed at the same jokes. But they were just friends…"

"Right." George smirked. "Typical chick thing to say. Guys are never *just* friends with women. They always want something."

"I don't think it was that way with them," she said, but he was still smirking as if she was naive. "It's hard to explain—"

"Is she attractive?"

Elizabeth considered. "Well, she's…I don't know. The intellectual type. No makeup, that sort of thing." She drained her margarita. "That was good."

"Want another one?" When she nodded, he waved his empty glass at the waitress. "She probably had the hots for your ex," he said after he'd ordered more drinks. "But he went for the best-looking woman."

"Thanks." Elizabeth smiled. "I did used to be good-looking."

"Still are," George said. "You're just carrying a few extra pounds, is all. I like that. Can't stand skin and bones."

"Then you wouldn't find Sarah attractive," Elizabeth said.

"Probably wouldn't." He stared into her eyes. "So your daughter's gone for a couple of days, huh?"

GEORGE WAS ALREADY IN BED and Elizabeth was in the bathroom wearing the silky robe and dabbing on perfume when the phone rang. She tied her belt, ran into the bedroom and answered it on the second ring.

"Lucy?"

"No. It's Sarah. Sorry to call so late. I tried to call Matthew, but he was at the hospital. Anyway, we're taking Lucy to Agate Beach tomorrow—"

"Fossils?" Elizabeth sat on the edge of the bed where

George was lying on top of the spread, naked. She felt his toes dig in under her thighs. She smiled at him, but moved farther away because it didn't seem right to be doing that sort of thing while she was talking about Lucy.

"…anyway, I just wanted to make sure Lucy has boots."

Elizabeth thought for a minute. "She's got this cute pair with fake fur around the tops and—"

"We're going to be in the water," Sarah said. "Actually, I might have an old pair that would fit her. She's about a size seven, right? If you have a pen, I also have a few other things she'll need…"

Elizabeth tried to think where a pen might be. George's toes had found the opening in her robe and were wriggling around in a sensitive area. She frowned at him, although she really didn't want him to stop. "Okay, found one," she lied. "Go ahead."

Later, as Elizabeth snuggled up to George's back—he'd started snoring five minutes after he pulled out—Elizabeth couldn't stop thinking about Sarah and how upset she'd been about whatever it was she'd said to Matthew. The difference between Sarah and herself was that she herself was like some uncomplicated kid's toy, wind it up and it chugs merrily along, but Sarah was like a difficult jigsaw puzzle. You always had to look at little pieces from different angles trying to fit them into the picture. Sometimes you'd think a piece was going to fit and you'd try to make it fit, but it wouldn't and you'd get frustrated and want to just knock the whole thing to the floor.

Still, it was good talking to Sarah. Except, knowing her daughter, she was pretty sure Lucy did not want to spend a day climbing over rocks. George moved in his sleep, reached back and patted her thigh. She smiled against his back. It felt good to hold someone again.

ON THE MORNING of the beach trip, Matthew woke before the alarm clock, which he'd set half an hour earlier than he usually got up. Sarah had left a message the night before.

"I just checked the tide tables," she'd said. "Low tide is at ten-fifteen and, if I remember correctly, it's a couple of hours' drive to Agate Beach. So we need to leave no later than eight. Oh, Lucy might enjoy looking for fossils. She'll need boots. Okay, never mind, I'll check with Elizabeth… Hey, Matthew. You think Lucy will like me? I'm not exactly a kid person…well, that's not true. The girls at Saint Julia's liked me, but…okay. I'm going to shut up. Good night, Matthew."

And then she'd left a second message. "Hey, I just wanted to say I'm glad we're doing this. Okay, now I'll really shut up. Good night again."

Matthew had played the messages twice, smiling as he listened to her. Talking fast, rapid burst of words. Just as she'd always spoken, he remembered, when she was nervous. It had been after midnight by the time he got home from the hospital, too late to call her. Although, knowing Sarah, the time wouldn't have mattered.

He lay with his hands behind his head. Lucy was still

at her friend Sierra's house where she'd spent the night. He'd left a message with Sierra's mother that he'd be by at seven to pick up his daughter. She'd laughed and said something about that being the middle of the night as far as kids were concerned. He'd said nothing about the beach expedition. He rehearsed his response to Lucy's inevitable protest. "Lulu, you need to do more than hang out at the mall. We live in one of the most beautiful areas in the Northwest and it's time we started taking advantage of it."

After a while he became aware of a new sound. Rain beating against the window. He dragged himself out of bed and shuffled downstairs to make coffee. It was not an auspicious start. He turned on the TV. The rain would clear, the relentlessly cheerful announcer informed him. He showered and dressed, then made two fried-egg sandwiches.

"Why couldn't we just go to McDonalds?" Lucy complained when he presented her with the sandwich, doubled wrapped in foil to keep it warm.

"This is just like McDonalds," he said, biting into his as they drove. "I even put cheese on it. And it's better for you."

Lucy, cocooned in a red goose-down coat, her hair hidden under a square hood, took a cautious bite. Then another.

Matthew shot her a sideways glance. "Good?"

"It's okay." She flipped the hood of her jacket, shook out her hair and turned to look at him. "So what's going on? How come we had to leave so early?"

"We're going to Agate Beach," Matthew said. "To check out tide pools."

"Huh?"

Matthew explained the day's itinerary, trying to make it sound every bit as exciting as a trip to the mall. Lucy's expression told him he'd failed. "You'll enjoy it," he said with more conviction than he felt. "There's a lot to see. Starfish, sand bars." He reached out to ruffle her hair. "Come on, Lulu."

"But I don't get it," she said as he parked outside Sarah's apartment. "Why do we have to do this?"

"I already explained." Matthew saw Sarah at the window as though she'd been watching for them. Knowing Sarah, she probably had been. A moment later, the front door opened and she appeared wearing a yellow oilskin slicker, black boots and carrying a large canvas bag. He smiled. A blue felt hat and she'd look like the Paddington Bear he'd once tucked into Lucy's crib. "Remember you were asking me about Sarah? Well, you're going to get a chance to meet her."

MATTHEW'S DAUGHTER LOOKED just as she had in the picture Elizabeth had shown her. Glossy dark hair, green eyes, a rosiness to her cheeks that, as it used to with Elizabeth, reminded Sarah of Disney's version of Snow White. But while Lucy had been smiling in the picture, the Lucy who greeted her from the backseat of the car, huddled into a bulky red parka, just barely managed to be civil.

"I've heard so much about you," Sarah said as she

reached to shake Lucy's hand. "And your dad was right, you look just like your mother."

Lucy frowned and met Matthew's eyes in the rear-view mirror.

"Sarah means when your mother was your age." Matthew started up the car and winked at Sarah. "Right, trooper?"

"MOM GOT the wrong socks for me," Lucy said some thirty minutes later. "I told her the kind I wanted and she got these weird ones."

"What kind did you want?" Matthew asked.

"The kind that wick the moisture off your skin. They have them in Brown's Outdoor, but they were ten dollars and Mom said that was too much."

"You know, I think I saw the kind you mean at Goodwill." Sarah turned to look at Lucy. "It's amazing how people buy stuff like that, spend a bunch of money on it and then decide they don't really need it after all. Lucky for us though, we can pick it up for a fraction of the price."

Lucy smiled politely.

You're talking too much, Sarah told herself. Shut up. Don't try to ingratiate yourself. Be cool. Looking at Lucy, she had the oddest sense of talking to the old Elizabeth. But unlike Elizabeth who, despite her formidable beauty, was always sweet and kind, Lucy had clearly been brought up to believe that she was the center of the universe. She's just a kid, Sarah reminded herself after Lucy had continued to complain about the socks.

"When I was in Nicaragua," she said when Lucy finally ran out, "I met this woman who was probably about my age, but she lived in a grass hut and washed her clothes in a stream."

Matthew shot her a glance, no doubt guessing where the story was going. Lucy seemed to be watching his face in the rearview mirror. Or watching her own, Sarah couldn't tell.

"Anyway," she forged on, "I started wondering what it would be to live like that, to have nothing—"

"Pretty hard for you to imagine that, huh, Lulu?" Matthew asked.

Lucy rolled her eyes.

"But the point is, I could see this woman was eyeing my backpack. I'd just bought it to go on the trip and it was really expensive, but I figured it would be like winning the lottery for her to have something like that so I thought, what the hey. I was just about to unstrap it, when she looked at me and shook her head. Then she asked me what it was like to have to carry such a heavy load around all day."

Lucy smiled faintly.

"*She* felt sorry for *me*," Sarah elaborated, not sure whether Lucy had understood the point.

"What d'you think about that, Lucy?" Matthew asked.

"I don't know," she replied, an edge of irritation in her tone.

"It must have been quite a culture shock for you, coming back here after all those years away," Matthew said. "Not that Port Hamilton is exactly a thriving metropolis."

"No, but you're right." Sarah turned back in her seat, grateful that at least Matthew seemed interested. "Even in a town the size of Port Hamilton, the quantity and variety of things you can buy is amazing."

"Port Hamilton needs a mall," Lucy said.

Matthew chuckled, then reached into the backseat to squeeze her knee.

Sarah felt oddly defeated. Reading the newspaper yesterday, she'd found herself turning from an article about the Manila slums, where mothers supported families with garbage salvaged from a dump, to an ad for Ikea. Worse, she'd been reading both with roughly the same degree of involvement. Maybe I should just volunteer for the Philippines, she'd thought. Or maybe I should buy some candles, some new sheets. Invite Matthew over. No, she had a better shot in the Philippines. If there was even an outside chance Matthew might reconsider the practice idea, complicating it with a personal relationship would be disastrous. If he'd made up his mind to join Compassionate Medical Systems, she still had all the work of setting up the practice, but without Matthew. Complications enough. Besides, she hadn't picked up the slightest hint that Matthew saw her as anything other than a friend.

Which, all things considered, was probably a good thing.

"Daddy, when we get home, can I stay the night at Brittany's?"

"We'll see," Matthew said.

"Daddy, can I see if your cell phone works out here?"

Matthew handed it back to her. "How did we ever get along without cell phones?" he asked Sarah with a grin.

"Pigeons," she said. "Remember?"

"Oh, right, but I always hated the mess they made. The way they'd poop on your hands when you were trying to retrieve a message."

"Oh, gross," Lucy said.

"Sarah taught her pigeon to play the piano," Matthew said. "Chopin, Beethoven. Her pigeon was much smarter than mine."

"Shut up, Dad." Lucy punched his shoulder. "You're crazy."

Sarah glanced at her watch. The rain hadn't let up and she was getting a headache. They still had a good forty-five minutes to go, which meant they'd miss low tide. Less beach to search on but, given the rain, it probably didn't matter a whole lot. She thought of the box of hammers and tools and shovels and God knows what that she'd carefully assembled. Matthew had loaded them into his car as Lucy looked on.

"How come we need all that stuff?" she'd asked.

Sarah tried to think of something to say, but nothing came to mind. Earlier, trying to fill what felt like a suffocating silence, she'd launched into a rambling explanation about the Mesozoic period. She'd intended it as an introduction to the dinosaurs—something she was sure Lucy would find interesting. Nerves had sidetracked her into a lengthy discourse on how the continents were formed and, even though she could see that Lucy was struggling to keep her eyes open, she hadn't been able to stop talking. She now gazed through the streaming passenger window at the stands of dark pines, at the relentless rain. Lucy was wearing some kind of perfumed cream that smelled like apples. She could smell her own wool sweater. The scents filled her nose, mixed with the stuffy warm smell of three bodies in a small space. She rolled down her window a crack, felt the rush of cool, wet air, then quickly closed it, afraid she might get Lucy wet.

Lucy didn't like her. But maybe Lucy didn't like any women Matthew was involved with. Except she wasn't involved with Matthew. Pepita had liked her though. All the girls at Saint Julia's Orphanage had liked her. Fighting for her attention, hanging on her hands. Resting their heads on her lap. Why could she talk to them and not to Matthew's daughter? The easy explanation was that Lucy reminded her of Elizabeth. But, come on, she wasn't that petty. Was she? Maybe it was *wanting* Lucy to like her.

Standing at the window that morning, waiting for Matthew and Lucy to arrive she'd felt as if she was waiting for a first date. She'd paced the room, changed from a navy parka that struck her as drab into a bright red one before deciding that wouldn't be warm enough and putting the navy one back on again. She'd added a scarf for color. And then because of the rain, she'd added the yellow slicker.

She glanced at her watch again.

"Only five minutes since the last time you looked." Matthew squeezed her shoulder. "Relax."

Sarah smiled. The gray skies seemed to lighten just a bit. They'd turned onto the road that ran along the coast and, through the pines, she caught glimpses of the ocean. "See that formation over there?" She scooted around in her seat to look at Lucy who was now in communion with her video game. "That tall pile of rocks?" Sarah gestured at the rugged seashore outside the window. "Formations like that are called stacks and they form when part of the headland is eroded."

"You know what *erosion* means, Lulu?" Matthew asked.

"Like when the sea washes stuff away?"

"Exactly." Sarah beamed at her. "Stacks also form when a natural arch collapses due to subaerial processes and gravity."

Matthew cleared his throat.

"What?"

He smiled. "Nothing."

"Was I rambling on too long?" she asked.

"That's okay," Lucy said.

"See, when a stack collapses or erodes, it leaves a stump. Or sometimes it leaves this small island, like that one over there." She pointed again.

"What's a headland?" Lucy asked.

"It's a piece of rocky land that juts out into the sea." Sarah smiled, feeling encouraged. *She likes me, she really likes me.* "You've heard of the Rock of Gibraltar, right?"

Lucy gave her a blank look.

"Sure you have," Matthew said. "Remember when we all went to Spain? That big rock—"

"Oh, yeah," Lucy said. "Cool."

"Interesting, Sarah," Matthew said.

"Can we get something to eat soon?" Lucy asked.

"It's early for lunch," Matthew said.

"Stacks are important sites for nesting seabirds," Sarah said, trying to regain Lucy's attention. "They're also ideal for rock climbing. Your dad and I used to have these great adventures rock climbing."

"We did." Matthew looked at Lucy in the rearview mirror. "Those are the kind of experiences you remember years later."

"Dad, really. I'm *so* hungry."

"I made sandwiches," Sarah said. "Two kinds. Goat cheese with red bell peppers on whole-wheat bread and—"

"Sounds good," Matthew said with a tad too much enthusiasm. "Right, Lu?"

Sarah sat back in her seat. Rose had stopped by while she was making the sandwiches. "Hardly kid's stuff," she'd said. "But you know best." Which Rose obviously didn't believe and, Sarah could see now, was obviously not true.

"Or…I don't know, it's kind of cold," Matthew said. "Remember that beach café that made really great clam chowder?"

"Yeah, let's go there," Lucy said, showing enthusiasm for the first time that morning.

"Hey, Sarah," Matthew said. "What about that rock formation just west of Agate Beach? One of the rocks was like a little cave, remember that?"

"I used to hole up in it," Sarah said.

"I wonder if it's still there…"

"One way to find out," Sarah said, and Matthew turned to smile at her.

"Dad," Lucy said, "I am seriously hungry."

"Let's put it to a vote," Matthew said. "I say rock formation, then lunch. Sarah?"

"I'm starving," Sarah lied. "Guess you lose, Matthew."

CHAPTER EIGHT

THE RAIN FINALLY STOPPED and by the time they'd had lunch, burgers for Lucy, clam chowder for him and Sarah—he'd been quite willing to eat her sandwiches, but she'd insisted—a few anemic sunbeams were illuminating the gloom. Encouraged by the break in the weather, they'd hiked a mile or so along a wooded trail, then clambered over barnacle- and mussel-encrusted rocks to check out the tide pools. But as they'd crouched on the rocks watching a hermit crab wind its way through ribbons of pale green seaweed, Lucy had grown bored and announced she was going off by herself to look for shells. He could see her red coat, a splash of color against the muted seascape.

"I guess my expectations were unrealistic," he said.

"About?"

"You and Lucy." He kept his eyes on his daughter's back. "You're not exactly getting along like a house on fire."

"Oh, come on. I'm this woman she doesn't know from Adam." Sarah's voice was heated. "She gets dragged along on some cockamamy trip with… Did you even ask her if she wanted to do this?"

"No."

She turned her head to look at him. "Figures."

"In my defense," he said, "I did think it would be good for her to do something other than shop." He straightened his legs. "And I wanted you two to meet each other. Elizabeth's always telling me I spoil her. I decided this time, instead of letting her choose, I'd set the agenda."

"It's a difficult concept to imagine," Sarah said thoughtfully. "Being spoiled. With Rose I tended to feel like a small and less intelligent adult she'd been stuck with but that she was trying to make the best of it."

"She used to intimidate me," Matthew said.

"She intimidated everyone. Once, she told me that my father died of a heart attack because he really wanted to leave her, but didn't have the guts to just walk out."

Matthew could hardly remember her father, a quiet, mild-mannered man, because his memories of Rose were so vivid. Sarah had baked a cake for, maybe, his tenth birthday. She'd called him over to her house on some pretext and it had been there on the kitchen table. Lopsided, frosted before it cooled sufficiently—Rose had pointed this out—but the first birthday cake he'd ever had. He'd hardly blown out the candles though before Sarah slipped into a gloomy funk. It was hideous, overcooked, revolting, on and on. And he'd imagined then, as he often did, a bird, a big black raven, perched on Sarah's shoulder, berating and judging her and continually finding her wanting. And he'd wonder what it was like being Sarah.

Today, at this very moment, he suspected it wasn't a whole lot of fun. The thought made him feel protective toward her. With any other woman he might have put his arm around her shoulders, pulled her close. But with Sarah, the simple gesture would turn complicated, require an explanation. He could hear her. *So you're feeling sorry for me?*

Down at the water's edge, Lucy was holding up a long strand of seaweed, her face in three-quarters profile, the wind tossing her dark hair.

"She looks like Elizabeth," Sarah said.

"Her personality's more like Elizabeth's, too," he replied. "She's creative and impulsive. Unlike me."

Sarah said nothing but, somehow, the silence spoke volumes.

Something wasn't working about the day. The chemistry was all wrong. He'd envisioned Lucy and Sarah forming this instant bond, chattering away about girl stuff, teasing him for being a guy. Instead, Lucy had hardly said two words and Sarah was most un-Sarah-like.

"So what happened with you and Elizabeth?" Sarah broke the silence to ask.

"Oh…" He considered the question. "We probably shouldn't have got married in the first place. We're very different. We tried to make things work, mostly because of Lucy, but it just didn't happen. Sometimes you just have to face reality." It might have been the moment to ask about her husband, but she felt closed off to him, contained.

"Do you see a lot of her…Lucy?"

"As much as I can. It was difficult for her after the divorce. I carried—carry—my share of guilt. You know how my childhood was. I swore I wouldn't impose that on my own kids, but…"

She smiled faintly. "I still can't quite get used to the idea of you being a daddy. How did we get to be so old?"

"Happens while you're not looking," Matthew said. "One minute you've got your whole life ahead of you, the next you're middle-aged."

The fog had slowly rolled in as they spoke, obscuring the horizon and the distant pines on either side of where they sat. Through it, he could just make out Lucy's red jacket as she walked toward them cupping something in her hands. He stood, reached for Sarah's hand to pull her up.

"Let's go see what treasures Lucy has discovered."

But as they walked down to the water, Sarah stopped to examine a shell and he walked on alone. By the time he reached Lucy and turned back to look at Sarah, he could barely make her out in the drifting fog.

"I WAS JUST THINKING about you," Curt Hudelson said when Sarah stopped by his stall at the Saturday farmer's market. "I went to an alternative-medicine seminar last week. Some of the things I heard there reminded me of your plan. What's happening with it?"

Sarah picked up a bunch of kale, feigned close inspection. "It... There's been a set back." She'd deliberately avoided Matthew in the week since the Colossal Fossil Failure, as she'd taken to thinking of it. "Someone I was hoping would be a key part of it isn't interested." She set the kale down, looked at Curt. "So now I'm doing some rethinking."

"Hold on." He bagged some red potatoes the size of marbles, handed the bag over to a man in a cloth cap. "Steam them, then eat them with chopped parsley," he said. "Good for the circulatory system." He turned back to Sarah. "Rethinking what?"

"The whole idea," Sarah said before she'd had a chance to choose her words. "Maybe Port Hamilton isn't really the place for it."

"You're wrong." Curt's pale eyes gleamed. "Port Hamilton is exactly the place for it. It's up to you and me—people who don't believe big medicine has all the answers—to fight the cancer that's spreading across the peninsula."

"Cancer?" Sarah fought back a grin. There was something almost evangelical about his fervor. Not difficult to imagine him in a preacher's pulpit. "You wouldn't be talking about Compassionate Medical Systems?"

"Compassionate Medical Systems!" He almost spit the words. "Let's see how compassionate they are when it comes to those who don't have the money to pay. Down where Debbi and I live on the west end of the peninsula. People in trailers and manufactured homes.

Men who used to work for the mill. My neighbor, for example. He lost his job, lost his home in town so he moved out where it's cheaper, but he's got no car, no money. I'll be interested to see how compassionate the system is when guys like him drop by for a visit."

"Hey." Debbi appeared at his side, smiled at Sarah then turned to Curt. "That woman with the bread stall needs help hauling boxes. I told her you'd go down and give her a hand."

"Off to do my Tarzan act." He pantomimed a show of strength, then fixed Sarah with another of his laser-eyed looks. "Port Hamilton needs you. The *world* needs you," he intoned theatrically.

Debbi rolled her eyes after he left. "He can be kind of fanatical, in case you didn't pick that up. I mean, he's got some good ideas, but sometimes he's over the top." She hesitated, her tentative manner in dramatic contrast to Curt's intensity. "I just made up that excuse to get rid of him, I wanted to talk to you alone. Do you have a minute?"

Sarah stepped aside to allow a woman in a navy parka to inspect a basket of mushrooms. "Sure."

"I took Alli to the E.R. a few weeks ago. Dr. Cameron saw her. He said she needs tests to see if she has kidney disease, but Curt keeps telling me it's just an allergy. I'm giving his herbal supplements another try, but…" She shrugged. "We'll see."

Sarah nodded. She'd seen enough examples of the power of natural healing not to scoff at the idea, but if the child did have kidney disease, she was probably going to need more than herbal remedies.

"I went to the library to look up stuff about kidney disease on the Internet. What really freaks me out is surgery. My mom died having surgery she didn't need."

"Well, it might not come to that," Sarah said. "That's probably why Matt—Dr. Cameron—wants her to come in for tests. Just to make sure."

Debbi nodded. "But I'm also worried about the Compassionate Medical Systems thing—what Curt was talking about. I'm scared that if they get their hands on her, they'll make me agree to surgery. Call me an unfit mother if I refuse."

"So," Sarah pressed, trying to see where Debbi was headed, "you're not completely comfortable with Curt's plan, but you don't entirely trust the alternative?"

Debbi nodded, clearly relieved at being understood. "What you were saying to Curt about the kind of things you wanted to do. That's what I want for Alli."

"You want me to have a look at her," Sarah said, a statement rather than a question. She dug into her purse for a business card, scribbled a number on the back. "Look, I'm licensed to practice here in Washington." She laughed. "I just don't have a practice yet." Or a place to practice, or equipment or a business plan. "Call me," she told Debbi. "We'll work something out."

"CURT IS DEFINITELY over the top," Elizabeth agreed when Sarah recounted the exchange over coffee at Mombassa that afternoon. "Debbi used to be a waitress here and he'd come in and pick her up. She used to hide her inhaler at work because she needed it for her asthma, but Curt would have a fit if he saw her using it."

Sarah nodded, remembering the almost fanatical look in his eyes. "Too bad, because a lot of what he said made sense." She stirred her coffee. "I think I might take on Debbi's daughter as my first patient."

Elizabeth smiled broadly, clinked her coffee cup against Sarah's. "Fantastic." She leaned across the table. "This is so great, Sarah. Even though I thought Matthew should go with CMS, I was still disappointed because, well, he had all these ideals—"

"He also had his reasons," Sarah broke in, not wanting to hear Elizabeth echo her own accusation that Matthew had sold out. "Matthew still has ideals. He's still a great doctor." She picked up her coffee cup, then caught Elizabeth's smirk. "And I'm not defending him because there's anything going on between us—"

"Damn," Elizabeth said. "I'm disappointed."

"Don't be. We're friends. But back to my first patient. Here's my plan. The new and revised version. I'll set up the practice here in town, hang out a shingle—"

"Where?"

She smiled. "Haven't figured that out yet."

"I can look around for you," Elizabeth said. "In fact, if you need an office manager—correction, when you need an office manager, receptionist, general gofer— I'm officially applying for the job."

"You've got it," Sarah said. "But don't talk to me about salary, at least not yet."

"I'm not exactly rolling in the dough waiting tables."

Elizabeth dipped a piece of biscotti in her coffee. "I am so stoked that you want to do this, Sarah. I mean, it seems like everything is falling into place. I was telling some friends about you going to Central America and taking care of patients down there and they said that what they really need is a doctor who would make house calls."

"House calls." Sarah stared at her. "That could be the answer, at least for now." She'd clipped an article from the *Seattle Times* just the week before about a physician in eastern Washington who'd decided to buck the trend and start an old-fashioned practice. No insurance companies—too time-consuming and it raises overhead—no paperwork. Strictly cash. And house calls. Maybe ten a week. Payment on the spot. The whole point was to keep the costs low and the services affordable. Her own version of that would include the integrated-medicine component. Deep in thought, she realized Elizabeth was watching her across the table. "What?"

"I was thinking about money. I mean, these people don't have any."

Sarah nodded, holding her mug in both hands, savoring the warmth. Spring had made a tentative appearance on the peninsula; daffodils bloomed in grassy roadside strips and pale green leaves covered tree branches, but the sun was deceptive and she inevitably ended up dressing too lightly for the weather. "I'm not in this to make a lot of money," she said. "I saved a little while I was in Central America. My dad left me some. It's enough to get started."

"When are you going to tell Matthew?" Elizabeth asked. "Or are you going to tell him?"

"Don't know," Sarah said. "To either of those questions. Right now, I have a million other things to think about."

MATTHEW HAD BEEN PAGED to the E.R. at around midnight. At two in the morning he'd started for home, but the fog was so thick it all but obscured the streetlights, creating a ghostly aura that would have been great for Halloween, except that it was mid-March and more of the same was forecast.

Socked-in fog was bad news on the peninsula.

The night before, he'd decided it wasn't worth going home and was napping on a couch in pediatrics when his beeper went off again. Car accident on 101, head injury. Fog had precluded flying the victim to Seattle.

As he'd walked down to the E.R., he'd imagined a conversation with Sarah. "While your ideals are all very well, this gets old. With CMS, there would be a trauma surgeon on call. The fog wouldn't be an issue."

But even as he'd worked up righteous indignation, he'd remembered her face after he'd dropped her off following the fossil trip. The same closed-off look, her voice with the same brittle quality.

"She's not very friendly," Lucy had remarked.

"You just have to get to know her," he'd said.

Now, thoughts of Lucy receding, he examined the young girl who lay drugged but conscious on a stretcher in the middle of the room, squinting against the bright overhead light. A nurse was adjusting the monitors that traced her heartbeat and respiration.

Matthew leaned over so that the girl did not have to turn to see his face. Her eyes were open and she looked responsive and alert. An X-ray tech at one end of the room fitted a newly developed picture of the skull into a manila folder and placed it next to the chart on a steel table. On the floor lay a brown paper bag with the clothes she'd been wearing.

After he'd examined her, he stepped out into the hallway to talk to the family and found them huddled in a corner of the waiting area across from the emergency room. Straight-backed chairs against cinderblock walls. Compassionate Medical Systems would have to be an improvement.

He finished reassuring them about their daughter, grabbed a few hours' sleep then, groggy and in need of coffee, he started down the corridor and ran into Sarah.

CHAPTER NINE

"YOU LOOK LIKE HELL," she told him. It had been over a week since the trip to Agate Beach, a week absorbed in the million and one details of setting up a practice. Long days and sleepless nights and still she had to look very closely to determine that she'd actually made any progress. On the other hand, she'd been too preoccupied to obsess about her relationship, or lack thereof, with Matthew. But now, although she'd sought him out on strictly professional terms, his gaunt appearance and shadowed eyes produced a rush of feeling she hadn't anticipated. "Seriously, are you okay?"

"Slept here last night." He ran his hand through his hair. "And the night before. I'm thinking of giving up my condo. Why do I need it?" He yawned. "What's up?"

"I need to talk to you about something." His eyes looked tired but very blue. She took a step backward. "A patient of yours."

"Okay." A moment's hesitation. "I was headed for a bite. Want to join me?"

"I'll even buy," she said.

In the cafeteria, the woman dishing out scrambled eggs and biscuits did a double take when she saw Sarah. "Aren't you Rose Benedict's daughter?"

"Yep. And you're…" The woman, who had worked there for years, used to serve her up extra portions of hash browns when she'd come in with Rose. "Betty."

"You could have just read her name tag," Matthew observed.

"Don't give him any food," Sarah told Betty, relieved that despite his obvious fatigue Matthew's sense of humor was still intact.

"So what are you doing these days?" Betty asked.

"Big plans in the works," Sarah replied.

"Sarah's always working on something," Matthew said. "Usually a way to improve the world."

"Too bad I haven't had time to start on you," Sarah shot back. He was fine, she decided.

"I heard about your husband," Betty said. "Sorry about that."

"Thanks." Sarah experienced the usual discomfort involved in not knowing quite how to respond to condolences. "He was definitely too young to die." A lame response, she thought, hearing the words. Is anyone ever the right age to die?

"You've never talked about Ted," Matthew said after they'd carried their trays over to a corner booth. "I just met him briefly when you came home after the wedding, but…"

"He was sweet and kind," Sarah said. "A good person." She started attacking her food, aware of Matthew watching her. Three years had dulled the pain of Ted's death, but it was still difficult to talk about him. Especially to Matthew. "You know, you married the wrong man," Ted had told her more than once, usually after she'd finished describing some shared escapade with Matthew, and she'd always reply that she and Matthew had been friends, nothing more. Ted had never seemed convinced. She drank some coffee. "Actually, I'm here in an official capacity."

"Let me put my official face on." Matthew affected an expression of extreme attention, leaning across the table, his eyes intent on her face. "There."

"You have egg on your lip." Sarah resisted the urge to reach over and remove it.

He wiped his mouth with a napkin. "Official egg, though."

"Okay, we can do this for—" she glanced at her watch "—another two seconds, then all jokes are off."

"Shoot." He drank some coffee. "Poor choice of words. Speak."

"It's about one of your patients. Debbi Kennedy's daughter, Alli." She saw the hesitation in his expression. "It's okay, Debbi gave me her permission to talk to you."

"I'm assuming you have a license to practice in the state of Washington?" Matthew asked, mock serious still.

"From beauty school."

"That'll work."

"Seriously." She set down her fork. "Debbi said you told her the baby needs surgery."

"I said she needed to come in to have tests," Matthew said. "I suspect she's going to need a kidney transplant. The tests would confirm that. Unfortunately, she seems to pay more attention to her boyfriend's medical advice."

Sarah nodded. "I've met them both. He's an organic farmer and—

"Crackpot," Matthew said.

"I didn't say that."

"You didn't have to. He's well-known around town. Last year he led a crowd of protesters against a condo project on the old Dungeness Highway. As I recall, he ended up in jail."

"He has strong convictions," Sarah said, irritated without quite knowing why. "Sometimes people have to take a stand. Go against the flow."

Matthew looked at her but said nothing.

"It's always easy to take the path of least resistance."

"Did you come here to defend Curt Hudelson? Or attack me?"

"I'm just making my point." She tried to calm her racing heart. "Okay, I realize he's got strong opinions. Debbi's a little…unnerved by him, too. She's torn between trusting the baby to him and fear that Alli will get swept up into the jaws of Compassionate Medical Systems."

Matthew's face tightened. "And you, of course, did nothing to reassure her that CMS is a reputable organization with hospitals all over the country."

"A lot of dirty little secrets about botched surgeries, patient dumping, that sort of thing."

"One thing I've always admired is your objectivity," Matthew said.

"That isn't stuff I made up, Matthew. You can go to the newspaper archives and see it for yourself. If you really wanted to know, that is."

Neither of them spoke for a few moments. Then Matthew met her eyes. "So," he said, "back to Debbi's daughter."

Sarah felt her face redden. "Look, could we start again? I didn't mean to get into a fight with you." She took a breath. "Here's the deal. I know I could provide the middle approach that Debbi would feel comfortable with. I know I could help Alli. But I also recognize that she might need surgery at some point and I just want to know that if that's the case, I can come to you and know that the child won't be…"

"Pulled into the maw?"

"Matthew."

"Where will you see Alli?" he asked. "You're going to open an office?"

"I'm going to make house calls." She saw his eyes flicker. "It's being done in other places throughout the country. It makes sense, Matthew. House calls are convenient for the patients and—" she leaned across the table "—they can also save thousands of dollars for taxpayers."

He smiled. "Vintage Sarah. 'Matthew, we open a lemonade stand. Five cents a glass. By the end of summer…'"

She sat back, folded her arms and glared at him.

"You can make light of it, but I'm serious. Research shows that patients who can't get to the doctor regularly are more likely to wait until they're really bad off, then call an ambulance. And what does that mean? Huge emergency-room costs, hospital-room costs and everything that goes with a prolonged illness. People out on the end of the peninsula—laid-off mill workers, single mothers—some of them qualify for welfare, some don't. But they can't get into town to see a doctor and even if they do, they can't afford the charges. Debbi's just one of many."

He carefully picked the foil off a pat of butter, then sliced open a biscuit. "Okay, let me just say something. I've had a brutal couple of days, I desperately need an uninterrupted night's sleep so if you're about to make another pitch, you've picked the wrong time. Again."

"I've asked you already, Matthew, and you've made your feelings pretty clear. You're obviously exhausted. Something clearly has to give and you think CMS is the answer. Fine. Maybe you'll enjoy practicing in an environment where the real focus is money. Go for it. I'm just looking out for Alli Kennedy's interests."

He spread butter on the biscuit, set the knife down and then, as though deciding he wasn't hungry after all, pushed the plate away and stood. "If you need to consult with me on Alli Kennedy's care," he said in a flat, expressionless voice, "I promise to honor your request." He reached for the tray, started across the room. "See you around, Sarah."

"Matthew." She got up, followed him across the cafeteria as he loaded his tray onto a conveyor belt. "Wait. Just talk to me for a minute."

He shook his head. "You got what you came for, now just go. Okay? Take your ideals and your sermonizing and your absolute convictions and peddle them somewhere else."

She stood there for a moment, watching his back as he walked down the corridor, not quite believing what had just happened. Then she raised her chin and walked out of the hospital into the cool air.

The hell with him anyway.

"...AND THEN SHE ACCUSED ME of being more interested in money," Matthew was telling his friend Roger Evans as they finished a bottle of Chianti over dinner the following night. "According to her, I've completely sold my soul to corporate medicine and, all in all, I'm a pretty poor excuse for a physician."

Roger laughed. A successful pediatrician with a practice in a Los Angeles suburb, he was visiting his adult daughter who now lived in Port Hamilton. Over antipasto, Matthew had filled him in on the Compassionate Medical Systems saga and segued into Sarah as they started on the lasagna.

"Who is this woman?"

"We grew up together," Matthew said. "She's two years younger than me and, as kids at least, she looked up to me." He grinned. "Although she'd choke if she heard me say that. She influenced me to go into medicine. Her parents and grandparents were doctors. We used to have all these high-flying ideas…"

"Didn't we all?"

"But Sarah never got over hers. She's just returned from Central America and now she's got some plan to start her own practice. Integrative medicine and house calls."

Roger looked amused. "Good luck."

"If anyone can make it work, Sarah can." Matthew pulled a slice of garlic bread out of the bread basket, bit into it and tried to recall the last time he'd had dinner at a restaurant with anyone but Lucy. "She asked me to go in with her, but…" He shrugged. "I've got a daughter. Upkeep. I hope she succeeds, but…"

"It's a long shot." Roger signaled to the waiter for more wine. "So, this woman—"

"Sarah. Strictly friends," he said, anticipating Roger's question. "Although, I don't know. Sometimes I look at her and wonder."

"Attractive?"

"In an offbeat sort of way. The odd thing is I know her so well on one level and yet she's this complete mystery to me."

Roger grinned. "Always fun solving mysteries."

"Yeah, I guess. These days though, I hardly have time to figure out my own life, let alone try to figure out what makes Sarah tick."

"Probably what you need," Roger said after the waiter had brought the wine, "is a simple, uncomplicated woman who looks at you adoringly and is good in bed."

Matthew laughed. "If you come across one, introduce me."

But long after he'd gone to bed that night, Matthew was still awake thinking. His relationship with Elizabeth had once seemed less complicated and sex had never been anything to complain about, but Sarah had always been there, on the edge of his consciousness. When he finally fell asleep, he dreamed about her standing on the beach, enveloped in fog just as she'd been that day on Agate Beach.

A CANVAS SATCHEL slung over one shoulder, Sarah rode her bike through town to her appointment with the Realtor to look at office space. If this all came through, she reflected, she would need to buy a car. Maybe a truck. The west end of the peninsula where most of her patients would probably live was too far to go by bike. The wind bit her face, blowing through the wool of the hat she'd jammed on as she left the apartment. It had rained during the night, a late spring storm that frosted the Olympics a sparkling sugar white—and made her think of Matthew. Of skiing down the mountain with Matthew years ago when anything seemed possible.

Everything made her think of Matthew.

At the east end of Port Hamilton, the highway split into two one-way streets. First Street ran through town. Front Street skirted the shore, before it headed west and, ultimately, off the peninsula. The day after the fight with Matthew in the hospital cafeteria, she'd seriously considered packing up and taking the road west.

Elizabeth had dissuaded her.

"So you had a fight?" Elizabeth had said. "And now you're going to let him chase you out of town? Sarah, he's always been smug and self-satisfied. Okay, okay, you didn't call him that, I did. But, listen to me. People are looking to you for an alternative. You can't let them down."

The next day she and Elizabeth had cleared off Sarah's kitchen table and begun a list of things they needed to take care of.

1) Location.
2) Patients.
3) Supplies and equipment.

Still, she missed Matthew. Thought about Matthew. Endlessly. Later, back at her apartment, she picked up the phone to call him. *I'm sorry. I said things I shouldn't have.* Dammit. She set the phone down. What had she really said that required an apology? She took a bubble bath. Cucumber melon to soothe the troubled soul. Except that it didn't. She climbed out of the tub, dried off. The doorbell rang. She grabbed the yellow terry-cloth robe from the hook on the back of the bathroom door and pulled it on. Her hair was wet, and water trickled down her back as she opened the front door.

"Even in Port Hamilton," Matthew said, "you should check before you open the door at night."

With one hand, Sarah lifted the hair off her neck for a moment. He'd come straight from the hospital, a parka thrown over his scrubs. Blue eyes, heartbreakingly blue like water in sunlight. She swallowed. "Lucky for you I didn't check."

"Can I come in?"

She stepped aside, then closed the door behind him.

"I can't stand being angry at you," he said.

"I don't like it much, either." Her arms were folded across her chest. She unfolded them, stuck her hands into the pockets of her robe. "Being mad at you."

"So—" he put his hands on her shoulders "—what are we going to do about it?"

"Don't know." She could hardly breathe. She felt the warmth of his hands through her robe, her body, naked, beneath it. He was so close. "Maybe we need to talk?"

He smiled. "Talking seems to get us into trouble."

She lifted her hands to cover his, to feel his skin against her own and then she moved toward him, or maybe it was the other way around, but they were holding each other and kissing, her mouth so hard against his that she felt his teeth. When she finally pulled away, she wanted to laugh but thought she might burst into tears instead.

"Why did this take so long?" Matthew, still wearing his parka, asked after they'd moved to the couch.

"I don't know." Feet curled up under her, Sarah couldn't take her eyes off his face. It was the Matthew she'd always known, but an altogether different Matthew that she hardly knew. "It wouldn't have if I'd had my way."

He frowned.

"Matthew, I think I've always been nuts about

you. I probably had a crush on you from when I was about ten—"

"You had a crush on me?"

She smiled. "Don't look so pleased with yourself. I was a dumb kid."

"Am I looking pleased with myself?"

"Very."

"I didn't realize that." He adopted a theatrically solemn expression. "All I can say is that if you had a crush on me, you certainly hid it very well. Mostly, I had the feeling you just wanted to prove that you could do anything better than me."

"And I could," she shot back.

"No." He shook his head. "I could arm wrestle you—"

"Well, there was that. You *were* three years older and on the football team, for God's sake."

"But *you* mispronounced *paradigm*," he said in a low voice,

"I did not."

"Yes, you did. You pronounced it *paradijum*."

"*You* didn't even know what it meant."

"Before I mention the time you said, without a shadow of doubt, that Tasmania was an island off the coast of England—"

"Maybe that's what happened," she said. "We've always had a competition going on. Like at the hospital. I feel this need to prove that my way is right and you—"

"No." He shook his head. "Maybe when we were kids. But that stuff at the hospital had nothing to do with me wanting to prove something about Compassionate Medical Systems. It's not what I'd be doing if…" He shook his head, his expression suddenly weary. "Let's not get into all that again, Sarah. Okay?"

She nodded, reached over to stroke his hair. "I'm glad you came by. I've missed you. A lot."

"How come you never… I mean, most women give off clues that they're attracted, but you…" He leaned his head against the back of the couch and closed his eyes. "I always had the feeling that if I'd made a move you'd have hauled off and hit me."

Sarah ran her finger under the elasticized cuff of his parka. "Maybe it was self-preservation. Maybe I was scared you'd reject me." He pulled her onto his lap and they kissed again. She felt the robe coming apart as they moved and, in a fleeting moment of sanity, decided that as much as she wanted to make love to Matthew, tonight wouldn't be the night. Things were happening too fast. She slid off his lap. Ironic, really, since they had taken a lifetime to progress to this point. Glancing at the small travel clock on top of the stereo, she saw that it was after midnight.

"Lucy's in a play," he said impulsively. "She's a fortune-teller. Clare Voyant. Which reminds me, I'm supposed to go buy her some tarot cards."

"I have some," she said.

"You have tarot cards?"

"I have a superstitious streak that I don't talk about."

"Tomorrow's opening night. Want to go with me?"

"Maybe she'd rather have you to herself."

"Of course," he said, feigning dismay. "How stupid of me. I wouldn't have figured that out by myself. Okay, I take back the invitation."

"Stop."

"You want to go, or not?"

"I want to go."

He smiled. "See how simple that was?"

CHAPTER TEN

BUT INVITING SARAH TO THE PLAY hadn't been such a great idea after all, Matthew realized. He was feeling beleaguered. First Elizabeth had given him a hard time for not consulting Lucy before extending the invitation—then Pearl, now Lucy herself. He'd picked her up from school and, as they were driving back to his condo, he'd casually mentioned it, confident that Lucy, unlike her mother and grandmother, wouldn't consider him some sort of insensitive clod who didn't understand the first thing about women.

Wrong.

"It's *my* play." Lucy folded her arms across her chest, her eyes fixed on the windshield. "I think I should be allowed to say who can come or not."

"So you personally invited everyone in the audience?" Matthew shot back, then immediately wanted to retract the words. *She's a fourteen-year-old kid.* "Lucy, I don't understand the big deal," he said slowly. "Sarah's just a friend—"

"*Girlfriend,*" she spit out. "Fine. Take her, I don't care."

He made an impromptu, conciliatory stop at the

Buzz where Lucy loved the homemade blackberry ice cream. "Come on." He caught her by the arm. "Let's go get a cone."

Inside, they sat at small iron tables in the window alcove and Lucy brightened a little. As he ate his ice cream, he attempted to sort things out in his own mind. Sarah was a friend, had always been a friend. He loved her as a friend. But was Lucy right in calling Sarah a girlfriend? Maybe not at the moment, but at some point?

Maybe.

"You're always talking about stuff you used to do," Lucy said after they'd sat in silence for a while. "Like in the car going to that dumb beach thing. *'Oh, Sarah,'*" she mimicked his voice, "*'Remember this? Oh. Matthew—'*" high pitched now "*'—remember that. Oh, wasn't it so fun?'*" She glared at him. "How d'you think that made me feel? Like I wasn't even there."

"Lucy, that's…" Frustrated, he shook his head. He'd been about to dismiss it as silly, but it clearly wasn't silly to his daughter who, he could see, was on the verge of tears again. "Look, sweetheart, I know this play is very important to you, so if it's going to upset you for me to bring Sarah, I won't."

She eyed him through her tears. "But you asked her."

"She'll understand."

She managed a tremulous smile. "She won't be mad?"

"No." Matthew felt his heart drop at the thought of breaking the news to Sarah. "She'll understand," he repeated.

SARAH SPENT the afternoon getting ready to go to Lucy's play.

She took a bubble bath, considerably more relaxing than the one she'd taken the night before, played Bizet on the stereo. After drying herself, she even painted her toenails then tried on clothes for the better part of an hour.

Attractive but not trying too hard—that was the look she wanted. At the mirror over the bathroom cabinet—the only mirror in the apartment, in fact—she considered her hair. Released from the braid, it came all the way down her back and the truth was, she was sick of it. Maybe she would call Debbi. Make an appointment to cut it all off. But not today, she decided.

In the bedroom, she kicked off her jeans and began pulling clothes from the closet. Discarding combinations, hating everything. It was as though three other people sat on the bed delivering commentary.

Elizabeth shook her head. "That drains your color."

Rose rolled her eyes. "What color you have."

Lucy smirked. "That's kind of old-fashioned."

"That one should have stayed in the jungle." Rose again.

"Not bad, but not with that skirt." Elizabeth.

Sarah banished them all from the room. This was ridiculous. Not just that her wardrobe was limited, but that it mattered. She was a forty-two-year-old woman.

A physician. Without a practice, without a patient, but a physician nevertheless. And she was getting ready to spend the evening with a man she'd known forever. Matthew. Her old friend Matthew.

Matthew, the father of a fourteen-year-old girl who hated her.

She sat on the bed and, without even thinking about what she was doing, picked up a pen from the bedside table. On the back of a grocery list, also on the table, she started a list of reasons she should halt this relationship before it went any further.

Number One, she wrote.

Not stepmother material.

She scratched out the words, crumpled the paper and tossed it in the trash. Maybe she was projecting just a tad? In the kitchen, she got a soda from the fridge, drank some and carried it over to the computer and immediately forgot everything else. Google had turned up several more articles on physicians who made house calls, mostly in rural areas like Port Hamilton. When the doorbell rang, she glanced at her watch, thinking at first that the time had gotten away from her and it was Matthew. But he'd said six.

She opened the front door. Matthew stood there, an expression on his face she couldn't quite read. "You're a little early," she said.

"I know."

"Couldn't stay away, huh?" She closed the door behind him and he followed her into the living room. He looked uncomfortable. Constrained somehow. "Have a seat." She gestured at the couch. "What's up?"

He scratched the back of his head. "I have to… disinvite you to the play," he said, the words all coming out on a breath. "I'm sorry, Sarah. I was looking forward to this. It's Lucy. I told her you were coming and she got bent out of shape. Maybe I shouldn't have caved in to her, but it's her play and…" He looked at her. "I'm sorry. I'll make it up to you."

"Hey." She curled her feet up under her. Even if going to the play meant more than anything else in the world—and it didn't—the look of sheer misery on Matthew's face was enough to convince her that it wasn't that important after all. "It's okay, really." He still seemed miserable and not entirely convinced so she scooted next to him and stuck her face under his. "Boo."

He smiled. "You're not angry?"

"Furious. Leave and never darken my door again."

"I'm torn between being angry at Lucy and—"

"Don't. She's a kid." She thought of the discarded outfits all over the bed and realized she was more relieved than disappointed. Having Matthew here with her now, rather than sharing him with Lucy later, was infinitely preferable. Although, she'd probably have to work on that—the concept of sharing Matthew. "I do remember what it was like being fourteen," she said. "The smallest thing gets magnified into gigantic proportions."

"I'm not going to start talking about the CMS thing again, but I just want to give you some context. When

Lucy was born, I remember feeling so awed at the responsibility of being a parent. I didn't take it lightly for one minute. I wanted her to have all the things I never had. Not just the material stuff, but a sense of security and the knowledge that she was really loved and wanted. Even after Elizabeth and I started having problems, I would have stayed with the marriage just so that Lucy had both parents. But then Elizabeth met this guy and I really had no other option but to move out."

Sarah watched his face. He'd closed his eyes and his voice was soft and almost faraway, as though he were thinking aloud. Except for the time when he'd asked her about Ted, they hadn't really talked about their other relationships. She'd spent so many years not letting herself think about Matthew and Elizabeth that, eventually, it required no effort. But now, she wondered. "Were you still in love with her?"

Matthew's brow furrowed. "No," he said after a moment. "Not for a long time." He opened his eyes, grinned at her. "But I never stopped loving her mother. I was just telling Pearl the other day, that I think she was part of the reason I fell in love with Elizabeth in the beginning—"

"Not to mention that every guy in school lusted after Elizabeth," Sarah said. "Including you."

He laughed. "Okay, I admit it. Including me. But it was more than that."

She slapped his arm. "You lusted after Pearl, too?"

"Yeah, it was those sheepskin bedroom slippers she always wore. Sexy as all get-out."

"Pearl's a good sort," Sarah agreed. "I liked her because she liked me."

"Same here. I missed out on having parents to confirm my self-worth, but Pearl always made me feel like the best thing that happened since sliced bread. It was addictive."

"Did Elizabeth make you feel that way, too?"

"Yeah."

Sarah picked at her fingernail. "And I was hard on you."

"You were just…you. I mean, what would you have done if I'd said something…sappy?"

"Like?"

"Like, I don't know. What if I'd said I loved you?"

"I'd have laughed."

"My point exactly," he said.

And then, in a replay of the previous night, he pulled her onto his lap and they blotted out the rest of the world. After a while, he nudged her around, but the futon was narrow and she was half hanging off, Matthew's body pressing down on hers, his head buried in her neck, his face covered by her hair. At one point, her feet touched the floor and she felt the edge of the futon cut into the back of her knees. The pain was no competition for the other sensations bombarding her body.

"It's about this couch," Matthew muttered when they finally came up for air. "Do you do a lot of entertaining on it?"

"Twice a day, sometimes more." She sat up but couldn't take her eyes off his. "If you'd done that when

I was fourteen, things might have turned out a whole lot different."

"If I'd done that when you were fourteen, I'd have been arrested."

"But I'm not fourteen now."

"I noticed," he said as they slid down onto the floor. Sometime later, he pulled his arm out from under her to look at his watch. Then he sat up. "God. I've got to go. The play starts in ten minutes."

At the door, he kissed her again.

"Go." She placed her hands on his chest, feeling the wool of his sweater. "Have fun."

"I'll call you." He reached for her hand, turned it over then took a pen from his jacket and wrote something on her palm. "Don't look at it until I've gone."

She waited until he'd driven off.

Keep the weekend free for me, he'd written.

"WHAT HAPPENED TO YOUR LIP?" Elizabeth asked as she slipped into the seat next to Matthew in the high-school auditorium. She fished around in her purse, then handed him a tissue. "It's bleeding."

"No idea." Matthew dabbed at his mouth as the lights dimmed.

Watching Lucy, he felt a complicated stew of emotions. Welling love and pride, mixing with a simmering irritation and disappointment. He would have liked Sarah to see for herself how Lucy was stealing the show and it bothered him that, even at fourteen, his daughter couldn't rise above her jealousy, or whatever it was.

Afterward, Elizabeth held a small party. The cast of eight and a dozen or so friends and family. Pearl found him in the kitchen, making a dinner out of the appetizers Elizabeth had set out. He realized as he piled Swedish meatballs onto a paper plate that he hadn't eaten since early that morning and he was devouring the food and only half listening to Pearl when he caught the word *manipulate*.

"Sorry?" He speared a meatball. "What was that?"

"Lucy manipulates you. Elizabeth said she's jealous of Sarah and giving you a hard time."

"Oh, I wouldn't say that," Matthew said, automatically coming to his daughter's defense. "Anyway, there's nothing…" He'd been about to tell Pearl there was nothing for Lucy to be jealous of. But he realized that was no longer true.

"You do more than enough for that girl," Pearl said. "You have a right to your own life, you know that."

Matthew watched Elizabeth and her new boyfriend, whose name he couldn't recall, and wondered why being a father seemed at odds somehow with having a personal life. It wasn't as though Lucy was completely sheltered from the facts of life. He realized Pearl was watching him.

"So?" She waggled her head. "You and Sarah got over your differences then? You told me she accused you of selling out."

"She apologized," Matthew said. "Not that she needed to."

"How's she doing?"

"Fine. She's going into practice for herself. Integrated medicine, she calls it. And house calls."

Pearl smiled. "Like her great-grandfather used to do. There's room for it."

"Actually, she asked me to join her."

"And?"

"I don't know," he said honestly. "Sarah talks about ideals and the kind of things we used to dream about. There's nothing she liked better than to get behind a cause. And I think she's found one that's challenging enough to suit her. The thing is, I don't know how realistic that is anymore. Money's more of an issue for me than for Sarah. I've got a daughter to support, house payments to make."

"Sell the house," Pearl said.

He laughed as though the suggestion were beyond consideration.

"Lucy doesn't need a swimming pool in the backyard," Pearl said. "If she wants to swim she can go to the beach just like you used to."

THAT NIGHT he hardly slept. The events of the day rattled around in his head, subsiding while he read, then springing to life again as soon as he turned off the lamp. Sarah was like a storm blowing and churning already turbulent waters. He'd lost his compass, unsure any more of the direction to take. Compassionate Medical Systems would provide financial stability. But with Sarah's input, he might have the chance to practice the kind of medicine he'd once dreamed about.

The next day, already tired and irritable when he got to the hospital, he discovered a six-month-old girl had managed to extubate herself and was struggling to breathe. The physician on call—a moonlighter—was long gone by the time Matthew found her. He checked blood gas, found the carbon-dioxide level sky-high and put her back on the ventilator. Then he walked across the hall to the nursing director's office and vented his anger and frustration.

"Well, good morning to you, too, Matthew," Carol Kirshman said after she'd listened to him rant for a good ten minutes. "I don't know whether you're interested in an explanation, but I'm going to give you one anyway."

Matthew wasn't interested in an explanation, but he owed her that. He sat down in the chair by her desk.

"…and the baby was doing fine, so Dr. Josephson left her off the ventilator to see if she would go on doing well if he kept her off. Unfortunately, he didn't follow up with her. Which meant no blood gasses were ordered. The nurse called him at six this morning to report the baby was having breathing problems, but he didn't get out of bed to come check her."

He nodded and they both looked at each other. "I'm sorry," he said, "for blowing up at you."

She shrugged. "We're short staffed, Matt. We're overworked. Stretched beyond capacity. But thank you for the apology. You did an excellent impersonation of acting like an asshole, but I wasn't entirely convinced. I was pretty sure I knew you better than that."

"Thanks."

"Things getting to you?"

"This whole thing with CMS. One day I think, okay, enough of all this. Let's just get on board, it can't be all that bad. And then—"

"New radiology department," she read from one of the CMS brochures in a stack on her desk. "More staffing, physician-recruitment effort."

"I've heard the sales pitch," he said.

"But you're still holding out."

"Something doesn't sit right." He hesitated. "And I've met this woman…well, I didn't just meet her, we grew up together…"

"Sarah Benedict?"

"Yeah. How—"

"One of my nurses lives in the same apartment building and she saw you over there. Plus, Rose mentioned something about her daughter being back. Rose was hoping she'd apply to CMS—"

Matthew shook his head. "Sarah's too idealistic for that. Joining CMS would be like selling out. I made the mistake of telling her how I'm leaning and she spent thirty minutes lecturing me about medicine as big business. Some of what she says makes sense, a lot of it actually. But Sarah isn't supporting a family, or making house payments. Although, I'm not sure that would make any difference. You've met her, haven't you?"

"Years ago when she was still in medical school." She leaned back in her chair. "Wasn't her husband killed in an accident?"

ag exactly how she would get staff privi-
Arthur General and explaining, or justify-
hew that it was just as close for people who
the west end of the peninsula and that se-
could be airlifted to Seattle, just as they'd
. When she tuned in sometime later, Rose
ring on about CMS and the new state-of-
that would replace the existing one.

n't happened yet," Sarah said. "So don't
eath. They'll say anything at this point."
tell Matthew your plans?"
e." She waited a moment. "He's not inter-

slept with him yet?"
Sarah stared at Rose, aghast. "I can't be-
ed me that. Anyway, what does that have
ything?"
ou should. Use a little bargaining power."

"Struck by lightning."

"And she hasn't remarried?"

"No." He suddenly realized he'd been led into a trap. "And quit looking at me like that. We're friends. We always have been." Now strictly speaking a lie by omission, but Carol didn't need to know that. "Sarah's this independent, self-sufficient woman. Determined to do her own thing, if only to prove me wrong." He smiled. "She hates losing, especially to a man."

"So you're good friends and…"

"Good friends."

"Well, friendship's a great start," Carol said. "Trust me, it's a whole lot better than sex as something to base a relationship on. Let me know if it turns into something serious, though, so the nurses can cross you off the eligibility list."

Matthew rolled his eyes. "Come on." And then he thought about the note he'd written on Sarah's hand. His plan had been to rent kayaks, like old times, but the scene on the futon was still vivid in his mind. "I have a question. Purely hypothetical." He scratched the back of his neck. "What would be your idea of a romantic evening?"

She laughed. "I can't, Matt. I'm married."

He waited.

"Okay, sit down." She slid a notepad across the desk. "Ready?"

SARAH, IMMERSED up to her neck in bubbling thermal water, was thinking about Matthew and their upcoming trip over to Victoria.

An overnight trip.

"So, I should bring a suitcase?" she'd asked.

"Not necessarily," he'd said in a suggestive way that, even over the phone, had sent shivers through her.

He'd called just before she left to pick up Rose—also immersed in water just a few feet away, her head tipped back, steam drifting up around her. After listening to Rose complain about her back, Sarah had suggested a drive up Sol Duc hot springs for a therapeutic dip. Located in the middle of an old grove rain forest with the Olympics towering in the background it seemed the perfect spot to do a little contemplating.

A door had opened leading out of the safe familiar place that had been her relationship with Matthew into to one where she didn't know the rules. He was a man, and she was turned on like she'd never been before—that part was easy enough to figure out. But the fact that the man was Matthew and they were tearing at each other's clothes required some adjustments to her thinking.

Although she'd loved Ted, she'd also known that he needed her more than she'd needed him. Not exciting, but it had been comfortable and nonthreatening. In the new place where she and Matthew seemed headed, the reverse could easily happen and it scared the hell out of her.

"Ah, this is bliss." Rose paddled over to Sarah's side. "Thank you, my dear, for taking the time to bring me up here."

"Glad to," Sarah said, pleased and touched by Rose's expression of gratitude. "I'm enjoying it, too."

"I apologize if I was
care proposal," Rose s

Sarah looked at her.
has softened your brai
isn't you."

"It's never too late
tell me some more ab

"You're pushing it

"Tell me anyway,"

Sarah breathed in
spirit of her mother's
cided to choose trust
explain her plans in n
saw the familiar quiz
voice, which had sta

"Makes no sense
against the tide. An
up with that farmer

Sarah leaned he
across the water, lif
for the new, accep
pected Rose's end
been tricked into
of security. Serve

"Why do you t
ing. "What if…"

Sarah tuned he
with Rose was an
thought that abo
make her mind g

was planni
leges at Po
ing, to Mat
lived out o
rious cases
always bee
was yamm
the-art E.R.

"That ha
hold your b

"Did you

"Of cour
ested."

"Have yo

"Mother.
lieve you as
to do with a

"Maybe y

CHAPTER ELEVEN

ELIZABETH WAS FEELING DREAMY. George had just called to say he'd made reservations at a hotel on the coast where they could watch the storms crash in without even getting out of bed. That sounded too romantic to pass up, even though it would mean calling her mother to look after Lucy. Matt had let it slip, when he'd called her to ask if they could swap weekends to have Lucy, that he was taking Sarah to Victoria.

"Does Lucy know?" she'd asked.

"Not yet. And I'd appreciate it if you wouldn't mention it to her."

"For God's sake, Matt." Sometimes it was as if he still lived in Victorian times. "She's old enough to realize that—"

"Just don't, okay?"

"Okay, calm down. I'll call my mom."

"Wait. You mean, you can't have her?"

"*I* have plans, Matt. I'm entitled to—"

"Forget it. I'll reschedule. I'm not having Lucy treated like a piece of lost luggage, carted from one place to another…"

"You know what?" Now she was getting angry. "This is ridiculous. We're talking about Lucy staying with her grandmother, not some stranger." In fact, Lucy wouldn't be too thrilled, mostly because Pearl didn't have cable, but so what? "And, frankly," she went on, "it might not be a bad thing for Lucy to learn that the world doesn't revolve around her."

Half an hour later, Matt called back to say that he'd drop Lucy off at Pearl's Friday night, so maybe some of what she'd said had sunk in. Then as soon as she'd put the phone down, it rang again.

"I have to buy some clothes," Sarah said. "I'm going to take a trip into Seattle, but the problem is I need something now. I was wondering if—"

"Sure. Come over, we'll find something," Elizabeth said. "I've got a whole closet full of clothes that don't fit me anymore." And then, very casually, because she knew why Sarah needed something besides jeans and a sweatshirt, she added, "Big date?"

"Oh…actually Matthew and I are going to Victoria."

"Just overnight?" Elizabeth asked ever so innocently.

"Well, yes…um, if you do have something that would be great. I'll see you in a few minutes."

As she hung up the phone, Elizabeth could imagine Sarah blushing like crazy. It was funny really, except Sarah had been very nice to her since she got back and she liked how Sarah seemed to take her seriously and listen to what she had to say. That had surprised her actually. So it wasn't like she was making fun of Sarah.

Ten minutes later, she was watching Sarah try on clothes and mentally giving her an extreme makeover.

"You should let me cut your hair," she said, after Sarah had disappeared into the walk-in closet. Elizabeth dug into her dresser drawer for the shears she used to trim her bangs when she didn't feel like looking at herself in a beauty-shop mirror. "I almost got a cosmetologists' license, you know."

She found the shears and looked at Sarah, who had reappeared wearing her off-white dress with the long sleeves and a low neckline. It would've looked a better with a push-up bra. Sarah wasn't exactly overloaded in the boobs department.

"I used to love that dress," she told Sarah. "About fifty pounds ago. It looks good on you. You need a different bra though."

Sarah frowned at her reflection. "I do?"

Elizabeth grinned. Sometimes it amazed her how clueless Sarah was about things that most women didn't have to think about. Even Lucy at fourteen was lot more savvy than Sarah. It made her feel protective toward Sarah. She needed someone to look out for her. "Seriously, you should let me cut your hair." She moved over to tug the rubber band from Sarah's ponytail. "Lucy does mine, it's no big deal."

"Yuck." Sarah frowned as the hair fell around her shoulders. "All I need is a wart on my nose and a broomstick."

"Stop it." Elizabeth caught the hair and arranged it around Sarah's face. "See?" She met Sarah's eyes in the mirror. "If I cut off about…four or five inches, it would frame your face and look really cute."

Sarah, still frowning at her reflection, looked doubtful.

"Come *on*." Elizabeth's fingers were itching to start. "It would make you look at least ten years younger."

For a minute Sarah seemed to be wavering, then she shook her head and moved away from the mirror. "You'll get it looking cute, but once I wash it, I won't be able to do anything with it." She grabbed the rubber band, pulled her hair back into a ponytail and grinned. "I need to control my hair," she said, "not have it controlling me." Then she disappeared into the closet again and came out with a black dress with spaghetti straps. "This is the other one," she held it against herself. "But it seems…out there."

Elizabeth, watching her, laughed. When Sarah bent over to shake off the dress, the tops of her breasts showed, and Elizabeth tried to imagine Sarah and Matt in bed together. Then she made herself look away. It was easier to imagine them the way she'd always seen them. Looking at each other in that conspiratorial way they had. *We have a secret.* She grabbed a hideous green shirt she'd meant to take to the Goodwill out of Sarah's hands.

"No."

"Why? I like it."

"Because it does nothing for you." She shook her head. "You are so strange sometimes, Sarah. It's like you ace everything you do, but—"

"Girly stuff. I know." Sarah sat on the bed. "What can I say? I'm no good at it."

"But you don't even try. It's like you're scared you'll fail."

"Maybe I am." Sarah looked thoughtful. "That never really occurred to me before."

Elizabeth picked up the black dress from the bed and held it up to herself, although she'd never fit into it in a million years. "What about Matthew?" she asked, not looking at Sarah because they'd never got onto this topic before. "I mean, I know you're good friends and you have a lot in common, but do you…have—"

"Have I slept with him?" Sarah was still sitting on the bed. "No."

"But you want to?"

Sarah laughed. *"Yes."* And then she lay back on the bed and started laughing more. "God, this is so weird to be having this conversation."

"No, it's not," Elizabeth said. "Women talk about this stuff all the time. It's not as if I still have something with him." She turned to look at Sarah. "You never talk to girlfriends about…dating, that kind of thing?"

"Nope." Sarah sat up. "But you know what? After Ted died, I mean, a couple of years later, just before I came back here, I met this guy who seemed interested in me. He was a reporter and he'd come to do an article on the clinic. We got along really well and then one night, we were drinking wine and solving the world's problems—"

"Like you and Matt," Elizabeth said.

"Well, yes, but I wasn't that attracted to him. It just made me feel better about myself that he seemed attracted to me." She chewed her lip. "I would have slept with him, I'd already decided, but he had an early appointment and left. And then he went back to the States and I never heard from him again. I sent him a couple of e-mails, he knew my phone number. Nothing."

Elizabeth rolled her eyes. "Men."

"Has anything like that happened to you?"

"Oh, God. Let me count the times. Show me a woman it hasn't happened to, and I'll call her a liar. It's just the way guys are."

"But I didn't know that," Sarah said. "I mean, it hadn't happened to me before and…what you were just saying about talking to other women? I don't do that. So I just carried on, feeling badly about myself."

"Aw." Elizabeth put her arm around Sarah's shoulder. "See, that's why it's good to share."

"Thank you," Sarah said. "Really."

"THIS IS A GREAT HOUSE," Sarah said after she'd finally selected a dress—the black spaghetti-strap number. Elizabeth had talked her into it, but she was also taking the off-white one, just in case.

She looked around the room—her entire apartment would have fit into one corner. One wall was an arrangement of floor-to-ceiling windows, of varying heights ranging from about ten feet to a soaring panel that reached the highest point of the cathedral ceilings. The design was clearly intended to maximize the panoramic views of water and sky and distant coastline. A massive floor-to-ceiling stone fireplace dominated another wall.

Elizabeth had gone to make cappuccino and Sarah sank into a sand-colored suede sectional which, like everything else about the house, was tasteful and obviously very expensive. Recalling Matthew's seeming indifference to his physical space—as reflected in the anonymous jumble of his boyhood bedroom—she wondered how involved he had been in the decorating.

"We used to have so many fights over the money when we were building this place," Elizabeth said, coming back in and setting two oversized black cappuccino cups on the glass coffee table. "When he found out what those windows cost, we didn't speak for a week."

Sarah sipped at the coffee beneath the froth. "Did you live here the whole time you were married?"

"No. We had it built after Lucy was born. We'd been living in a house on Peabody. I was always complaining that we needed something bigger, but Matthew was busy at the hospital and it was as if he didn't really hear me until Lucy arrived." She grinned. "I could pretty much buy anything as long as I could somehow make it seem it was what Lucy needed."

Sarah thought of Matthew's defense of Lucy on the fossil trip. *I wanted my daughter to have the things I never had.* Most parents felt that way, she guessed, but it saddened her to think that Matthew could be so easily manipulated and that he apparently couldn't see that he was doing his daughter no favors. *But then I don't have kids.* "He moved out after the divorce?"

"Yeah. I suggested we sell this and look for a smaller place. Lucy and I didn't need all this room, but it was the same old story. Sometimes, even now, I walk through the rooms and instead of seeing how beautiful everything is, I can almost hear all the arguments we used to have about money."

Sarah looked at her. "So you'd spend the money, Matthew would worry about it, but then justify it because of Lucy?"

Elizabeth nodded. "Go figure." She got up from the couch and returned with a slip of paper. "Before I forget, I was talking to this girl who came into the restaurant. I was telling her that I have this friend who's an incredible doctor and she's going to start making house calls."

Sarah smiled. "You don't know how much I appreciate hearing that. Actually, you're the only one I've told who doesn't think I'm out of my mind."

"Don't feel bad about Matthew's attitude," Elizabeth said. "Maybe if it was just him, but it's Lucy and—" she waved at the living room "—all this. I mean, Lucy could live in a house half this size and be happy, but—"

"It's the way he grew up," Sarah said. "His dad never had anything."

"Tell me. I remember when we first started dating, his clothes were so horrible. Polyester shirts that had been washed so many times they had these little bumpy things all over them. Wal-Mart sneakers."

Sarah laughed. "I never even noticed."

"It's with Compassionate Medical Systems," Elizabeth said. "He's been dragging his feet about joining because he doesn't really believe in it, but if I say it would give him more time to spend with Lucy, or if Lucy wants something he can't afford now, that's when he starts thinking it might not be a bad idea."

Below them, on the street level, she heard a door slam, then the sound of feet on the wooden staircase leading up to the living room.

Elizabeth smiled. "Lucy's home."

Sarah arranged her features into a smile.

"Mom…" Lucy stood in the doorway, her face, as she spotted Sarah, darkening dramatically.

"Hi, sweetie," Elizabeth said.

"Hi, Lucy," Sarah added.

Lucy ignored them both, then left the room. "Mom, can I talk to you for a minute?" she called from the kitchen.

"Sure, go ahead," Elizabeth replied.

"Can you come here, please?"

Elizabeth glanced at Sarah. "Be right back."

Sarah tipped her head back against the sofa's plush upholstery. From the kitchen, she heard Elizabeth's low voice and then, loud and shrill enough that it might have been intended for her to hear, "Daddy's going to Victoria with…her. And I have to stay with Grandma. It's not fair, I hate everything."

ON THE AFTERNOON of his overnight trip with Sarah, Matthew left the hospital two hours earlier than usual with the intent of helping Lucy understand that Sarah in no way posed a threat to the love he felt for her. He'd rehearsed the words so many times he worried that by the time he actually said them, they'd sound rehearsed and insincere. It was ridiculous, of course, that Lucy could doubt him in any way.

On the way over to Pearl's, she refused to speak to him.

When Pearl opened the front door, Lucy burst into tears and retreated to the room she'd be using. Pearl took his face between both her hands.

"Go."

"I hate leaving her like this," he said as they stood in hallway of Pearl's little cottage. From the bedroom, the sounds of Lucy sobbing as though her heart would break. "Maybe—"

"You do that, Matthew Cameron, and I'll throttle you with my bare hands."

Despite himself, Matthew grinned. "You don't even know what I was going to say."

"Oh, for heaven's sake." Pearl took him by the arm and steered him toward the front door. "You just go and have a good time. She'll be fine."

Matthew nodded. That she was right didn't make him feel any better. Didn't change the fact that he alone had the power to make his daughter happy again.

"I want you to promise me you won't think about her for the next two days," Pearl said.

Matthew grinned. "I'll do my best."

"Sarah's a good girl."

"Pearl, I don't want a good girl."

She smacked his arm. "Buy her some flowers. Women like that."

CHAPTER TWELVE

"ROSES?" SARAH SAID when she opened the front door to find Matthew standing there with a pale pink bouquet. "So this really is a date?"

"As opposed to?"

"I don't know." It was the first time she'd seen him since they'd kissed and now everything was different. Different and difficult acting in the same jokey, good-pals way they always had when all she really wanted was to tear off his clothes. "A fig?"

He considered. "So as opposed to dating you, that would mean I'm figging you?"

"That sounds rather obscene." She led him inside. "But not altogether unpleasant. Anyway, I think the term *dating* has become… well, dated."

"Only old farts like us use it. Is that what you're saying?"

"Watch who you're calling an old fart." She filled a drinking glass—the only thing in the apartment that vaguely resembled a vase—with water and attempted to arrange the roses. "I'm two years younger than you."

"A veritable child." He came up behind her, nuzzled her neck.

She caught a whiff of the perfume she'd dabbed on, felt the beat of her heart. Then she relaxed in the warmth of Matthew's body for a moment before turning to look at him. "You look very nice, by the way."

"So do you. I didn't realize you had legs."

"Oh, the dress." She glanced down at herself. At the last moment, she'd decided against Elizabeth's castoffs and splurged at Port Hamilton's only boutique, a pricey little place frequented mostly by tourists. "Wait." Hips swaying, her version of a model parading down the catwalk, she strutted across the room. When she turned, Matthew was leaning against the counter, smiling.

"Zees?" She gestured at her dress. "A little number I picked up in Paris, dahling. Terribly chic, *non?*"

"Yeah." He pulled her hard against him. "Terribly."

"Just trying to do my girly girl best," she said.

And then they looked at each other and started laughing.

"I'd rather stick a lizard down your top," Matthew said.

"Don't even think about it."

"Or we could go kayaking," he suggested.

"So this thing. Us. This date—"

"It takes some adjustment. I think I missed most of Lucy's play. I mean, I was there, sitting in the auditorium, but my head was somewhere else."

She reached up to kiss him and he put his arms around her and they kissed until it seemed she would melt into him and nothing else mattered, and the rest of the world and everyone in it could just fall away and—

His cell phone rang.

He broke away to look at it. "Lucy." Indecision played across his face, then he put the phone away. "Let's go."

HALF AN HOUR LATER, as they stood in the chill night air waiting for the ferry, Matthew felt his cell phone, which he'd slipped into his overcoat pocket, vibrate. One arm around Sarah's shoulder, he debated what to do. He'd considered leaving it in the car but compromised by turning off the ring. Out on the water, a splash of light appeared as the ferry made the turn into the harbor.

"Six minutes," Sarah said.

"Six minutes and thirty-five seconds," he countered. They'd both seen it cross the straits so often that timing was predictable. The crowd started milling around them. His phone continued to vibrate.

"Just to show how accommodating I've become," Sarah said, leaning into him, "I'm going to give you the last word. Even though I know it's actually thirty-*four* seconds. And by the way, you look incredibly sexy."

He laughed. "Come on."

"I've always thought you looked sexy," she said. "I never had the guts to admit it."

Matthew decided to ignore the phone.

Sarah kissed his neck.

"Keep that up," he said, "and...I will stick a lizard down your back."

The phone, which has stopped vibrating, started up again. "Hold on." He removed his arm from around

Sarah's neck, fished the phone from his pocket. Lucy's cell-phone number. He felt Sarah watching him. "You know what?" He turned the phone off, took Sarah's arm and they joined the foot passengers filing down the narrow walkway to get on the ferry. And tried not to think of what Lucy was doing at that very moment. Probably crying as she waited for him to call back to say he'd be there for her.

MATTHEW HAD MADE reservations at Dickens, a restaurant on the Victoria waterfront. All timbered ceilings, cozy nooks and waiters in period costumes. They'd walked there from the ferry, the night cool and sparkling with light, the wind in their faces. The tables were set with pewter dishes and flowers and over Matthew's shoulder Sarah could see the lights along the waterfront and the illuminated spires of the Empress Hotel. He looked great, broad-shouldered and handsome. She felt terrific in her stylish little black dress. Life was good

After a waiter brought the wine, Matthew raised his glass and smiled across the table. "To...what?" He thought for a moment. "New beginnings."

"New beginnings." She raised her glass and clinked his. "Not to ruin your toast or anything, but aren't beginnings new by definition? Could you have an old beginning?"

"Probably not." He set his glass down. "I don't know why I said that. It just came to me."

"Although I guess you could begin something," she amended, "a discussion, say, but it's not really new, just a continuation of the one you had the day before."

"Or a relationship," Matthew said. "It's a new beginning to…" He shook his head, reached across the table and took her face in both hands. "Damn it. Why can't you just smile prettily and clink your glass and not tax my brain?"

She smiled prettily. "Because that wouldn't be me."

"Okay, you make a toast."

She raised a glass. "To us. All grown up."

"To us," he said. "All grown up."

"It's funny," she said after a moment. "I'm looking at the Empress and trying to remember the last time I was there and I'm pretty sure it was when my mother took me for my fourteenth birthday. We had afternoon tea. The china cups were so thin you could see the tea through them and there was a silver tray of cucumber sandwiches, which I actually hated. Plus, I was upset because you were hanging around Elizabeth constantly and that's all I could think about. Finally I told Rose I had a stomachache and we took the next ferry back."

"I remember that," he said. "Your birthday, I mean. In fact, I seem to recall it was Elizabeth who suggested the Empress to Rose. It was an Elizabeth thing, having tea at the hotel. If Rose had asked me, I'd have suggested snowshoeing or something."

"Except that my birthday's in June," she said.

"I know that, Sarah," he said solemnly. "But I would have manufactured snow. For you, I'd have done that."

She smiled. "You gave me a glass sea horse."

"I did?"

"Yep. I kept it for a while and then…" She took a breath. "I smashed it with a hammer."

"Why?"

"Because you were acting as if I didn't exist and then one day I saw you holding Elizabeth's hand."

"I'm surprised you didn't take the hammer to me," he said. "Or Elizabeth."

"Trust me, I thought about it."

"But Sarah…" He frowned. "I mean, it was different. You were my best friend, my pal. Elizabeth was, well, my teenage love."

She stared at him. His hair was slightly ruffled from the wind.

"What?" he asked.

"Your pal."

"We were kids, Sarah."

"But I wanted to be—" she paused, trying to think of the right word "—your love object." The words sounded so ridiculous she burst out laughing, and then Matthew started laughing, too.

"Tonight, my dear," he leaned across the table, leering at her, "your dream will come true. Tonight you will be my love object."

She grinned. "Be still, my heart."

"Perhaps we should look at these." He picked up the menus the waiter had set down and handed one to her.

Sarah scanned it. Salmon, steak, chops. Beef-and kidney pie in a herb-infused gravy with creamed potatoes. She shifted and her knee brushed against Matthew's. Sensation shot through her body.

"I'm going to have steak," Matthew said. "Blood-red," he growled. "Man food. What about you? Gonna go for the steak, too?"

It was exactly what she wanted, but she closed the menu and smiled demurely, or her version of demurely. "No, I think I'll have the salmon."

The waiter arrived and they ordered. And then Matthew ordered more wine. "A cabernet for me this time and—" he looked across the table "—the lady will have a…"

"A chardonnay, please," the lady said.

AFTER DINNER, they danced. The band and the small dance floor in the bar of the restaurant was one of the reasons he'd chosen it in the first place. They'd fed each other dessert—crème brûlée—and drank champagne, so by the time he led Sarah onto the floor, they were both feeling pleasantly woozy and he didn't have to wonder whether Sarah would laugh hysterically at the idea of the two of them locked in dance step together.

"See?" Her arms around his neck, Sarah smiled up into his eyes. "I *can* dance."

"But you're leading,"

"Shut up and kiss me."

They were still kissing when the music stopped.

"Let's get out of here," he said.

HE'D BOOKED A ROOM at a hotel a short walk away and, although he occasionally thought of Lucy, anticipation of the night ahead banished concerns to the far recesses of his brain. Sarah was unlike any other woman he'd known, the connection he felt to her, the comfort of being completely in tune with another person. But then in an instant, that Sarah would slip away and she was a woman, complex and unfathomable. Like most women, he thought ruefully.

"You planned a good date," Sarah said as they got off the hotel elevator and walked, arms entwined, down the carpeted hallway to their room.

"Yeah?" He slid the plastic key card into the lock. "Listen, babe, it hasn't even started yet. The real test is yet to come."

"I'm going to ace it. No sweat."

He laughed. The old Sarah, all laughter and challenge, face pink from the wind, was back in force. He tipped her chin with his finger. "Talk is cheap."

INSIDE THE ROOM, they stood looking at each other. Behind her was the bed. *The bed.* She should have asked Elizabeth about hotel protocol. Were you supposed to just disappear into the bathroom and return a few minutes later in a fluffy peignoir? Or naked? No, not naked. She'd never seen Matthew naked. Well, actually she had. Once, at her house after they got back from the beach, she'd walked into the bathroom while he was showering.

The room felt cold. The drapes were pulled wide and all the lights of Victoria were glittering in the night sky. Everything seemed slightly unreal, as though they were actors playing unfamiliar parts.

She realized that Matthew was laughing.

"What?"

"Just you. The look on your face."

"Well…" She tried to think. "Don't you have some champagne, or something?"

"In the fridge. But first you have to take your coat off."

"No *problema*." She slipped off her coat, threw it on the bed. And then her heels, which were killing her. The carpet felt good under her bare feet—she'd drawn the line at panty hose. "You look very tall now," she said, peering up at Matthew. "Now, can I have some champagne?"

"Take off your dress," he said.

She hadn't expected that and the words shot through her like an electric jolt. She stared at him for a moment and then without taking her eyes from his face, slipped the spaghetti straps off her shoulders. The dress required a tug or two before it slid down her body, but finally she was standing there in her bra and panties—ecru lace, not borrowed from Elizabeth—feeling more turned on than she'd ever been in her life.

"Hey." She moved toward him, slowly undoing his belt buckle. "Your turn. Except that I get to undress you."

"Just can't play by the rules, can you?"

"Nope." She slid his pants down over his hips, slipped her hands into the elastic of his shorts and then, suddenly, all bets were off. They ended up down on the carpet and Matthew, still wearing his shirt, had unclasped her bra, and the last conscious thought she had was that the apartment dwellers in Victoria were probably getting quite a show.

CHAPTER THIRTEEN

WHEN SHE OPENED her eyes the next morning, Matthew's arm was across her body, and her hair, which he'd unbraided, was spread out over the pillow, strands of it across her eyes, in her mouth. She brushed it off her face and, careful not to wake Matthew, rolled onto one side to look at him.

Tomorrow or the next day, or a year from now, waking up alone, I will remember exactly how he looks at this moment. His head on the pillow, sunlight falling across his face.

The thought, sudden and unbidden, filled her with a vague melancholy. Why the image of herself alone? Where would they be a year from now? Five years from now?

"Yes?" His eyes were still closed; a faint smile curved his mouth.

She touched her finger to his lips. "You can feel me looking at you?"

He opened his eyes. "For the past fifteen minutes or so." He pulled her on top of him and kissed her. "This is a great way to wake up," he said, his mouth against her neck. "Definitely beats the alarm clock."

Sarah disentangled herself and rolled over onto her back. "I was just thinking—"

He stroked her hair. "Don't. No thinking allowed."

She watched the play of sunlight across the foot of the bed. "You know what was so great about last night?"

Matthew laughed. "Nothing. It sucked."

"Shut up. I'm serious. So much of the time we're together we're talking about the past. What we used to do, how we used to be. And then there's the future, the stressful situation with Lucy and what I end up doing professionally, it's vague and cloudy. But last night was just us. Right in the moment and…" The words that had spewed out uncensored, unedited, dried up. Moments went by before Matthew put his arm around her.

"If your suggestion is that we stay in bed and have sex day and night, I'm all for it."

She smiled, although she felt on the verge of tears.

"One thing I always admire in Elizabeth," he said, "which also drives me nuts, is her refusal to look beyond the present moment. Her reasoning is that what's passed has passed, tomorrow may never happen, so why not enjoy what you have while you have it?"

Sarah nodded and moved in closer so that their hips touched. Matthew's leg covered hers. She sighed. "I understand that, intellectually, but it's difficult to…get out of my head."

"I know," Matthew said. "It is for me, too."

"I love you," Sarah said.

"I love you, too. I always have. You know that."

"I do." Tears began spilling down her face. *Do we*

have a future? The question begged to be voiced. But she knew the answer wasn't entirely Matthew's to give.

"Food," Matthew said sometime later. "And more sex, not necessarily in that order."

"I vote for room service." She slid her foot over the sheet and rested her leg on his thigh. "And while we're waiting for the food to arrive…"

THEY CAUGHT the four-o'clock ferry back and spent most of the ninety-minute crossing on the outside deck watching as Port Hamilton gradually came into sight on the horizon. From a distance, the hardscrabble appearance of the town, with its empty, shuttered shops along Front Street and dark waterfront bars, fused together into the vision of the idyllic coastal town she'd nurtured during homesick moments in Central America.

A cold wind had driven most passengers inside, but by unspoken agreement, they'd stayed outside, huddled in their coats, wind whipping around their heads. Matthew kept his arm around her, but neither of them said much, and she wondered more than once what Matthew was thinking.

"Lopez Hook," she said as they rounded the bend into the harbor.

"The old lumberyard where my father used to work." Matthew pointed to the smokestacks.

"And…one, two, three. The fourth house at the top is Rose's."

"Fifth," Matthew said. "You need glasses."

"And there's the hospital."

"That's too much reality," Matthew said. "I'm not ready for that. Let's jump overboard and swim back to Victoria and get a room."

"Can we have champagne for breakfast every day?"

"Champagne and whatever else your heart desires," Matthew said. "God, I really don't want to go back."

Something in his voice made her turn to look at him. She linked her arms in his, moved up close. "That tough, huh?"

He shrugged. "Well, that, and Lucy."

"It's a tough age, fourteen," she said. "I know from personal experience."

"I feel guilty for ruining your fourteenth birthday."

"I got over it. Don't knock yourself out trying to solve her problems. She'll get over what's bothering her now."

He hunched into his jacket. "She's jealous of you. Mad that I left her with her grandmother. I've never done that sort of thing and I think she feels insecure."

"She's not bothered by Elizabeth's relationships?"

"Doesn't seem to be. She's with Elizabeth more than she's with me. Anyway." He pulled her ever closer. "We'll work it out. I'll take her for pizza tonight, talk things over."

Sarah waited for him to invite her along, but he seemed to have retreated into his own world, and they said nothing more for the rest of the trip. As they filed off the ferry in a drizzling rain, he reached into his overcoat, pulled out his cell phone and, as they walked, he flipped the lid.

"Four calls from Lucy," he muttered. "Three from Elizabeth."

In the car, he listened to his voice mail. Sarah stared through the windshield at the rain-slicked street. She heard his intake of breath and turned. His face was ashen.

"Pearl's dead," he said. "She had a heart attack last night."

"GRANDMA'S DEAD and it's your fault!" Lucy was screaming at him, her face contorted with rage. "I hate you. Go be with your girlfriend, I don't care." And then she ran up the stairs and he heard her bedroom door slam.

Matthew looked at Elizabeth, red-eyed and wan. They were standing in the hallway where, the moment he'd opened the door Lucy had attacked him. She'd grabbed a book off the sofa, hurled that at him, then cushions and then a backpack before her fury finally subsided into sobbing.

What seemed like an eternity later, Elizabeth filled him in on the details as they sat side by side on the living-room couch.

"She had heartburn," Elizabeth said. "It got worse, then she started complaining about chest pains. Lucy called me around midnight. George…"

"Heartburn," Matthew said. "I spoke to her."

Elizabeth shrugged. "Anyway, they got worse and around midnight Lucy called me—George couldn't get anyone to look after his dog, so we ended up not going to the ocean. We were in bed when Lucy called in a panic. Grandma had a pain in her shoulder and she couldn't breathe. We took her to the E.R., but the doctor who was supposed to be on call had his beeper on Vibrate and they couldn't find him. The E.R. was packed and Mom was getting worse and then—" she shook her head "—it was too late."

She'd started to cry and he put his arm around her, but she pushed it away.

"Leave me alone, Matt." She blew her nose. "Maybe it's not fair of me, but I can't help thinking if you hadn't dragged your feet about the CMS takeover, there would have been enough staff and… Just get me some more wine, okay? There's a bottle in the fridge."

He went out to the kitchen and refilled her glass then took it back out to her.

She sniffed. "I know how you felt about Pearl and I don't want to make you feel worse, but you need to accept some responsibility for this, Matt. Not for going to Victoria with Sarah, but for Compassionate Medical System. This is a horrible wake-up call."

By the time he left later that night, the clouds that had seemed so benign as he and Sarah left Victoria had broken and the rain was coming down in torrents.

MATTHEW WAS UNAVAILABLE when Sarah tried to reach him the next morning. She'd stayed awake much of the night, expecting that he would call after he left Elizabeth's. She'd offered to go with him when he got the news, but he'd dropped her off at the apartment.

She got in the car and drove over to Elizabeth's.

Lucy answered the door. She wore skintight blue jeans and a red sweatshirt. Her face was pale, but her eyes were dry. When she saw Sarah, her expression darkened. "My mom's upstairs."

"I've come to see how you're *both* doing," Sarah said.

"Okay," Lucy mumbled.

Sarah stood awkwardly in the doorway. "Do you mind if I come in for a minute?"

Lucy shrugged but pulled the door open. "I have to go to school," she said. "And my mom's still asleep."

"I can give you a ride if you want," Sarah said.

Lucy looked uncertain. "Okay," she said after a moment, "I guess."

Hardly a ringing endorsement, Sarah thought, as she ran upstairs to tell Elizabeth. But at least the girl hadn't said no. Sarah had expected to find Elizabeth sleeping, but instead found her hugging a pair of old lamb's-wool slippers and sobbing. "She got these at Wal-Mart," she said when Sarah walked in. "Because I didn't want her walking over my rugs in her outdoor shoes. And the backs were all worn down so she shuffled around in them. It drove me crazy. Was it too much trouble to just put them on properly? And now…" Her voice broke off.

Sarah sat on the edge of the bed beside her. "Come here." She stretched her arms out and Elizabeth, the slippers still on her lap, fell against her, sobbing on Sarah's shoulder.

"Listen, I'm going to take Lucy to school," Sarah told her. "Then I'll come back and we can talk."

"She doesn't have to go. I'll call and tell them."

"I think she wants to," Sarah said. "She was ready when I got here, and it might be better for her to keep her usual routine."

"Whatever," Elizabeth said.

"I WAS TEN when my grandma died," Sarah told Lucy as she drove her to school. "One of the things that made me feel really bad was that I hadn't spent a whole lot of time with her. She was always asking me to come over, but…" She glanced at Lucy, stoic and unyielding. "She was very deaf and she talked too much—you couldn't get a word in, so I always made up excuses about why I couldn't go. After she died, I felt awful."

"I spent a lot of time with my grandma," Lucy said.

"I know. Your mom said you baked cookies with her all the time."

"And cakes. Mom's terrible at baking."

"Me, too." Sarah laughed, encouraged by what seemed like a breakthrough in their relationship, but then Lucy—as her father had on the ferry—seemed to retreat into her thoughts. Sarah's further attempts to draw her out were met with polite one-word responses. There will be other opportunities, Sarah decided after she'd dropped Lucy off and stopped at Safeway to pick milk, bread and eggs. This is just a first step.

Elizabeth was in the kitchen making coffee when Sarah got back.

"You should go home and hug your mom and tell her

you love her," Elizabeth said without turning to look at Sarah. "I'm serious. I feel guilty for just about everything to do with my mom. I even feel bad about telling Matthew it was his fault my mom died."

"That's ridiculous," Sarah said, her voice sharper than she'd intended. "Why would you blame him?"

"Well, they were short staffed and Pearl had to wait. Then they couldn't find the doctor on call. I can still see his face, the way he looked when I accused him. He loved Pearl. I know he was hurting, too, but…I don't know, I just wanted to attack him. If he got hit by a car or dropped dead of a heart attack, I'd never forgive myself."

Sarah stuck the milk and eggs she'd bought over for her friend in the refrigerator and tried to ignore the cold sense of dread that clutched at her.

SARAH ENDED UP staying at Elizabeth's that night and the next, cooking meals, helping Elizabeth with plans for the funeral and generally trying to keep things together. Matthew stopped by a couple of times to see Lucy, who still refused to speak to him. He looked gaunt and beaten, and Sarah's heart broke for him.

"I appreciate you being here with Elizabeth and Lucy," he said as they stood in the kitchen. "I'm concerned that Elizabeth will start drinking too much again and Lucy's already got enough to contend with."

"Hey, Matthew." She put both hands on his arms and looked into his eyes. "Take some time for yourself, too. Don't beat yourself up."

"YOU SHOULD CALL your dad, honey." Elizabeth sat on the edge of the bed, stroking Lucy's hair. Downstairs, she could hear Sarah vacuuming. What she would have done without Sarah, she didn't know. "He keeps calling to talk to you and I know it makes him feel bad."

"Who cares?" Lucy said.

"Honey, even if he had been here, it might not have made any difference," Elizabeth said.

"I hate him."

"No, you don't."

"Yes, I do. And don't tell me what I feel. I hate him."

Elizabeth's head was aching. "Well, I don't know what else to say except that your not talking to him is tearing him up." She rose and left the room, closing the door behind her.

In the kitchen, Sarah had found the breadmaker that Matthew had bought years ago for Christmas and was at the counter reading the recipe book that came with it. "I've used that thing once," Elizabeth said. "But it makes this fantastic honey-wheat bread."

Sarah smiled. "I was just looking at that recipe. Do you have honey?"

"Yep." Elizabeth found a jar at the back of the cupboard and set it on the counter. And then she burst into tears. Sarah grabbed a paper towel from the roll and handed it to her.

Elizabeth blew her nose into the towel. "It's just seeing you here, doing all this. I couldn't have managed—"

"Sure you could." Sara looked embarrassed. "Um, let's see, I also need…"

"No, I'm serious. Come on, you don't need to do that now. Talk to me. I'll make some tea." She microwaved two mugs of water, stuck in a couple of bags of Lipton tea and pushed one across the table to Sarah. 'When I heard you were back, I had mixed feelings. You were always so perfect."

Sarah laughed. "Right."

"No, Pearl was always comparing us. She used to hold you up as this example of what I could be if I studied harder. Why can't you be like Sarah? Sarah gets straight A's, Sarah swims faster than most boys, Sarah's going to medical school. Looks fade, blah blah blah. But I mean, I could have studied day and night, which I never would have because I wasn't that interested, and it wouldn't have made any difference."

"We should have traded mothers then," Sarah said. "*My* mom thought I should be more like you. She never wanted a tomboy daughter."

"You want to know the truth? Not that I didn't love Matt, I mean, he's a really good guy, but I first set my eyes on Matt because I didn't like you." She drank some tea. "When he and I started going out, I felt as if I broke you guys up. Matt always said that you were just friends, but—"

"That's what we were."

"But didn't you ever want it to be more than that?"

"I don't know. I guess I didn't feel confident about

myself. The way I looked. I wasn't a very feminine girl." She grinned. "Like some people I could mention."

Elizabeth laughed. "Remember when I tried to fix you up?"

"Oh, God, that pale pink lipstick and the black eyeliner. I hated makeup. I just wanted to be me. But obviously Matthew was interested in girls and he was good-looking and after a while he left me behind. I couldn't compete with the kind of girls I knew he liked and it used to eat at me."

"You mean, you were jealous."

Sarah rolled her eyes. "I used to cry myself to sleep every time I saw him with someone."

"That's so strange. I remember when I started to like him. You two were talking about something in the science lab. Your heads were close together and you were laughing. And then I came in and asked if he wanted to get a soda. I had this feeling you liked him. But you acted as if you were just fine."

"I missed my calling. I should have gone into the theater," Sarah said.

"But why didn't you do something?"

"Like what?"

"I don't know. Let Matt see that you wanted more than friendship."

"Matthew and I talked about that. I was afraid he'd reject me."

"I'm sorry if what happened made you feel…bad."

"Thanks," Sarah said.

"No, really. I didn't understand, but—" she sighed

"—when I found out George has been seeing one of the waitresses I thought was my friend, it killed me. And then I thought, that's karma. I did it to Sarah—"

"That's okay," Sarah said. "Truly, just hearing you say you understand makes me feel good."

Elizabeth smiled. The connection they'd made since Sarah got back had just got even stronger. "So did you guys have a good time in Victoria?"

"Yeah." Sarah got up from the table, ran water at the sink. "It was great."

Elizabeth tried to think of something else to ask. Well, actually she could think of tons of things to ask— what it was like, for instance finally having sex with Matthew. But even though she and Sarah were closer, it wasn't the kind of question she'd feel comfortable asking. It's just the way Sarah was. The door never opened all the way.

CHAPTER FOURTEEN

SARAH HELD her mother's rusty black umbrella high enough to shelter Rose and herself as they hurried through the pouring rain from the parking lot of the First Unitarian Church to the chapel for Pearl's memorial service. The service had already started as they squeezed into a pew in the back. In the front row, she could see Matthew sitting next to Elizabeth, Lucy on the end.

She'd slept in Elizabeth's guest bedroom again that morning and awakened to the phone ringing and then Elizabeth yelling to Lucy that her father was on the phone. Sarah had strained to hear Lucy's response, but, after a moment, heard Elizabeth tell Matthew that Lucy was still sleeping.

"She blames him," Elizabeth had said over coffee in the kitchen. "I feel terrible for him, but I can't get through to her. And Matthew's walking around like a zombie."

Deep in thought, Sarah heard Rose sniff. She turned her head slightly to catch Rose dabbing her nose and she looped her arm around Rose's shoulders. They'd probably never bond the way the perfect mother and daughter would, but she had the sense that they'd grown closer in the past few weeks. And perfection, she was beginning to believe, was pretty much an illusion. If nothing else, witnessing Rose's imperfections had given her some new insight into her own.

Afterward, there was a small gathering in an anteroom and the Sweet Adelines sang a medley in memory of Pearl. Sarah watched Elizabeth, glassy-eyed, drift in and out of clusters of mourners. Lucy, in a short black skirt and tight sweater, her dark hair pulled severely away from her face, hung back on the sidelines looking heartwrenchingly young and alone. But when Sarah walked over to talk to her, Lucy was politely distant and after a moment excused herself and drifted away.

Sarah greeted people she hadn't seen for years, answered questions about Central America, gave vague responses about her plans, aware all the time that she was looking around for Matthew's dark head. At one point, she glimpsed him standing with Lucy, but when she looked again Lucy had gone.

She saw him talking to a stooped gray-haired man in a black suit jacket that hung like a cape over the curve of his spine. Matthew's back was to her and she tapped his shoulder. When he turned around his expression was unreadable.

"Sarah," he said, "I meant to call you, but…"

"That's okay. How're you doing?"

He shrugged. "Fine."

She kept looking at him until he smiled faintly.

"I'm fine. Really."

"You're not invincible."

"Don't spread that around." The smile flickered then faded. "Listen, I need to talk to Pearl's sister. I'll…I'll give you a call."

And then he'd disappeared into the crowd. Sarah hung around for a few more minutes, then went to look for Rose. She found her talking to a middle-aged couple.

"My daughter, Sarah," Rose said. "She's been in Central America for the past…what, five or six years?"

They smiled. The woman had a cap of white hair as soft and flyaway as dandelion seed, and lipstick on her teeth. "We were in Costa Rica last year." She glanced at her husband. "Beautiful beaches, weren't they, honey?"

"Beautiful," he agreed. And then he turned to Rose. "So you sold your practice?"

"Yes, well, it was time." She glanced at Sarah. "Listen sweetheart, Bill and Maude said they'd give me a ride home. They've invited me to dinner, okay?"

In the car, Sarah felt water trickle down her neck. She'd left the umbrella with Rose. Wet and shivering, she started the ignition. Through the fogged-up windows, she looked out at a cluster of pines at the edge of the parking lot and, beyond that, a canopy, metal folding chairs and a carpet of plastic grass, vibrant green in the monochrome landscape. She watched a woman in a long black coat and rubber boots with fur around the edges dodge a puddle. Matthew came out of the church with his arm around Elizabeth's shoulders. Lucy walked next to Elizabeth, her hand in her mother's. Sarah started the car and drove off. The last time she'd felt so completely alone was after Ted died.

"I'M SORRY, Daddy," Lucy said the night after Pearl's funeral. Her mouth quivered and her eyes were red and swollen. I didn't mean all those things I said to you."

"I knew you didn't." He'd finally coaxed her out of her room and they'd gone out for pizza. On the table between them, a candle in a Chianti bottle flickered, throwing shadows on her face. "We sometimes say things in anger that we don't really mean."

Lucy reached for a slice of pizza. "I was also mad because you went to Victoria and I told you a bunch of times that I wanted to go. Remember we were going to see the movie at IMAX? And then you just went with Sarah."

Matthew regarded his own pizza: he'd suddenly lost his appetite. Despite the sense of déjà vu the topic gave him, she was still recovering from the death of her grandmother and he didn't want to further muddy the emotional waters by talking about his relationship with Sarah.

"We'll go to IMAX," he said. "I promise."

Lucy nodded, but still seemed to have something

on her mind. "Sometimes even after you stop being angry with someone, its kind of hard to trust them because they're still the same person, so what if they do it again?"

TEN DAYS AFTER Pearl's death Matthew stood in the darkened radiology room, the only illumination coming from the CT scanner. An angiogram showed arteries wriggling, twisting and branching much like his own thoughts. He was sleeping fitfully, if at all, and other than their brief conversation at the funeral, he hadn't spoken to Sarah.

Intellectually, he knew Pearl could have—and with her medical history—probably would have died regardless of whether or not he'd been working for Compassionate Medical Systems the night she went to the E.R. He also recognized that Sarah's low regard of the program had influenced his thinking.

Okay, he didn't blame her. But neither could he make himself call her. And, always, there was Lucy. He thought of Sarah, lying next to him, talking about the future. "It's all vague and cloudy," she'd said, "but last night was just us. Right in the moment." And now a part of the past, which so much of his relationship with Sarah had been.

A technologist behind him said something and Matthew dragged his attention back to the screen.

Later, up on the patient floor, he reassured the patient's mother everything about her son's angiogram appeared normal. Then he headed for administration.

"Morning, Dr. Cameron," Heidenreich's secretary greeted him. "Mr. Heidenreich has someone in his office. He should be through in a few minutes."

"I'll wait," Matthew said, but then the door to the administrator's office opened and Rose Benedict walked out. When she saw Matthew, she put her hand on his arm.

"So sorry about Pearl," she said. "It hit me hard personally—she and I were about the same age." She peered into his face. "You taking care of yourself? You look as though you haven't slept in weeks."

"I'm fine." Matthew realized he hadn't spoken to her since hearing that she'd sold her practice and added, "I understand congratulations are in order."

She beamed. "Yep. I'm now officially an employee of Compassionate Medical Systems."

"How does that feel?"

"I haven't had much time to think about it yet. I do know they produce a lot of paperwork. More manuals and guides and lists of procedures than you could shake a stick at. I've left the lists conspicuously around the house, hoping Sarah would look at them when she dropped by. It's very organized, compulsive. Sarah's style, I would have thought."

Matthew smiled.

"Unfortunately, she doesn't take the bait," Rose said.

"CMS isn't Sarah's kind of thing," Matthew said. It isn't mine, either, he thought, but he'd made his decision. "How is Sarah lately?"

"Haven't seen her since Pearl's funeral," Rose said. "Sarah has a tendency to crawl into her shell when things aren't going well. And I sense they're not going very well for her right now. You know Sarah."

Matthew didn't answer, in part because he wasn't sure he really did know Sarah. He was also remembering how Rose had always made him feel as a child. Not the sort of mother you'd want if your heart was breaking.

"Have you seen her?" she asked.

"I tried to call a couple of times, but there was no answer and—" he scratched the back of his head "—I never left a message."

"She's got a lot of things on her mind these days. I do know she was a bit down after the fossil trip. Sarah's not exactly the warm and cuddly earth-mother type. Poor girl, she takes after me in that regard. All crusty and impenetrable on the outside, but mush in the center."

He laughed. "I've yet to see your mushy center."

"Oh, it's there, trust me. It just requires someone with enough imagination to bring it out."

"Matthew." Heidenreich appeared from his office. "You here to see me?"

"Yeah." He looked at Rose. "If you see Sarah, tell her I said hi."

Rose smiled archly. "Why don't you tell her yourself, Matthew?"

A moment later he was sitting across from Heidenreich trying to face down the odd sensation that his life was flashing past him. Or perhaps just life as he'd known it until now. "I'm ready to join the opposition," he told Heidenreich.

SARAH WAS THE LAST PERSON Elizabeth ever thought she'd have a pity party with, but here they were sitting in Cup o' Joe, which was about to close down, feeling about as gloomy as the weather. Sarah's nose and cheeks were red from the wind—and maybe a session with the tissue box—and she was wearing a red parka and a black woolen cap pulled down over her hair. Like she usually did whenever she looked at Sarah, Elizabeth wanted to give her a makeover, except that right now she needed some advice.

"I think George is avoiding me," she told Sarah, who had just blurted out that she was feeling depressed about Matthew, but she wasn't about to go to the hospital and beg him to talk to her.

Sarah drank some coffee. "Why do you think so?"

"He didn't call for a week, then when I called his house, his roommate said he was out. But I had this strange feeling she was lying. But then I thought, well, maybe he's just busy and he'll call me when he has time."

Sarah nodded. "And?"

"Okay, there's this online-dating site where I met him. I thought I'd just check it out to see if… And he was online."

"But so were you."

"But I wasn't looking. He was. Looking for someone else. I feel horrible."

"Remember what you said when I told you about that reporter I was attracted to? The one who never called me again?"

"The one you said you wanted to sleep with?"

"I didn't say I *wanted* to sleep with him," Sarah corrected, "I said I would have. Anyway, you told me I wanted him to be attracted to me so I'd feel better about myself. Maybe that's how it is for you with George."

"But he did make me feel better about myself. He respected what I said. Not like Matthew—"

"Listen to me—" sarah leaned across the table "—no one can *make* you feel better about yourself. You have to feel it in here." She stabbed at her chest. "You have to know that you're a good, worthwhile person."

Elizabeth sighed. "I wish I could be like you."

Sarah rolled her eyes. "Oh, please."

"So, what if you never saw Matthew again?"

Sarah chewed her lip. "It kills me to even imagine it. But, if that did happen, I'd still be the same person inside."

"Yeah?"

"Yeah." She nodded slowly. "I mean, I'd have to do a sales job on myself to believe it, but yeah." A pause. "Maybe not so lovable though."

They both laughed. Through the window, Elizabeth watched the foot passengers file off the ferry, all bundled up against the wind whipping off the strait. There were days when it seemed as though the sun had forgotten about the Olympic Peninsula altogether.

"You know the strange thing?" she said. "We seem so different. You're a doctor, you do all this interesting stuff. And I'm…about to be an unemployed waitress. But underneath, we're pretty much the same. We both want someone who sees us for what we are and loves that about us."

"Well, I'll tell you what. We're going to get my practice up and running, and I can't think of anyone I'd rather have help me than you."

"Wow, thank you," Elizabeth said, so touched by what Sarah had just said, she thought she might start bawling.

Sarah smiled.

"By the way, Matthew finally did it," Elizabeth said.

"Did what?"

"Joined CMS. I thought maybe you'd heard."

"No." Sarah shook her head. "When did this happen?"

"He dropped by last night to see Lucy and he told me then."

She saw Sarah shut down, the way she sometimes did. "It's like I told you," she said after they'd sat there in silence for a few minutes, "Matt's first priority is always going to be to Lucy."

"Well, naturally. She's his daughter."

"It's more than that. I know you think you know him better than anyone, but let me tell you, I know him, too. He's beating himself up because Pearl died while he was in Victoria with you. Even though he hasn't taken a weekend off for God knows how long and my mom might have died whether he was there or not, he sees it as his fault. And Lucy blaming him was fuel on the flames."

"He's been leaning toward CMS all along," Sarah said. "I guess this just pushed him over the edge."

"Does it make you feel bad?"

"Not really." Sarah straightened her shoulders. "In a way, it makes me more determined to make my idea work."

"Yay for you," Elizabeth clinked her coffee cup against Sarah's. "Who needs men, anyway? Let's talk business."

SARAH HAD FELT pretty chipper when she left Elizabeth, but as the day wore on, she started to feel less and less confident about her plans and, ultimately, about whether she even wanted to stay in Port Hamilton at all. First Rose had dropped by to inject her own brand of negativity into things, and then that night, while Sarah was on the Internet, Matthew called to tell her his decision.

Just hearing his voice, she had felt her resolve crumble.

"Congratulations," she said, her voice clipped and brittle. And then, unable to resist. "I guess."

"Sarah, I had to. You—"

"I don't understand. I know." Her temper got the upper hand. "You have a family to support. Ideals don't pay the mortgage." There was silence on the line. "I'm sorry, I shouldn't have said that. I hope things work out for you, really."

"You could give it a try yourself," Matthew said.

"I'd rather fry hamburgers."

"So you're still going ahead with your plan?"

"Why wouldn't I? Because you've decided to join the opposition?"

"It's unrealistic, Sarah."

"For you maybe. But that's what I intend to do." She wanted to sound certain, but to her ears her voice sounded full of a ten-year-old's bravado. *Fine, I'll start my own game.* "And don't tell me all the reasons it won't work, I've heard them all from my mother. It only makes me more determined."

"Same old Sarah."

"There'll always be room for you," she said. "If you ever change your mind."

"I'll remember that. Listen, I hear my name, I've got to go. I'll…see you around, Sarah."

"Yeah, see you around, Matthew," she muttered as she hung up the phone.

The following day and for most of the next week, the *Peninsula Daily*'s front pages were full of Compassionate Medical System's takeover. In the kitchen, Sarah cradled a coffee cup in both hands and stared at the newspaper spread out across the counter. A picture of a smiling Matthew in surgical scrubs extolling the benefits of practicing on the peninsula. On the next page, a feature about the new state-of-the-art scanning machine. On the editorial page, one letter of dissent lamenting the good old days before corporate medicine.

Sarah cut that one out and stuck it on the refrigerator.

CHAPTER FIFTEEN

A WEEK WENT BY, then two, then a month. Matthew left a couple of messages on Sarah's voice mail. Once she'd been riding her bike past the hospital and she saw him in the distance and rode the other way. It seemed there was nothing to say to him, no way to bridge the distance. A cold sort of emptiness filled her heart. Despite Elizabeth's daily reassurances, she found herself wondering more than once whether staying in Port Hamilton was really the right thing to do.

She said as much while they were walking out on Lopez Hook one morning.

"I thought I could come back here and just pick up where I left off. But everything's changed. I've changed. I'm not so sure anymore that this is really where I belong. Maybe Matthew and my mother are right. Maybe I'm being hopelessly naive."

"Hey, you can't back down," Elizabeth said. "There are people on the other end of the peninsula just waiting for you to get started."

"I realize that, but—"

"Is it the money?"

"No, I wasn't making much in Central America, either. Besides, I have some my dad left me."

"Matt?"

Sarah wiped her eyes. "I felt…feel, I don't know, it seems crazy…"

"First me, then Lucy. Right?"

"Yeah. I want him to choose *me*." Tears in her eyes, she grinned. "Choose *me,* or I'll have a hissy fit."

"Give him time. He's got his own stuff to work out. Plus he's a guy. They do things their own way." She grabbed Sarah's arm with both hands. "Listen, toots, you can't run away again. Port Hamilton needs you. Not to mention I need a job. How would Elizabeth Cameron, receptionist/office cleaner/supply buyer/ general gofer look on my business cards?"

"Great," Sarah said. "Go order them."

A few days later, after a restless night, she dressed and walked out into the thick morning fog that had drifted in from the strait. Shoulders hunched, hands thrust in the pockets of her parka, she trekked the mile to the Olympic National Park and then down a winding trail into the woods.

The deeper into the thicket of trees she walked, the cooler the air around her felt. With the soft mulch of the trail under her feet, the quiet cathedral-like hush was broken only by the twitter of birds. From the harbor, she heard the ferry's horn. And then she looked up and, through the highest branches, still veiled by mist, a pale gleam of sunshine had broken through. She tipped her face up and felt the faint warmth. It seemed as good a sign as any that she should stay.

And then, later in the day, she saw Debbi at the farmer's market. Her now white-blond hair was cut close to her scalp. Her left eye sported a fading bruise that had turned the colors of a tropic sunset. Curt was nowhere in sight.

"What happened?" Sarah asked.

"Oh…" Debbi shrugged. "I fell." Clearly uncomfortable, she busied herself rearranging a pyramid of red peppers. "I broke up with Curt," she said. "Well, he walked out. He's moved in with this woman who does colonics."

Sarah met her eyes for a moment. "So how are you doing?"

Debbi shrugged again. "Okay. I miss him though." She wiped her eyes with the back of her hand. "He's difficult to be around sometimes, but…we kept fighting about Alli."

"How is she?"

"Doing great now. Whatever it was cleared right up and she hasn't had a problem since. I guess the herbal stuff worked. Curt was right."

"Good." Sarah wanted to say more, but customers where jostling for position around the stand. "You have my number. Call me. Even if you just need to talk," she said with a glance at Debbi's bruised eye.

"Great. I probably have some other patients for you, too. I know a bunch of people who don't have cars to get into Port Hamilton. They'd think they'd died and gone to heaven if a doctor made house calls."

Sarah smiled. "Well, that's a deal then."

THAT EVENING Rose dropped by carrying Deanna in a huge cage. "He's lonely," she said. "And since you're here all day, I thought the two of you could keep each other company." She set the crate down on the kitchen floor. "If you have tuna, I'll feed him."

Sarah looked at Deanna. Deanna hissed. Sarah bared her teeth.

"He isn't usually so touchy," Rose observed, her back to Sarah.

"Perhaps he doesn't like being called Deanna." Sarah found a can of tuna in the cabinet. She got the can opener from the drawer. "How's he going to pick up a mate with a name like that?"

"He doesn't seem to have much trouble in that department," Rose said. "I don't think they bother exchanging names. By the way, I ran into Matthew at the hospital the other day. I was complaining that you wouldn't listen to reason, this whole solo practice thing, and he said I should be proud of you."

Sarah tried to keep her face expressionless.

"You can't exist on house calls alone," Rose said. "Eventually, you'll need to have an office."

"First I need to find one I can afford."

"Use the old consulting room," Rose said. "Rent free."

Sarah gaped at her. "Are you serious?"

"Perfectly. There's a certain synergy to it. Family tradition and all that. Your great-grandfather used to make house calls in a horse-drawn cart."

Sarah didn't trust her voice.

"Actually, I am rather proud of you." Rose handed Sarah a set of keys. "I still think it's an absurdly impractical idea, but I've grown quite used to having you around and I would prefer that you don't go gallivanting off to Central America again."

"EVERYTHING'S GOING SO well, it's almost scary," Elizabeth said a few weeks later as she drove Sarah out to a trailer park on the west end of the peninsula to visit Debbi Kennedy and some of her friends and neighbors who'd signed on as Sarah's patients. Neil Diamond was singing "Sweet Caroline" on a moldy-oldies radio station. George had called last night and the weather had finally turned warmer.

She dug into the bag of fat-free white cheddar cheese potato chips tucked into the console between them. Every day it seemed either she or Sarah heard from someone who wanted to be added to the list of patients.

Lucy was doing better, too. Matthew was spending a lot more time with her now that he was working for CMS and, although she'd never say this to Sarah, she suspected Lucy was happier now that Sarah was out of the picture. Just about the only person who didn't seem chipper right now was Matthew. Maybe he missed Sarah. Maybe they missed each other. But Sarah clammed up whenever Matthew's name came up.

Pine trees flew past the window. Pine trees and more

pine trees. Elizabeth glanced at the speedometer and realized she was doing eighty. She let up on the gas and grinned at Sarah. "Easy to speed out here where there's no traffic."

"Fine with me," Sarah said. "I've been looking forward to this." She took a handful of chips. "So you know most of these people?"

Elizabeth made a face.

"What?"

"I hate talking about this, especially to you." She ate a couple of chips. "Mostly they're people I met in counseling. Rehab, to be honest. After the divorce, I drank too much. Dabbled in a few things I shouldn't have. Matt threatened to take Lucy unless I straightened myself out. So I did. Debbi used to do drugs a few years ago, nothing major, but then she had her little girl. Plus all the stuff with that Curt character."

Sarah didn't say anything and they drove along in silence for so long it started to feel uncomfortable. "You're not sorry I talked you into this?" Elizabeth finally asked.

"No, of course not," Sarah said. "These people have kids who get sick. Someone needs to take care of them." She grinned. "I'll be fine until I run out of money."

THE FIRST PERSON she saw when they pulled up outside Debbi's trailer was Curt, jeans loose on his hips and a floppy straw hat shading his face. He walked over to meet them. "If it isn't the good doctor herself," he said. "Come to dispense her medical wisdom on the unwashed masses."

Sarah, reaching into the backseat of the truck for her medical bag, felt a sense of foreboding. A few feet away from where he stood, two goats were grazing among what looked like rows of spinach. It occurred to her that Alli's intestinal troubles could have stemmed from some sort of E. coli contamination and she made a mental note to look into it later.

"Hey, Curt." Ignoring his sarcasm, she stuck out her hand. "How's it going?"

"Everything is bloody marvelous," he said. "My woman has left me, taken my child." He gestured at a row of raised planting beds. "My crops are suffering from neglect, through no fault of my own, I might add. This, of course, means that my livelihood is essentially down the toilet, but—" with one hand, he swept off the hat, bowed low "—other than that, no complaints. And yourself?"

From where she stood, Sarah could smell alcohol on his breath, see the enlarged pupils that made his pale eyes look almost dark. Hadn't Debbi told her that Curt had moved in with another woman? She tried to remember, then decided ultimately the domestic issues didn't matter. "Is…Debbi here?"

"No, Dr. Sarah," he said, "Debbi is not around. Didn't I just explain? Debbi has taken a powder. With our daughter." He laughed. "My God, I do have a way with words. Debbi, my constant companion, has taken a powder with our—"

"I heard you the first time," Sarah said. "Do you know where she is?"

"Haven't the foggiest," Curt said. "And if I had, I certainly wouldn't tell you since you, Dr. Sarah—" he stabbed her chest with his forefinger "—are indirectly, or perhaps directly, a cause of our…shall we say *estrangement?*"

Sarah glanced around, reassured to see Elizabeth coming toward them. The borderline quality to his personality, which had struck her as eccentric but harmless, now seemed ominous.

"I'm not sure I know what you're talking about," she said.

Curt stroked his chin and appeared for a moment to be deep in thought. "Well, let me explain, Dr. Sarah. Once upon a time, two happy hippy people and their small child were leading a quiet and simple life selling the fruits of their labor at the local farmer's market. But then one day a serpent crawled into their world, masquerading as one of them when, in fact, she was an emissary of evil. Soon, the serpent had lured half of the happy couple away, promising to rid the small child of some imaginary ailment while all the time conspiring to poison her with a cache of evil drugs."

"He's nuts," Elizabeth muttered in Sarah's ear. "Let's get out of here."

"Look," Sarah started, but Elizabeth grabbed her by the arm and practically marched her down the dirt path to the asphalt road that led to the other trailers. When she peered over her shoulder, Curt had disappeared.

"Did you hear that?" Sarah asked.

"I heard enough." Elizabeth still held Sarah's arm as though she was afraid Sarah might bolt and go back. "He's on something. You don't want to mess with him in the state he's in right now."

"I'm concerned about Debbi and the baby," Sarah said, recalling the bruises on Debbi's face.

"Maybe one of the neighbors will know where she's staying," Elizabeth suggested.

But no one in any of the other trailers, including the mother of a toddler with a eczema on his back, knew anything of Debbi's whereabouts. "They were having some problems," the woman said as she took the sample tubes Rose had donated to Sarah. "But what couple doesn't?"

DRIVING BACK TO Port Hamilton, Sarah took some comfort in the knowledge that if the child had been seen in Rose's dermatology office, the charges would have exceeded a hundred dollars. Instead, she'd scribbled out an invoice and, reluctantly, accepted the ten dollars the women gave her. It would hardly pay for her gas, but that wasn't the point.

"Our instinct is to feed ourselves first," an old village healer in Mexico had once told her. "And to only make friends with others if they can feed us. But if we are willing to feel hunger, something more valuable comes out of that discomfort which is that we can help somebody else at the same time."

She tried to keep this in mind. Tried not to worry about Debbi. Tried not to think about Matthew.

"I ALREADY POSED for a picture," Matthew told the public-relations woman, a young pretty blonde in a figure-hugging red suit, who had arrived in his office, camera and digital recorder in hand. He wondered, as he had more than once since he joined Compassionate Medical Systems, how many public relations and marketing people the organization employed. They seemed to be everywhere.

"That picture was for the print media," the woman said. "This is for our employee magazine."

"You can't use the same picture?"

"Dr. Cameron." She laughed the way you'd laugh at a naughty but appealing child. "You're the cover story for our next newsletter. Not only do we need more pictures, we also need to do an interview about the rewards of practicing medicine here in Port Hamilton. You don't have the interview down on your calendar?"

Matthew tried to recall. Actually his calendar had been taken out of his hands. Literally. He now had a secretary who kept his appointments on her computer, coordinating them with the BlackBerry he'd been given by CMS executives as a token of appreciation for his work in encouraging the medical staff's en masse acceptance of the new regime.

In one sense, not having to keep track of his appointments was a relief. Although he saw fewer patients, he was constantly taking overnight trips to the company's headquarters in Seattle to attend meetings. He was also on numerous local committees. Compassionate Medical Systems, he was learning, was very big on committees.

This morning, he'd met with the committee to plan a new doctors' dining room. He'd asked what was wrong with the old doctors' dining room before he realized that the hospital had never had a separate doctor's dining room. Physicians ate with everyone else, an arrangement that had always suited him fine. It was just a matter of not having patient conversations during meals where they might be overheard.

On the plus side, three more physicians had been brought in from Seattle to provide temporary staffing until permanent replacements were found. And he no longer had to be on call over weekends and holidays.

Still, he couldn't sit in a committee meeting and listen to the administrative team drone on about team spirit and team building, and God knows what else, without imagining Sarah's reaction. Reading the newspaper, something he actually had time to do these days, he'd come to the full-page picture of himself and wondered if she'd seen it.

That night, he tried to call her. He was in the kitchen making risotto with braised lamb shanks. He and Lucy had started taking cooking classes together at the Y and, to his surprise, he found the chopping and sautéing and stirring a relaxing way to shake off the stress of the day. Lucy also enjoyed it, to the point that they'd quickly grown bored with the Y's offerings and had started checking out books from the library, following increasingly complicated recipes.

But he missed Sarah and thought of her constantly. On a flight back from Seattle, he'd struck up a conversation with a woman in the next seat. An artist. She'd invited him to visit her when he was in the area. He'd briefly considered calling her, but it was Sarah's face he saw as he fell asleep each night.

Since Pearl's death, he could no longer see their relationship, or whatever it was, with any degree of clarity.

A relationship with Sarah would force Lucy to accept—or not—a new version of Lucy's relationship with him. He'd had endless discussions in his head. *Love isn't like a cake that you divide into pieces. It can be divided endlessly.* Ultimately though he'd decided that Lucy needed more time to adjust to the death of her grandma. Which didn't stop him from missing Sarah.

And then, stirring the risotto, he decided to hell with it. He wanted to talk to her. He heard the phone ring on her end and then her answering machine picked it up. He had opened his mouth to speak just as Lucy appeared in the kitchen.

"Who are you calling?"

He shook his head. "No one."

She narrowed her eyes. "You're calling no one."

"Right. But no one's home."

"Dad. You're losing it."

"I've lost it, Lulu."

"You're also supposed to be stirring the risotto. Constantly."

He started stirring.

"Dad. I have something very important to ask you."

"Ask ahead."

"Could I come and live here with you?"

"Why?"

Her face darkened. "What kind of question is that? *Why?* You don't want me to live with you?"

"That wasn't what I said," Matthew said. "I want to know why you're asking right now."

"Because I like living here better than living with Mom."

Matthew kept stirring. "Well, let's think about it, okay?"

"That means no."

"I didn't say that." He turned the burner down. "Lucy, I've had a long day. Don't give me a hard time, okay?"

"I don't like George."

"George?"

"Mom's boyfriend. He's weird."

Alarm bells going off, Matthew turned to look at her. "Weird, how?"

"He just is."

THE NEXT MORNING, before he saw his first patient, he called Elizabeth.

"This guy you've been seeing—"

"He has a name, Matt. It's George. What about him?"

He plunged right in. "Lucy said he's weird."

Elizabeth laughed. "She said *you're* weird."

"He's a musician, isn't it?"

"So?"

"So…she asked if she could live here with me. The reason she gave was that she didn't want to be around George. It raises some concerns in my mind…"

"Let's talk about how Lucy gets along with Sarah," Elizabeth said.

"That's different."

"No, it's not different. She's jealous of Sarah and she's jealous of George. She wants to be the center of our attention and anyone else is competition. You can let her dictate your personal life, Matt—that's your business—but she's not doing it to me."

A talk with Lucy was clearly overdue, he decided, but then calls from former patients started trickling in.

The first was from the mother of a five-year-old daughter he'd operated on a year ago to correct problems with her esophagus. "I tried to make an appointment with your office," she told him, "but I got switched to this eight-hundred number in Seattle. They told me that because Roberta has existing medical problems, we can't enroll her in Compassionate Medical Systems. They said I'll have to find another doctor."

By the end of the day, he had a stack of similar messages, forwarded by his secretary. Parents complaining that CMS wouldn't insure their children because of one thing or another and now, as a last resort, they were calling him. "It's not even a question of money," one mother had said. "I'm more than happy to pay the premiums, but Compassionate Medical Systems won't touch us because my son has medical problems."

Before he left for the day, Matthew walked up to the

administrative suite, now renamed Compassionate Medical Systems, Port Hamilton branch. Heidenreich, demoted to general flunky, had been moved down the hall, his former office now occupied by a patient services representative who smiled regretfully when he told her about the calls.

"We can't accept everyone, Dr. Cameron," she said. "Compassionate Medical Systems' goal is to extend affordable coverage to as many people as we can, but in order to keep costs under control, we simply have to exclude some conditions."

CHAPTER SIXTEEN

NO ONE AT THE CURLY Q HOUSE of Hair knew where Debbi Kennedy might be. "She quit, oh, about two weeks ago," the receptionist said when Sarah stopped in to ask. "She said the drive was getting to be too much."

"Does she have parents in town?" Sarah asked. "Anyone she might be staying with?"

"Not that I know of," the receptionist said. "If you want to leave a message for her, I'll give it to her if she stops by."

On her way back to Rose's house, where Elizabeth was painting the old consulting room, Sarah stopped in at the police station.

"The last time I saw her about ten days ago," she told the officer at the front desk, "she had facial bruises that I gather were inflicted by her boyfriend."

"Did she tell you that?"

"No. She said she fell. But…maybe you know her boyfriend? Curt Hudelson? I think he spent some time in jail—"

"Assault?"

"No, he was protesting a development, but he's a loose canon. When I went out to see Debbi, he said she'd moved and wouldn't tell me where."

The officer seemed unimpressed. There had been no calls, no domestic complaints. If they could, they'd send someone out. "But it's a long way to go on a wild-goose chase."

"There's not much else you can do," Elizabeth said when Sarah returned. Paintbrush in hand, she stood on the stepladder surveying the results. "What do you think?"

Sarah looked at the wall Elizabeth had just finished. They'd chosen a pale yellow and, with the late-afternoon sun coming through the windows, the place looked bright and cheerful. Exactly the effect she'd been after.

"It looks terrific," she said, trying to shake her concerns about Debbi. For all she knew, Debbi and Curt fought constantly and Debbi routinely took off. She grabbed the bandanna she'd taken off earlier and tied it over her hair. Things were going better than she'd dared even hope. An article in the local newspaper had brought in a few new patients, but, better still, a couple of physicians who had decided not to go with CMS had offered their services. One was a surgeon with staff privileges at the hospital in the next town. She'd also applied for a business loan and, since the bank manager was a friend of her mother's, felt pretty optimistic about getting approved. All in all, she was beginning to feel that coming home had been a good decision.

Except, of course, that it had hurt her friendship with Matthew. The usual solution for insoluble problems—just not thinking about them—didn't work for this one, in part because of Elizabeth, whom she saw every day. Elizabeth's conversation tended to revolve around George or Lucy and Lucy was inextricably linked to Matthew. In fact, she realized now, Elizabeth had just said something about Lucy that required a response.

"Sorry."

"I asked what you would do?" Elizabeth said. "If it was your daughter."

On the top step of the ladder, Sarah reached to dab a spot she'd overlooked. "Do about what?"

"Lucy. She wants to live with Matthew so she's hinting that it's because of George and now Matthew is giving me the third degree about George."

Sarah stared at her. *If it was your daughter.* The words slammed around in her brain. *If it was your daughter.* How the hell would she know what she'd do? She didn't have a daughter. She'd probably never have a daughter. Or a son, for that matter. She had causes. And she was ready to give up everything else for them. Including a man she truly loved.

"Sarah?" Elizabeth had set her paintbrush down. "Are you okay?"

"I'm fine." She pulled off the bandanna. "I'll see you later."

MATTHEW HAD CALLED in sick that morning, one of the few times he could ever remember doing so. His throat was sore, his head felt full of cotton. Overriding it all was the feeling that if he slept around the clock, he still wouldn't shake off an all-consuming fatigue, exacerbated by the fact that once he laid down to sleep, his mind immediately went into overdrive.

He forced himself to stay in bed till noon then, thirsty, he pulled on sweats and shuffled into the kitchen. As he stood at the sink, he heard footsteps outside and then a faint noise at the front door. Glass in hand, he went to investigate.

Sarah, about to slip a note under the door, was caught by surprise as he pulled it open, and she stumbled against him. She wore jeans with rips in the knees and a big white cotton shirt that might once have belonged to her father.

"Matthew." Her expression changed to one of concern. "I thought you'd be at work, I was just leaving you a note. What's wrong? Are you sick?"

"A cold, I think." She had a smudge of paint on her forehead and one on her chin. "Come in. If you're not scared of catching whatever it is."

She followed him inside and they both sat on the couch. He set the water glass on the coffee table. Sneezed. Sarah jumped up. "What are you doing for that, Matthew? Have you eaten?"

He hadn't thought he was hungry but suddenly realized he was ravenous. He sneezed again. "There's stuff in the fridge. Some eggs, cold cuts. If you want to fix something."

"I can do that." Sarah walked over and opened the

fridge. "I've been painting," she said as she pulled items out. "Rose is letting me use the old consulting room. Rent free."

He smiled. Rose had apparently taken his pep talk to heart. "So we should be drinking champagne then."

"When you're up to it." She opened a jar of mayonnaise, sniffed the contents, then spooned some into a bowl. "Things are going surprisingly well. A bunch of new patients. I'm not going to get rich, but—"

"That was never your intention," he said.

"Exactly." She found the chicken breast he had cooked the night before and began cutting the meat from the bone. "By the way, you haven't seen Debbi Kennedy's daughter lately, have you?"

"Not since she brought her into the E.R. about a month ago, maybe longer. Why?"

"I'm concerned about her. Elizabeth and I drove out to her place, and her boyfriend said she'd left with their child and claimed not to know where she was. He seemed… I thought he might be on drugs. No one appears to know where she might be. I even went to the police."

"You've done all you can then." He leaned his head back and closed his eyes. He didn't feel like talking about Debbi Kennedy. A thump on the couch beside him signaled Sarah's return.

"Chicken salad." She set the bowl on his lap. "It probably should have been chicken soup, but I didn't think of that until right now." She stuck two forks in the bowl. "Eat."

He took a mouthful, then set the fork down. "I've missed you, Sarah," he said finally. "A lot."

"Me, too." Sarah picked at the salad.

They both looked at the bowl as though it contained the secrets to the universe.

"Can we pick up where we left off?"

"I don't know." She wouldn't look at him. "I don't know what happened when we left off. I've thought and thought about it and I still don't know. It's me. I'm like a turtle. I sense danger and go into my shell."

From the couch where they sat, he could see through the French doors and out to the street where two boys were riding skateboards. One he recognized as a kid he'd operated on eight or nine months ago for a shattered foot. Sarah moved closer and dug her chin into his shoulder.

"What danger did you sense this time?"

"Maybe coming between you and Lucy. The feeling that I'm competing with her somehow."

"It'll take time, Sarah."

"I know."

"And nothing we say here, right now, is going to make any difference in the long run. I *know* Lucy manipulates me. Enough people have told me so. But knowing it and doing something about it are two different things."

She nodded. "It's easy for me to talk, I don't have kids, but—"

"Lots of people who do have kids also manage to have successful relationships. I'm sorry I flaked out after Pearl died. So much was going on and I just opted out. I'm truly sorry, Sarah."

"I want you in my life, Matthew." She shifted to look at him, a faint smile on her face. "Not necessarily in my practice, but in my life. I mean, you always have been, but I want—

"A more integrative approach?"

She laughed. "Yeah, you could say that. Damn." She glanced at her watch. "I need to get going."

"I'll walk you out. Sick as I am." He slung his arm around her shoulder, nudged his hip against hers as they walked down the narrow hallway to the front door. Outside, they stood on the sidewalk, neither of them making a move to leave. Over the rooftops of the houses on the other side of the street, the Olympics were purple against the pale blue sky. Still, neither of them moved, and then suddenly they both moved and he put his hands on her shoulders and pressed his forehead against hers. He closed his eyes.

"Sarah."

"That's me."

He sighed. "I'm feeling better already."

"Well enough to go dancing?"

He pulled away to look at her.

"I'm serious. There's a fiddle band playing at the Grange tomorrow night. I was planning to drop in anyway. Can't let the grass grow under these feet." She stuck out one of her sneakers. "Want to go?"

THE WOODEN GRANGE BUILDING had been built back in her grandfather's days for potluck suppers and community meetings about this and that. As a child, she'd practically drool as she checked out the covered dishes of hamburger casserole and chicken stew and the endless array of pies and cakes lined up on the trestle tables along one side of the room.

Matthew—looking incredibly sexy in jeans and a red flannel shirt—had been delayed at the hospital and by the time he picked her up and they'd driven to the west end, the music had already started and the dance floor was filled. Sarah stood with Matthew's arm around her, eyeing the flouncy skirts and elaborately tooled boots and wished she'd done better than what was essentially a version of Matthew's outfit, except her shirt was yellow. Then she decided that the only thing she really cared about was standing right at her side and to hell with her costume.

"Want to dance?" she asked.

"I thought you'd never ask," he said as he took her hand.

Afterward, in the cranky elevator of her apartment building, he kissed her. When the elevator groaned and creaked to a stop, he took her hand and they walked to her apartment. Inside, he closed the door behind him and she heard the lock click. Then he led her to the bedroom and kissed her again. Moonlight shone through the French doors that led out to the balcony, illuminating Matthew's face as he slowly undressed her.

SHE WOKE in the night to find him watching her, his hands pillowed behind his head. "Hey." She leaned to kiss him. "Can't sleep?"

"I never can in strange beds." He nodded at the scarves and fabric tacked, tentlike, on the ceiling and walls around them. "And this one is definitely strange."

"So am I," Sarah said. "We match."

He laughed.

"Anyway, how often do you sleep in strange beds?"

"Not often, actually. I usually carry out my trysts in the linen supply closets."

"Or the doctors' lounge," Sarah said. "Isn't that the cliché?"

"I don't know." He sat up, caught her by the shoulders and pulled her up on top of him. "I'm working on just enjoying the moment, but…"

"What?"

"I've been lying here trying to think how…I don't want dates with you, Sarah. I've known you too long for that. I want to wake up in the night next to you. I want to come home to you."

"Or maybe *I'll* come home to *you*."

"You're accusing me of being a chauvinist?"

"No." A strand of her hair had fallen down across his face and he pushed it away. "I'm just saying—"

"I know what you're saying," Sarah said. "It's what I was thinking about in Victoria. Trying to imagine a future together. It's not as if we need time to get to know each other. But, well, there's Lucy."

He nodded. "I'm working on that."

"I think we need to take it very slowly. She needs to feel confident I'm not going to steal you away. And I need to work out some things too…"

"Such as?"

"I felt shut out, Matthew, after the funeral. I wasn't prepared for that. I didn't think that was your way of handling things."

"It isn't," he said. "Usually."

"That's what I mean. We both have things to work out."

"Come over for dinner tonight," he said. "Lucy and I have been taking cooking lessons. I want to wow you."

WHEN THE PHONE RANG, soon after Matthew left, Sarah thought he was calling about his billfold. She'd found it on the floor under the bed and immediately called his cell phone but the call went through to voice mail. She'd been unable to resist flipping it open with one finger. A plastic insert contained about a dozen pictures.

Every one an image of Lucy. She'd closed it again.

The call was from Elizabeth, who wanted to know whether she'd seen Matthew. Lucy had been trying to call him for hours the night before and, Elizabeth said, was now completely stressed and refusing to go to school until she spoke to him.

"Sorry," Elizabeth had finally said. "I didn't mean to burden you with our problems."

"You didn't," Sarah said. A future with Matthew meant Lucy was her problem, too. "If I hear from him, I'll tell him to call Lucy."

She showered and dried her hair, pulled on a pair of sweats, made coffee and drank it at the kitchen table.

No house calls today, just a couple of hours of paper-work then, to reward herself, a run.

The phone rang again.

"Dr. Cameron, this is Debbi—"

"Debbi. Where are you? I've been worried about you."

"I'm staying with a friend in Edwardsville. It's kind of far away, but—" she lowered her voice "—I had to go somewhere Curt wouldn't find me. Alli's been throwing up all night and she's running a fever. This isn't like the other times. Her tummy is hard and—"

"I'll be there in as long as it takes me to drive." Sarah glanced at her watch. Edwardsville was a blip on the map, more than an hour from the nearest hospital. She could get to Alli in less time than it took Debbi to arrange transportation. "Just give me directions."

She made it in thirty minutes, but standing in the tiny bedroom of the small frame house, looking at the flushed toddler with the distended abdomen, she realized she was dealing with something she couldn't handle by herself.

"I think we may need to get her to the hospital for a specialist to look at her."

Debbi, chewing her lip, was clearly on the verge of tears. "But I don't have insurance."

"It'll be okay," Sarah said with far more confidence than she felt. "Look—" her brain sorting through various options, she put her hand on Debbi's arm "—why don't you and Alli come back to Port Hamilton with me? I'd feel better if she was closer to the hospital. I'm going to see Dr. Cameron tonight," she said, remembering Matthew's dinner. "Between the two of us, we'll be able to work something out. You can both stay with me—"

"Or you could drop me off at my mom's," Debbi said, her expression clearing. "If that's all right with you."

In the car, she used her cell phone to call Port Arthur General Hospital where she'd been notified she had admitting privileges. Port Arthur, she learned, was not taking new patients. Not enough nurses.

It was dark by the time she'd dropped off Debbi and a sleeping Alli at Debbi's mother's with instructions to call if Alli's condition worsened. Back at her apartment, she felt a wave of exhaustion. Still wearing her parka and boots, she flopped down on the couch for a quick nap before she changed for dinner with Matthew. And fell asleep.

LUCY HAD DECIDED on the menu for the evening. Lasagna, salad and garlic bread. Matthew had been relieved when she told him. Anything more ambitious would lead to the possibility of failure and add to the tension he already felt. Had there been any way he could lock both Lucy and Sarah in a room together with the order that they were to stay there until they liked each other, he would have done it. Instead, he was trying not to talk too much about Sarah because he didn't want the evening to start off with Lucy feeling jealous. When Sarah arrived, he decided he wouldn't be overly solicitous with Lucy, the way he sometimes was, for fear of Sarah feeling left out. And now Lucy was making noises again about wanting to move in with him.

The whole thing made his head spin. Half an hour before Sarah arrived, he considered breaking into the Chianti he'd bought for dinner. Instead, he showered and shaved and changed into the pants and shirt Lucy had bought him for his birthday. Banana Republic, she'd said as he'd opened the box. "Mom let me use her charge card." He surveyed himself in the mirror. The black pants were…twill, he thought. And the shirt was cotton suede—Lucy had told him—and the color of milky coffee. It wasn't a combination he would have picked out, but even Elizabeth had complimented him when he'd worn it to parents' night at the school.

"Check you out, Matt," she'd said. *"Styling."*

Smells wafted up from the kitchen. Onion and garlic and tomato. Lucy's music also reached him. She was always talking about this band or trying to get him to listen to that band. They all sounded alike and way too loud. As he ran downstairs, he considered how to tactfully suggest switching to something more suitable for a couple of doddering ancients.

"Taste this." Lucy, her face flushed from the kitchen's warmth, held a spoon to his mouth. "Does it need more garlic?"

He tasted. "Wow. No worries about vampires around here."

She frowned. "You're saying there's too much garlic?"

"No. *No.* It's great. Perfect." He glanced at the

clock. Sarah would be here any minute. "So, what else has to be done?"

"Nothing." She smiled. "I set the table and…" She led him by the hand into the dining area. "Flowers. Cut from mom's yard, but that's okay. And I even got dessert. Tiramisu, from the bakery. That was Mom's idea, but I grated extra chocolate on top."

"You are incredible, Lulu." Overcome by a surge of paternal pride and love, he caught her face in his hands. "You are so capable and grown-up and I love you a whole—"

"Don't get mushy," she said as she pulled away. But then, her back to him, she said, "You're a pretty good dad, okay?"

Smiling, he glanced again at the clock. Sarah was late.

CHAPTER SEVENTEEN

THE TELEPHONE WOKE Sarah up from a deep dream in which she was piloting a helicopter with Debbi's daughter on board to a hospital in Seattle, but something had gone wrong with the blades and she thought they might have to make a crash landing. Groggy and disoriented, she bolted upright on the couch where she'd collapsed and grabbed the phone.

"Hello?"

"Sarah. It's Matthew. What's going on? You were supposed to be over here forty-five minutes ago. Lucy's made dinner and we're sitting around waiting for you."

"Oh, God." She rubbed her eyes. "I completely forgot. I had to drive out to the west end to see Debbi's little girl. I finally heard from her and...well, I need to talk to you, Matthew—"

"Can we talk about it later?" There was an edge of impatience in his voice. "Lucy's been working all day on this dinner."

"Of course." She stood. "I'm sorry, I just meant to shut my eyes for a few minutes. I'll be right there. Hey, Matthew," she started to say, but he'd already hung up.

Thirty minutes later, her hair still damp and pulled back into a ponytail, dressed in faded jeans and an equally faded University of Washington sweatshirt, she realized she'd blown it. The table was set with flowers and twinkling candles. Lucy, in an off-white dress, looked like a model from *Teen Magazine* and Matthew...Matthew was sophisticated and just plain handsome.

"Jeez, I wouldn't have dressed up if I'd known we were going casual," she quipped, covering her embarrassment with a joke that produced the faintest of smiles from Matthew and a stony look from Lucy. She accepted the glass of wine Matthew handed her. "I'm really sorry for being late," she told Lucy. "It's been a long day and I just closed my eyes—"

"I know," Lucy said as she carried the lasagna to the table. "Dad told me."

"Wow." Sarah leaned over the table to get a closer look at the lasagna. "That looks amazing. Smells amazing, too." She hadn't eaten all day, but instead of feeling ravenous, she felt slightly queasy. "What can I do?"

Matthew grinned at her. "Very clever, Sarah. Wait till everything's done, then ask." He glanced at Lucy, who had taken her place at one end of the table and was using wooden tongs to toss a salad. "Does it matter where we sit, Lulu?"

"Nope." She nibbled at a lettuce leaf she'd pulled from the bowl, considered momentarily, then ground pepper into the salad. "Sit, you guys," she commanded. "Let's eat."

"So your dad said you've been taking cooking

classes together," Sarah said after she and Matthew had, excessively she felt, admired the brilliant flavors of the sauce, the masterfully blended salad dressing and the perfect crispness of the garlic bread.

"Introduction to cooking," Lucy said with a look at Matthew. "But next month we're starting the intermediate course. And—" another glance in her father's direction "—after that, Foundation of French Cuisine."

"Well, let's finish introduction first," Matthew said.

Lucy's expression darkened. "You *said,* Dad. Plus, if I move in, I'll be able to cook for you."

Sarah met Matthew's eyes across the table. He looked away.

"So, Lucy." Sarah felt a need to change the subject. "What else do you like to do—besides cooking, which you do very well, by the way."

Lucy shrugged. "I don't know. Hang out with my friends…"

Sarah rushed to fill the conversational void. "I'm trying to think back to when I was fourteen, which was a long time ago—"

"Very long," Matthew said.

"Even longer for you," Sarah said.

Matthew winked at her.

"Anyway…" The wink had shot a charge through her body, which she was trying hard to ignore. "Let's see. I used to ride my bike everywhere, that much I do remember."

"And she got more flat tires than you could believe," Matthew said.

"Which I was able to fix myself," Sarah added.

"After I showed you how," Matthew said. "'*Oh, Matthew,*'" he imitated a girl's voice, "'*could you please fix my tire?*'"

Laughing, Sarah wondered if he was picking up on the telepathic message she was trying to send. *I love you.* "How about you, Lucy?" she asked. "Do you fix your own flats?"

"I don't ride bikes that much."

"Lucy's more the creative type," Matthew said. "*Theatuh* and that sort of thing. Right, Lulu?"

Lucy, picking at her salad, shrugged again. "Whatever."

"I heard all about your play," Sarah said. "Do you have any other productions coming up?"

"Huh?" Lucy's look suggested Sarah had just lapsed into Greek.

"Are you going to be in another play?" Matthew clarified.

"No."

Matthew reached for a piece of garlic bread. "I thought you were trying out for—"

"I changed my mind."

"How come?"

"Dad." Lucy shot him a warning look. "Pass me the bread please."

Regarding her empty plate, Sarah realized she'd eaten the entire meal and, despite the lavish compliments, hadn't tasted a thing. Her head was throbbing and the tension at the table was palpable. The rest of the evening plodded on for what seemed like hours. Sarah watched Matthew asking Lucy questions to which she either professed not to know the answer or didn't want to discuss. Sarah also tried to keep the conversational ball rolling but eventually grew impatient with Lucy's sullenness. By the time they'd all finished dessert, she was feeling so bad for Matthew that it was all she could do not to banish Lucy from the room and take Matthew in her arms and tell him it wasn't his fault.

"SARAH AND I CAN DO the dishes, Lucy," Matthew said after they'd cleared the table and stacked everything on the counter next to the dishwasher. "You knocked yourself out making dinner, now it's our turn."

"I don't mind doing them," Lucy said.

Sarah affected astonishment. "You're getting a chance to skip out on the dishes and you're not taking it?" She shook her head at Matthew. "These kids today. Go figure."

Lucy ignored her. "I said I don't mind," she muttered, rinsing off a plate.

"I know you don't mind." Matthew took the plate from her. "Don't you have homework?"

"No."

He gave her a warning look. "Lucy—"

"Fine." Glaring at him, she kicked the dishwasher shut with her foot. "Do the stupid dishes yourself."

Sarah was at the sink, rinsing off the rest of the dishes. From the set of her shoulders, he would have bet money he knew exactly what was going through her mind. He imagined himself as Sarah had probably seen him at dinner. Apprehensive, conciliatory—exactly the way he'd promised himself he wouldn't be.

"It's going to take time," he said.

"I think you may have said that once before." Sarah kept rinsing dishes. "The truth is, I want to go up and have a long heart-to-heart talk with Lucy," she said. "But I also think she needs to learn that the world doesn't revolve around her."

"She wants you to like her." Matthew thought of all the effort Lucy had put into making dinner. "I think she might be a little shy around you," he said, not believing the words even as he spoke them.

Sarah turned from the sink, raised her hand, still damp from the dishes, and placed it against his face. "Poor baby."

He smiled. "That helps."

"Any more of that Chianti?" she said.

"Yep." He filled their glasses and they carried them out to the balcony. The moon was hardly more than a sliver, with just the lights from the ferry landing and an oil tanker at anchor to punctuate the darkness. He put his arm around Sarah. "So what's this with Debbi's daughter?"

Sarah leaned into him. "We don't have to talk about that right now."

"Talk. Whatever it is has got to be easier than talking about my daughter."

"Matthew." Sarah raised his hand to her lips. "I feel so bad for you. Do you want me to go up and talk to Lucy? I will." She turned to look at him. "I'll tell her I

know what it's like to be fourteen and feeling alone…"
She laughed. "I won't mention I also know what it's like
to be forty and alone."

"You're not alone now," Matthew said. "Unless you
choose to be."

Sarah said nothing. Maybe, right at this minute, he
meant that. Would he always? She wanted to believe it.

"So about Debbi's daughter?" he prompted.

"Debbi called me this morning to say Alli had been
vomiting all night. I drove out to see her. I think her kid-
neys are failing, Matthew."

"I've suspected that all along."

"She needs to be hospitalized for tests. Port Arthur
isn't accepting new admissions because of a staffing
shortage." She drew a breath. "I need your help."

He feigned shock. "Let me call the public-relations
department. They'll want to alert the press."

"I'm serious, okay? This could be where my grand
solo practice scheme falls apart. I'm pretty sure she'll
need dialysis. Debbi has been trying various remedies,
but nothing is working. I want you to have a look at her.
I know Debbi doesn't belong to Compassionate Medical
Systems, but I wondered if you could pull some strings."

"Have Debbi bring her in," Matthew said. "They
owe me. Actually, a new kidney specialist just signed
on. I'll give him a call tomorrow."

Sarah kissed him. "*They* owe you?"

SITTING ACROSS an expanse of mahogany the following
day trying to gauge the expression on the face of the

woman who had replaced Heidenreich, he felt less confident. Carolyn Calhoun, the fiftyish, power-suited chief executive officer and director of business administration, Compassionate Medical Systems, Port Hamilton branch, listened to his appeal with her arms folded and her lips pursed. Matthew was not encouraged.

"This is a dangerous precedent, Dr. Cameron," she said when Matthew had finished. "Compassionate Medical Systems is a closed operation. Potential members are screened beforehand. To arbitrarily admit a patient, particularly one suffering from a chronic condition—"

"We don't know that yet," Matthew interrupted.

"Regardless. The point is, we had a lengthy open enrollment period in which anyone who chose to, could enroll in Compassionate Medical Systems—"

"Anyone who could pay the premiums."

"If this child's mother is unable to afford the premiums," she said, "there are other options."

"Unsatisfactory options," Matthew said, recalling his own response to Sarah. "And I think you know that, Ms. Calhoun. There is a free clinic, staffed by paraprofessionals, but that's about the extent of it. This was one of my objections to CMS coming to the peninsula in the first place. There's CMS for people who can afford it, inferior care for everyone else."

She raised an eyebrow. "Then perhaps you should have stayed in private practice, Dr. Cameron."

Matthew held her glance. "Perhaps I should have."

"Which, in cases such as this—" she glanced at the

file on her desk "—this Kennedy child, wouldn't address the issue of hospitalization."

"When I agreed to join CMS," Matthew said, "I brought in most of the medical staff with me. I could do the same if I left…" He saw her eyes flicker and pressed on. "One consideration had been a physician purchase of the Port Arthur hospital. That remains a possibility."

Carolyn Calhoun unfolded her arms. "One scenario comes to mind. I would have to check with our legal council and, of course, the internal-affairs department, but I seem to recall that we do have compassionate care funds for selected needy cases." She allowed a faint smile. "It might make a nice human-interest story."

An hour later, he got a call from William Cone, a pediatric nephrologist with Compassionate Medical Systems in Seattle who agreed to discuss the case. "Does this town have a decent restaurant?" he asked Matthew.

Matthew assured him that it did, but they ended up in the cafeteria anyway. "Show me a hospital anywhere in the country that has a better view than this," Matthew said as they stood at one of the windows looking out at the glittering blue waters of the straits and the distant shore of British Columbia.

Cone laughed. "I guess there's not much else in this town but the view." He made his way over to a far table and sat down. "Seems it would make more sense to move the hospital and build condominiums on this site. Patients don't need million-dollar views."

"It's part of the community," Matthew said. "People

in this town are proud of their hospital, even though it does need serious upgrading. That's why CMS has had such a hard sell."

"No room for sentiment in medicine," Cone said.

"Let me tell you about Alli Kennedy."

"*If* I agree to see her," Cone replied after Matthew had explained the details, including Sarah's involvement, "she's my case. I want to make that clear. I don't take kindly to interference."

"HOW DID DINNER GO last night?" Elizabeth asked Sarah, trying to sound casual. They were having coffee in the consulting room between patients. Lucy had told her that morning that Matt said she could move in. If it was true and she wasn't sure it was, she wondered what Sarah thought about it. "Lucy said she made lasagna."

"She did."

Elizabeth waited.

"The lasagna was great. Me and Lucy?" She waggled her hand. "Not so great. Was she like this with other women he dated?"

Elizabeth laughed. "I don't know about other women. If he saw any, he kept them away from Lucy."

"Probably a good idea," Sarah said. "No offense, I know she's your daughter."

"Hey, I'll be the first to tell you, she can be a brat. But you just have to hang in there. Let her see who's boss."

"I guess." Sarah looked doubtful. "But Matthew and Lucy are happy together...well, maybe not so much lately. She's only fourteen, right now she needs him. Maybe I came along at the wrong time."

The phone rang, Matthew for Sarah. From Sarah's end of the conversation, Elizabeth figured that Matthew had managed to get a hospital bed for Alli.

When the phone range again Sarah held up her hand as Elizabeth reached for it. "Unless it's an emergency or Matthew, I'm not here for—" she glanced at her watch "—another ten minutes."

A man with an English accent asked for "Dr. Sarah."

"I can take a message for her," Elizabeth said, looking at Sarah.

"Right. Well, here it is. Please inform Doctor Sarah that I'm on to her game. She's well aware that I have no faith in her Big Medicine treatment; she knows, too, that she's a charlatan who has temporarily succeeded in brainwashing my daughter's mother into—"

"Hold on." Elizabeth covered the receiver with her hand and looked at Sarah. "I thought I recognized that accent. It's Curt Hudelson, rambling on like he did when we were out at the trailer."

Sarah groaned. "Oh, God, I don't want him mixed up in this. Alli needs to be in the hospital. Matthew's trying to set it up with CMS, I'm just waiting to hear from him. If Curt gets involved it could really mess things up."

"Curt." Elizabeth spoke into the receiver. "Are you with Debbi and Alli right now?"

"All you need to know," he said, "is that I know exactly where to find them."

Elizabeth hung up the phone.

"I don't like this," she said after she'd filled Sarah in on the converstion.

"Neither do I," Sarah said.

CHAPTER EIGHTEEN

Matthew had managed to arrange for one of Seattle's top nephrologists to look at Alli. Before she left to see Alli herself, Sarah called the hospital security, explained the situation and asked if a guard could be posted outside the child's room. The guy who answered the phone didn't exactly laugh at her request, but did explain that there was only one guard on each shift to serve the entire hospital. If nothing else, Sarah decided as she left to walk over, she would stay in the room herself.

One advantage of having the consulting room in Rose's house, Sarah reflected, was that she could just walk over to the hospital after she'd finished seeing patients. That, of course, had been her grandfather's idea when he started the practice. A windstorm had blown in from the north, chilling the air and whipping tree branches and scouring the sky. The stars were out as she struggled against the wind to cross the road, the Olympics black shapes against a darker sky.

In her grandfather's time, the hospital had been housed in a two-story wooden structure which had gradually been expanded over the years. The latest word was that most of the original structure would be pulled down to make way for a state-of-the-art facility. No room in medicine for sentiment, she guessed. Still, she averted her eyes from the Compassionate Medical Systems logo that now ran across the front of the hospital.

In the front lobby, she smiled at the gray-haired woman in the pink volunteers jacket, took the stairs up to Matthew's office, learned he was in surgery and headed straight to the pediatric floor. Alli's bed was at the far end of the room, and as Sarah approached, she could hear a child's loud wailing. The curtains were partly pulled around the bed and she could see Debbi seated in a chair, Alli sobbing as a nurse tried to administer medication.

It was several minutes before she saw Curt sitting quietly in the shadows. He'd spotted her first and he slowly smiled at her startled gasp.

"Well, well, Dr. Sarah. Long time no see."

"Curt." Debbi frowned at him from across the room. "I'm warning you." She turned to the nurse. "She's not tolerating it. She's been crying and spitting up and gagging for more than an hour. Can't we just give her a break?" Then she, too, saw Sarah. "I told him that stuff would give her diarrhea, but he just ignored me."

"Surprise, surprise," Curt muttered.

Sarah looked at the nurse. "Let's hold off for now."

The nurse seemed doubtful. "Dr. Cone ordered—"

"I'm Dr. Benedict, Alli is my patient. I'll talk to Dr. Cone," Sarah said.

The nurse hesitated for a moment then, clearly disapproving, left the room.

"You didn't tell me they would want to do surgery," Debbi said accused her. "You said this was just for tests."

"Oh, my poor naive child," Curt said softly. "Will you ever learn?"

Sarah glared at him before addressing Debbi. "Who said anything about surgery?"

"Dr. Cone. He said they needed to do surgery right away so that they could connect her to a dialysis machine when the time came."

"Clearly, the good doctor divined the need," Curt said. "Doctor God, and all that. Is that not true, Doctor Sarah?"

"Listen, buddy." Sarah walked over to his chair, leaned down and poked her finger in his chest. "This is your daughter we're dealing with. Go play your smart-ass games somewhere else, or I'll have you thrown out."

Debbi started crying. "I feel bad complaining after all you've done, Dr. Benedict, but I don't like this guy. He's talking about way more tests than I thought she was going to need and I don't feel comfortable with it. Can't we just wait and see what happens?"

"Maybe you should tell Dr. Sarah what you told me just before she arrived," Curt said, and paused. "Right, then I will. Debbi said she wishes she hadn't let you talk her into bringing Alli in."

"You had no choice," Sarah addressed Debbi. "Dr. Cameron said this guy is the best nephrologist in Seattle—"

"What else would he say?" Curt scoffed.

"He talked to us like we were stupid," Debbi said.

"Tell you what—" Sarah looked from Alli, who was sleeping fitfully, to Debbi "—I haven't met Dr. Cone yet, but I'll have a word with him and see what's going on, okay? And I'll also talk to Dr. Cameron. We'll get things straightened out."

She left the room, started down the corridor and almost ran into a small man with sparse, colorless hair and complexion the color of putty. Talking on his cell phone, he glared at Sarah after their near collision and then she caught the name embroidered on his white coat. William Cone, M.D.

"Dr. Cone." Momentarily forgetting he was on the phone, she put her hand on his arm. "Just the person I need to talk to."

He muttered something impatiently into the phone before hanging up, then eyed her through clear plastic framed glasses. Under his white coat, he wore tan slacks and a white shirt with a beige tie. "May I help you?"

"I'm Sarah…Dr. Benedict. Alli Kennedy is my patient and—"

"Are you on staff here?"

"No, but Dr. Cameron—"

"Anything I have to say about the patient I'll say to Dr. Cameron. Now, if you'll excuse me."

Shocked, Sarah stood there for a moment. By the time she'd recovered, Dr. Cone had turned the corner out of sight. She fought the urge to run after him, before deciding that Alli's continued care and treatment was her primary consideration and, hospital politics being what they were, silence might be the best response. But she was still fuming when she stormed toward Matthew's office a few moments later.

MATTHEW RUBBED his eyes with his knuckles. If he'd had worse days, he couldn't recall them right now. They never used to see cases like this at the Port Hamilton hospital. Traffic pileups with multiple injuries. Two ambulance deliveries from a crash on Highway 101, a sixteen-year-old kid with a gunshot wound. Even with Compassionate Medical Systems the teen would have been airlifted to Seattle, but the winds prevented the helicopter from taking off.

He had three messages from Lucy on his desk, the last marked *urgent*. And the director of social services had just given him an earful, which he was trying to digest when Sarah burst into his office, eyes blazing, spots of color on her face.

"What an insufferable jerk." She plonked down onto the chair by his desk. "I'm sorry, but—"

"How come you didn't tell me Debbi Kennedy doesn't have custody of her daughter?" Matthew blurted, his mind still on the call from the social worker. "She's been legally in the custody of state child protective services since the middle of March when I stopped seeing her."

"Maybe because I didn't know she didn't have custody?"

She was glaring at him and he glared right back at her. She probably didn't know, he decided, but he felt ambushed and Sarah was a convenient target for his anger. "You didn't know Debbi was treating her with herbs?"

Sarah's eyes flickered. "She might have said something about it. It's one approach. Maybe something else is needed now. That's the whole concept—openness to other approaches."

Matthew nodded, his anger abating somewhat. Kidney disease in young children could be tricky to diagnose without tests. He hadn't been convinced himself that that's what they were dealing with. "According to the social worker, the treatments were putting Alli at risk."

"One, that's not necessarily true. And two, the fact that alternative treatment might be valid for Alli doesn't negate the fact that even if Debbi had chosen to go the conventional route, she couldn't afford to take her to a doctor."

"There's a free clinic in Port Hamilton," Matthew said, "but Debbi chose to move her daughter out to the middle of nowhere."

"Because she couldn't pay her rent," Sarah answered, her voice rising. "That doesn't give Cone the right to act like an asshole. I just ran into him in the hall and he informed me that anything he had to say about Alli, he would say to you." She got up from the chair and began pacing his office. "Debbi was in tears; she said he made her feel like an idiot."

Matthew thought of something Cone had said when they'd been discussing Alli Kennedy's case. *There are times when we ask parents to make decisions. This should not be one of those times.*

"Look, I wasn't thrilled with Cone's personality,

either,' Matthew said, "but he's still the best in his field. If he decides Alli needs surgery, then I think we have to take his word for it."

Sarah sat down again and leaned forward in her chair. Her elbows on his desk, face cupped in her hands, she looked at him. "I'm sorry for yelling at you, Matthew."

He reached for her wrist. Her nose had reddened and she looked on the verge of tears. "You've been yelling at me for most of your life. If you stopped now, I'd be confused."

She smiled faintly. "There's more at stake this time. I know you went out on a limb for me and…it's just that I hate being condescended to."

"If it's any reassurance, I'd trust Cone if it was Lucy."

"Yeah." She reached for a tissue on his desk, blew her nose. "I'm concerned about Debbi, too. Her mother died during surgery and she's scared to death something will happen to Alli."

"Something could," Matthew said. "We have to be prepared for that."

"But this whole thing about her not having legal custody makes it worse, doesn't it? I mean, they could overrule her objections anyway."

He nodded. The social worker had said as much. "The wheels were essentially set in motion when she came into the hospital," he said. "Now I think the best thing we can do is accept that even though Cone isn't going to win any personality contests, he will do what's best for Alli."

Sarah sighed. "You're right, I know."

"Wait! Say that again, I'm not sure I heard…"

"Shut up, Matthew."

But she was smiling now and things were okay between them again. It had been hours since he'd eaten and he was about to suggest they go find something other than cafeteria food to eat when his eyes fell on the pink slips with Lucy's messages. "What are you doing tonight?" he asked.

"Right now, I'm going to talk to Debbi. Then back to the apartment. My mother has essentially relinquished custody of Deanna."

"Deanna?"

"That ugly old tomcat. I know," she said when he grinned. "You'd be ugly too with a name like that, but what can I say? Rose always said to keep him in a cage, but I felt sorry for him so he has the run of the apartment. If I don't get home, he'll start ripping up the sofa."

"Think Deanna would mind if you had some company?"

"He probably would, but I'll stick him in his cage."

He got up and walked around to where Sarah was sitting and held out his hand. "I'll see you as soon as I can leave this place."

"Don't eat," she said. "I'll make something yummy. Any requests?"

He grinned. "Surprise me."

After Sarah left, he dialed Lucy's cell phone.

SARAH RETURNED to Alli's room to find her sleeping peacefully. The nurse who had been trying to administer the medicine earlier said Debbi and Curt had gone home.

"Dr. Cone will be in to see Alli first thing in the morning," the nurse said. "So I told the mom the best thing she could do for herself and her child was to get a good night's sleep."

Sarah thanked her and headed downstairs. She could use a night's sleep herself, although Matthew wouldn't exactly guarantee that. Not that she was complaining, of course. She walked through the lobby and out into the parking lot. The winds were still howling and, as she walked along the row of parked cars to her car, she huddled into her parka. She would make something that could be eaten out of one dish. One dish, two forks, in bed.

Smiling, she unlocked her car. And then someone tapped her on the shoulder. Startled, she turned to see Debbi's boyfriend. Curt wore an army-surplus jacket, a woolen cap pulled down low on his forehead and seemed amused by her reaction.

"Not a good idea, sneaking up on people in a dark parking lot," she said, her heart still pounding. "You might get surprised yourself."

He smirked. "Oh, Doctor Sarah, you frighten me."

Sarah glanced over his shoulder. Did security patrol this lot? Her car keys still in her hand, she geared herself to gouge them out if she had to. "I just stopped by to see Debbi. The nurse said she'd already left."

"Her asthma was troubling her. Stress tends to do that. I took her to her mother's where she's sleeping like a baby."

"Well—" she moved to open her car door "—I'll see you both in the morning. Dr. Cone—"

"Your betrayal infuriates me." In the darkness, his features under the knit cap were shadowy and indistinct, except for his eyes. They glimmered. "How in good conscience could you do this to her and our child?"

Sarah said nothing, suddenly on alert again.

"If she dies, the fault will be entirely yours. We were fine, all three of us. Debbi's asthma was under control. Alli was a healthy two-year-old. If she had the occasional upset stomach, it was nothing that couldn't be easily remedied. I can't forget how earnest you seemed that day at the farmer's market. I believed you—"

"Curt. There is no one right, absolute approach. Alli had reached a point where more had to be done."

"You don't know that. You act as though you're certain, as though you have all the answers, but you don't." He moved closer. "I want her out of that hospital," he said in a low voice. "So does Debbi."

"I can't do that," Sarah said. "I don't have the authority—"

"You had the authority to get her in there, didn't you? Use it to get her out." And then he walked away, without a backward glance, and disappeared into the darkness.

CHAPTER NINETEEN

SHAKEN, SARAH STOOD beside the car, uncertain what to do next. Matthew wouldn't have left yet... She walked briskly toward the lights of the main entrance and took the stairs up to Matthew's office. The door was locked, the lights out. From a phone in the lobby, she paged him. Dr. Cameron was in emergency surgery, the operator said. She ran back down the stairs, stood for a moment in the lobby, considered requesting an escort, then told herself this was Port Hamilton and ran, keys at the ready, across the parking lot to her car.

Driving back to her apartment, she passed Matthew's condo building and saw the lights were on. On an impulse, she parked at the curb, rang his number on the security system.

"Yes?" a female voice answered. A young female voice.

"Lucy? It's Sarah. I saw lights in your dad's place and—"

"Yeah, I'm moving in."

Shivering and fatigued, Sarah only hesitated for a moment. "Would you mind if I came up for a while?"

"Um, I guess."

After a few seconds, the buzzer rang and the glass front doors swung open. Lucy stood in the entrance of Matthew's apartment, one hand on the doorjamb as though to slam the door shut if Sarah had any ideas about forcing her way in. She wore skintight jeans and a top that exposed several inches of midriff.

"Dad's not home yet," she said. "He had an emergency surgery."

"I know." Sarah nodded at the door. "Can we go inside and sit down? It's been a long day."

Lucy shrugged and went inside, Sarah following. Packing boxes were stacked at one end of the coffee table. She wondered when the move had been decided and when Matthew planned to tell her about it.

"So how does your mom feel about you moving?"

"She's okay with it," Lucy said. "Mostly she wants to be with her boyfriend anyway."

And your dad? Sarah wondered. Lucy was in the small kitchen, fishing around under the sink. Sarah watched her, the tumble of dark glossy hair, the exposed skin above her jeans. "Lucy, how about you come and sit down here with me for a few minutes? It's difficult to talk to your rear end."

With a sigh suggesting great imposition, Lucy came over to sit on a chair opposite Sarah. Her eyes were heavily outlined with kohl and her lips were pink and glossy.

"I've never been very good at subtleties," Sarah said. "So I'll just plunge right in. I love your dad. A lot. I've always loved him, but it's different now." Lucy's expression was impassive, unreadable, her lips in a glossy pink pout. "I know you love your dad, too. I think we both want to make him happy, to do what's best for him and I know things are strained between the two of us. You—" she nodded her head at Lucy "—and me, and that doesn't make him happy. I wondered if you had any idea how we could make things better."

Lucy, twirling the ends of her hair around one finger, said nothing.

"Lucy?" Sarah said after the silence grew uncomfortable. "Any thoughts?"

"Not really."

"Oh, come on," Sarah coaxed. "I don't believe that."

The silence stretched agonizingly long. Sarah pictured herself grabbing the girl by the shoulders, marching her into the bathroom, scrubbing off the lip gloss and the eyeliner to see if possibly there was something underneath all the artifice.

"My mom said you're jealous of me," Lucy finally said.

Sarah felt her expression freeze. If Lucy had physically delivered a body blow, the effect couldn't have been more profound. It wasn't just Lucy's words, but the sense of betrayal that Elizabeth, who she'd come to see as her best friend, would have said this. Or had she? Maybe Lucy was lying. Or could it be that you *are* jealous? a small voice wondered.

"What do *you* think?" Sarah said.

"I don't know."

"Lucy." Sarah wanted to scream. "We can't get any-where if you—"

"I think you want Dad for yourself," Lucy said. "It's like you've got all these jokes and things you used to do together and I'm just a kid and I get in the way."

"First of all," Sarah said, trying to gather her thoughts, "that's not true about me wanting your father for myself—"

"Yes, it is." Lucy jumped up from the table. "Yes, it is true." Her face contorted with rage and, perhaps with the effort of holding back until now, she glared at Sarah. "Like that stupid fossil trip. You didn't want me there, you just wanted to talk to Dad so you can have your stupid jokes." She burst into tears. "Why don't you just leave and go back to wherever it was? I hate you." And then she was across the room, into one of the bedrooms, the door slamming behind her.

WHAT HAD SEEMED LIKE a routine appendectomy had turned complicated and it was nearly ten by the time Matthew scrubbed up. He called Sarah from the hospital lobby to say he was on his way and reached her machine. And then, because he hadn't reached Lucy when he'd tried earlier, he called her at home.

Elizabeth answered. "She's at her friend Brittany's house. I dropped her off; she had all these boxes to give to Brittany's mother for a church sale. Did you try her on her cell?"

"Yeah, I got her voice mail." After he hung up, he walked out to the car and tried Sarah's number as he turned the key in the ignition. "I'm ready for whatever you're cooking up," he said to her answering machine. At the top of Sarah's street, he remembered that he had surgery first thing tomorrow morning and no change of clothes or shaving gear. As he drove, he grinned, picturing Sarah's reaction to his request for space in her closet and a shelf in her bathroom. He could just see her, hands on her hips, pretending indignation. "If I let every man who spends the night store his clothes in my closet, there'd be no room for my stuff." Outside his building, he hit the garage opener on the visor, parked the car and made his way upstairs.

Even before he turned on the lights, he sensed something was wrong. A flick of the lamp switch confirmed it. Blood on the white kitchen tiles, over the pewter-colored carpet, an exclamation point of blood outside the bedroom door.

SARAH SAT in a chair at the kitchen table, still shaken up by the scene with Lucy who, ultimately, had refused to be coaxed from the bedroom. Back at her own place, she'd listened to a couple of messages from Matthew, the last saying that he was on his way. Now, it was after midnight and he was almost certainly a no-show.

She made herself a mug of peppermint tea and carried it into the bedroom where Deanna had made himself at home on the bed. He still hissed and spit occasionally, but he seemed quite happy with his new digs and, although Sarah told herself she loathed him, in fact, she was quite pleased to see his malevolent green eyes peering at her from behind the curtains when she got home.

Just an old lady and her cat, she thought gloomily. She looked at the phone, willing it to ring but then hoping it wouldn't. Matthew would defend Lucy, explain away her behavior, deliver his assurances that everything would be fine. Tell her it would just take time. Which, for the most part, was why she wouldn't pick up the phone to call him. That and picturing the phone ringing in Matthew's apartment. Lucy would sneer.

My mom said you're jealous of me.

She swung her legs onto the bed and lay back against the pillows. The thing was, she understood Lucy's behavior, even empathized with it. A year or so after her father died, she'd suspected Rose was seeing someone. Even though she'd been older than Lucy and not nearly as close to Rose as Lucy was to Matthew, she'd felt displaced somehow. Once, she'd come home to find him sitting at the kitchen table in the same spot her father had always sat, eating dinner with Rose. Candles were lit, something Rose had never done for her father, and there were wineglasses. She'd stood in the doorway for a moment, watching them. He'd said something and Rose had laughed and then he'd looked up to see her there.

She'd barely been civil to him. Weird, she couldn't even remember his name and he'd been a semipermanent fixture for one entire summer.

Maybe years from now, Lucy would try to recall the name of that woman she'd gone fossil hunting with.

"Some old friend of my father," she could imagine Lucy explaining. "They were going hot and heavy for a while, then she just took off again like she did when he married my mom."

And Matthew? Would he have moved on? Remarried perhaps to a woman who had immediately hit it off with Lucy?

The idea hurt. A lot. But maybe it would be for the best. Maybe she didn't have the patience. Or the inclination. Maybe she didn't want a relationship with Matthew enough to spend the rest of her life walking on eggshells for fear of upsetting his daughter.

A car passed by, seemed to slow. She got up, thinking it might be Matthew, and peered through the window. It moved on.

She got back into bed. Maybe she *should* move on. It had seemed brave and independent striking out on her own, but maybe it was also foolish. Eventually the money her father had left her would run out. Even a bank loan would eventually run out. Rose wouldn't care if she left. Not really. Elizabeth seemed to want her to stay, but could she trust Elizabeth? Lucy, of course, would be elated. And Matthew?

"You're not alone," Matthew had said. "Unless you choose to be."

But who would Matthew choose if push came to shove? Her or Lucy? Lucy, of course. That was the way it should be.

She scratched Deanna's neck. "Is anyone ever going to choose me first?"

The cat purred.

"What was that? No way? And quit feeling sorry for yourself?"

She got undressed, pulled on sweatpants and an old T-shirt and crawled under the covers. Not that she had any hope of getting to sleep.

The phone rang. Her heart went into overdrive. She reached for it on the second ring, then glanced at the caller ID. Matthew's number. She withdrew her hand. Not tonight. If he came over as he'd said, fine, but she wasn't up for a heart to heart over the phone. Whatever he had to say could wait till tomorrow.

Somehow she managed to drift off. And then the phone woke her. Groggy, she lifted the receiver. "It's late, Matthew." She opened her eyes to glance at the clock. The numerals flipped over to 3:36 a.m.

"Dr. Benedict," a woman said, "this is Debbi."

Sarah sat up in bed so abruptly she felt dizzy. "Debbi. Where are you?"

"I'm…I'm in the hospital parking lot, by the emergency room entrance." She started crying. "Can you pick me up, please?"

Sarah threw on some clothes and grabbed her keys. The streets were deserted, rain shimmered in the headlights. There was one other car in the emergency lot, a black van close to the E.R. doors. Her mind racing, she pulled up beside it, got out and glanced around for Debbi. And then things happened so fast she had the sensation of watching a movie in fast forward.

The gun in her back, the quick glimpse of a black stocking cap and then a cloth around her eyes and a surge of pain in her left knee as someone hoisted her up into what she guessed was the black van.

CHAPTER TWENTY

"I PROBABLY SAID some things I shouldn't have," Lucy told Matthew the next morning as she sat at the breakfast nook, spreading peanut butter on a slice of toast. "But she acts likes she's the smartest person in the world and she had this look on her face like everything I said was really stupid and then I just blew it."

Matthew, on automatic pilot, went to the freezer for coffee beans then decided he couldn't be bothered with the whole process and microwaved a cup of instant. The blood had clearly been meant to impress, and it had.

He'd seen the knife flung on the kitchen floor, followed the trail to the guest bedroom and found Lucy sound asleep. He'd shaken her awake and she'd told him about the fight with Sarah who, his daughter said, had been mad because she was moving in. Matthew decided to deal with that issue—which he'd known nothing about—at a later date. By that time, the self-administered nicks to her wrist had dried.

When he finally remembered that he'd been on his way over to Sarah's, it was nearly one, too late to go over and he didn't want to leave Lucy alone. He'd called but hung up without leaving a message.

He called again just after seven and, once again, got her answering machine. It seemed unlikely she wasn't home at this hour. More likely she didn't want to talk to him. He glanced at his watch, considered stopping by her apartment before he went to the hospital, then decided he needed more than a few rushed minutes to straighten out the mess they—he—had made of things.

"Dad?" Lucy came up behind him as he stirred sugar into his coffee. "Don't be mad."

"I'm not mad, Lucy." He turned to look at her. "I'm concerned that two people I love very much are finding it so difficult to get along."

"It wasn't *my* fault."

"Sweetheart, I've seen you around Sarah. I saw you at dinner the other night. Before she arrived, you were fine. Terrific. Helpful. Cheerful. Then it's like you turn into your evil twin."

She laughed. "Oh, right."

"I'm serious. I've been tiptoeing around, scared to hurt your feelings, but this has gotten out of hand. It *is* your fault if you choose to behave like a spoiled brat around Sarah, and it's my fault if I go on letting you do it."

The phone rang.

"Matthew. Carolyn Calhoun. Alli Peterson, the child in Two west wasn't in her bed when the nurse made the 6:00 a.m. rounds. No one has seen the parents. Security has searched the grounds, but there's no sign of either of them. The police have been called."

"I'll be right there," Matthew said. He looked at Lucy. "There's an emergency at the hospital. If Sarah calls... No, never mind. Well, just tell her to call me."

By the time he reached the hospital, a news helicopter was circling the roof.

ELIZABETH, AT THE RECEPTION DESK, was trying to reach Sarah. Some sort of bug was going around and already four people had called for appointments and home visits. She'd called Sarah's house phone, her cell phone, left messages, and now she was getting this awful feeling something was wrong.

The office phone rang.

"Mom," Lucy said, "I'm watching TV. Debbi Kennedy's baby has been kidnapped from the hospital. And there's an Amber Alert."

THE POWERS THAT BE were huddled behind closed doors in the administrative conference room. Matthew arrived in time to hear Cone describe his last exchange with Sarah.

"...and there is no doubt in my mind this Benedict woman..."

"Dr. Benedict," Matthew said as he sat at one end of the long polished conference table. Security had just identified Sarah's car in the parking lot, a development that bolstered Cone's conviction and steered his own thoughts in a troubling direction.

"I had an encounter with her yesterday." Cone ignored Matthew's interruption. "She struck me as somewhat unstable."

"Unstable? You mean, she's more concerned with her patient's welfare than navigating through bureaucratic channels?" Matthew snapped.

"Has anyone spoken to Dr. Benedict this morning?" Carolyn Calhoun asked.

All around the table they shook their heads.

Matthew spent another five minutes listening to the details of Alli Kennedy's case, then decided he could be more useful elsewhere.

Out in the corridor again, he ran into Rose Benedict. She looked more frazzled than usual, her gray hair escaping from the bun, her white coat open over a blue plaid dress.

"My God, Matthew, what on earth is happening? I just heard the news."

"Have you seen Sarah?" he asked.

"No. I was coming to ask you the same thing." She stepped closer, inclined her head. "This Kennedy child? Father runs a stall at the farmer's market. Fanatical type. I tried to tell Sarah…"

"That's the one," Matthew said. "Sarah thought she needed tests and I got her admitted. They weren't too happy with the nephrologist assigned to the case." He stopped, aware from the look on Rose's face, that their thoughts were running along parallel tracks. "I called Sarah's apartment," he said.

"So did I. Before I knew about this. She's been keep-

ing Deanna. I think she gets lonely. Sarah, not Deanna.
Deanna's a male—"

"I know." Already it seemed ages since he and Sarah
had stood in his office joking about her mother's cat.
"Listen, Rose, I need to go."

She put a hand on his arm. "Sarah's headstrong, but
she'd never do anything to endanger a patient."

"That's what's bothering me," Matthew said.

Down in the O.R., a check of the day's surgery
schedule confirmed what he already knew: he had back-
to-back surgeries until late that afternoon. For a moment, he struggled with his conscience and then decided
if he were suddenly stricken with a heart attack, everything would have to be rescheduled. This was a crisis
of similar proportions, he reasoned as he called to leave
instructions with his secretary.

From the hospital, he drove directly to Sarah's
apartment. He banged on the door—no answer; not
that he'd expected one. He ran down the stairs at the
side of the building to the manager's office. The
manager hadn't seen her, but thought he'd heard a car
start up outside, early that morning.

"How early?" Matthew asked.

"Oh, around three-thirty or so."

Back in the car, he called Sarah from his cell phone.
The call went immediately to her voice mail.

He sat with his hands on the steering wheel, trying
to think.

His phone rang.

"Matt, what's going on?" Elizabeth's voice was

shrill. "I heard about the kidnapping and I can't get hold of Sarah. I'm worried—when we went out to see Debbi, Curt said she'd left him. He has…well, you know. He's always been kind of weird and—"

"Do me a favor," he said, already constructing a scenario, "get me Debbi's address from the file."

"She lives more than an hour from here."

"I know. Just get it for me, okay?"

While he waited for her to come back with the address, he switched on the radio and turned the dial to the all-news station. Top story: the kidnapping of a two-year-old girl from Port Hamilton Hospital. An Amber Alert issued. Police were also seeking the whereabouts of the child's physician, Sarah Benedict. "And this just in. The Rite Aid pharmacy on Lincoln Street in Port Hamilton was broken into sometime during the night."

"THIS WASN'T my idea, I assure you." Curt momentarily took his eyes off the road to glance at Sarah in the passenger's eat. "My goal was merely to rescue Alli from the clutches of Big Medicine and Doctor God. This—" he gestured at the gun that Debbi, in the backseat, was holding to Sarah's head "—was a safety measure. You've managed to worm your way into her confidence and now she seems to think you can perform miracles."

"I didn't say that, Curt," Debbi protested. "Why can't you admit that maybe someone knows more about medicine than you do? Just admit that you don't know everything. I wanted Dr. Benedict here in case Alli got really sick again."

"But she is really sick." Sarah tried to twist around in the seat to see Debbi's face. She couldn't see Alli, bundled up on the seat beside Debbi, but she could hear her uneven breathing. "Right now, she should be in the hospital. There's nothing I can do, especially not under these conditions, to help her."

"But you're her doctor," Debbi said. "There must be something else you can try."

"Had you listened to me…" Curt began. "But why waste my breath." He glanced at Sarah again. "A veritable cornucopia of pills and potions in that bag by your seat, should you wish to avail yourself. Common and not so common."

"I told Curt to get everything he could find," Debbi said. "Maybe you should take a look in the bag."

"I don't know how many ways I can say this," Sarah said. "Alli needs more than what we've been doing. We have to take her back to the hospital."

"I think not," Curt said. "A plan will ultimately present itself, but a hospital is not part of it."

"They'll take Alli away from us," Debbi said. "The social worker already said that could happen. And that doctor was horrible. He didn't care about Alli, he frightened her. I'd rather…" She shook her head, unable to finish. "I'm so scared."

Sarah watched the dark trees fly past the window. The hospital would have discovered Alli missing hours ago, and by now the police would be searching for them. But the van's heater wasn't working, and she was seriously concerned about how long Alli could make it without medical intervention.

"Look, she's not going to get better without treatment." She waved her hand at the bag of drugs. "And none of this is going to help. Every hour we delay puts her in more jeopardy. Here's my suggestion—" she looked directly at Debbi "—let me call Dr. Cameron. I'll tell him everything you've told me… You can talk to him yourself, if you want. But let's at least give him a call and get his thoughts." She looked at Curt. "You have to do something, you guys. Or else Alli's going to die."

"If she dies, so do you," Curt said.

"That's ridiculous," Sarah said, then felt the gun against her head. *Keep your mouth shut.* But then she felt the light pressure of Debbi's finger on her shoulder. She turned involuntarily and in the next instant the gun was in her hand and Debbi had propelled herself into the front seat, startling Curt, who fell against the driver's door, which burst open. With the gun in one hand, her other against Curt's shoulder, Sarah pushed him out of the truck and moved behind the wheel.

"Okay, here's the plan," Sarah said, as she and Debbi sped off into the night.

CHAPTER TWENTY-ONE

"IF I CAN OFFER you a piece of advice, Dr. Cameron," the detective said. "Leave the police work to us in future. You could have saved yourself a tank of gas driving out there. That's our job."

"I know." Matthew nodded wearily. There had, of course, been no sign of Debbi or the child at the trailer park. And no word from Sarah. They were sitting around a table in one of the hospital conference rooms that had become the temporary nerve center. Every ten minutes or so, a public-relations type would come in with the latest press release. Compassionate Medical Systems bigwigs in droves. Endless recitations of the known facts.

As he got up to get coffee, his cell phone rang. He glanced dispiritedly at the screen, expecting either Elizabeth, who had called several times, or Lucy. His heart lurched when he saw the number.

"Sarah."

Around the table, everyone seemed to freeze.

"Okay, Matthew, listen," Sarah said when he answered. "I'm with Debbi, Curt and the baby. Alli's not doing well. We need to get treatment for her as soon as possible. She needs to be in the hospital, but…" She paused. "This is really important, okay? Debbi is going to bring her in. She wants *you* to look at the baby. You. Not Dr. Cone or anyone else. Okay?"

"Okay." Matthew leaned against the wall. "Where are you?"

"It doesn't matter. But Matthew? You have to promise that nothing will happen to Debbi. That she won't be arrested or anything. Because…I'm the guarantee."

"Okay," he repeated. "Tell me—"

"I suggested that Debbi brings Alli in through the basement. There are probably reporters hanging around the lobby and E.R. She'll be there in about an hour." Sarah paused. "Matthew, please promise me. Don't let anything happen to Debbi."

AN ETERNITY LATER, Matthew stood before a bank of reporters. "I am Dr. Matthew Cameron, Alli Kennedy's physician." He breathed deeply to still the nerves created by the microphones thrust at his face. "She is responding well to treatment and is in stable condition. Yes," he answered to a shouted question, "her mother is with her."

He glanced at the police chief to his left. "Charges? I think that one's for you."

SARAH SHOWED UP at his apartment later that night. "It was a joint effort really. Once Debbi gave me the gun, getting Curt out of the van was a piece of cake. But then we had to decide how to make sure Alli got treated by you and not Conehead. So we concocted the story. I wasn't sure you'd fall for it."

She scooted around on the couch, so that she lay stretched out, feet hanging over the arm, her head in his lap. "The only good thing that came out of this, I guess, is that Curt is in jail for kidnapping. Hopefully they don't press any charges against Debbi."

Matthew stroked her hair. She seemed on the verge of tears and, knowing Sarah, he guessed she was beating herself up for her role in this. "That isn't the only good thing," he said. "Without your intervention, without you to turn to, Debbi would have gone on trying to treat Alli herself. Or gone to the free clinic and possibly seen someone not sufficiently trained to recognize Alli's problems. So things aren't all bad."

"Maybe not." She sounded unconvinced.

He yawned and leaned down to kiss her forehead. "I don't know about you, but I'm ready for bed."

"Me, too."

But long after Sarah had fallen asleep, he was still wide-awake. He'd reached a crossroad, he realized. To continue down the path he'd been on before Sarah came back. Or head into unfamiliar, fog-obscured territory. Lying there with Sarah beside him, her arm across his chest, he considered what would happen if he continued along the known road. He decided to risk the unknown.

THE FOLLOWING MORNING, he received a visit from Carolyn Calhoun. She was not happy.

"You exerted considerable pressure to get this child into the hospital, Dr. Cameron. In doing so, however, you chose not to disclose the full facts of the situation. Namely that the state had taken custody of her. You assured Dr. Cone he would enjoy your full support and cooperation, but you did not keep your word. As a result of this unfortunate turn of events, Compassionate Medical Systems has been subjected to a great deal of unfavorable publicity. I've been in conference with our legal counsel and, on his recommendation, I must regretfully ask for your resignation."

"No regrets," Matthew said. "I was about to offer it to you anyway."

Back in his office, he called Lucy and then Elizabeth and told them he'd see them both that evening at the house.

"What's wrong, Matt?" Elizabeth had asked.

"Dad, just tell me why," Lucy had insisted.

"Just be there," was all he would say to each one. "Six, sharp." And then he called Sarah.

"I was walking out the door," she said. "I have some errands to do. Are you okay?"

"Fine," he said. "Will you be home tonight?"

"Yeah." He heard her pause. "Really, Matthew. Is everything okay? As okay as it could be under the circumstances?"

"Everything's okay," he said. "I'll see you later."

AFTER SHE HUNG UP, Sarah packed Deanna in her cage and drove to Rose's house.

"All I can say is it's a good thing you're a dermatologist," Sarah said as she set the cage on Rose's living-room floor. "If you were an ob-gyn, I'd seriously wonder about your competence."

Rose, reaching into the cage to remove Deanna, looked up at Sarah.

"What?"

"Deanna's a she. And, what's more, she's pregnant."

"*No.*" Rose rolled the cat over in her arms, cradling it like a baby. "Come here, poky. Let mama check what's under all that pretty fur."

"You can save yourself the trouble," Sarah said. "I already checked."

Rose grinned. "What a little slut!"

"I assume you're talking about the cat."

"Of course, my darling. You know, I did think he—she—was rather, well, touchy for a boy." She set the cat down on the carpet. "Coffee? I was in the middle of making some."

Sarah followed her into the kitchen and sat at the table. Rose set a coffee mug in front of Sarah and sat down beside her.

"Well?" Rose asked. "What's the latest?"

"Debbi called a while ago. Alli's doing better, but she's still undergoing tests. Debbi's apparently had a change of heart about Dr. Cone. She's still not thrilled with his bedside manner apparently, but she says he's a good doctor." She drank some coffee. "She thanked me for all I'd done, but said that Alli would be seeing Dr. Cone from now on. And one of the PR people is going to write an article for the employee magazine—about Alli's care and how Compassionate Medical Systems really is compassionate."

Rose raised an eyebrow. "She's been thoroughly indoctrinated, eh?"

"*I* didn't say that."

"You didn't have to."

Sarah suddenly felt close to tears. She watched the play of sunlight across the top of the table. Spring, after a few tentative starts, had finally come to the peninsula. On the way over to Rose's, she'd noticed daffodils blooming everywhere, the pink clouds of cherry blossoms, but her mood felt leaden and gray, the tender shoots of her fledgling practice withering before they could grow into anything meaningful. "Debbi's got a hearing next week about the custody issue," she said, mostly to fill the silence. "We'll see what happens after that."

"Cone wields a lot of influence," Rose said. "As long as Debbi keeps all the appointments and doesn't start feeding her dandelion tea, they'll probably grant her custody." She peered at Sarah. "How are *you?*"

Sarah considered how to answer the question, not sure she wanted to confide in Rose.

Rose raised a brow. "That bad, eh?"

"Debbi also said Matthew had resigned from CMS." Tears stung her nose and throat and she waited a moment, trying to get control. "He didn't mention it when he called, but he's coming over tonight. I guess, to tell me."

"I'd heard rumors," Rose said.

"I feel like a tornado that blew into town," Sarah said. "Lucy, Debbi, Matthew." She got up from the table, grabbed a tissue and blew her nose. "Well, maybe not so much Debbi. She's getting the proper treatment for Alli, which is a positive, I guess. But Matthew."

"And what's your solution?"

Sarah moved to the window. The mock cherry at the edge of Rose's yard was in full bloom, blossoms like pink confetti fluttering in the breeze off the straits. Out in the water, a red coast-guard boat left a wake as it rounded the harbor.

"I think I want to get out of Dodge," she said. "Well, I don't exactly *want* to, but I think that would be best for everyone."

"Very noble of you."

Sarah felt the words like a slap. She'd turned from the window to glare at Rose. "Why *is* it so difficult for you to act like a mother?"

Her expression unruffled, Rose met Sarah's angry stare. "Sarah, I don't *act* like a mother. I *am* a mother. Maybe I'm not your idea of what a mother should be, but I'm me. I'm the way I am. And I refuse to beat myself up because I don't meet your standards."

Her anger dissipating as quickly as it had flared, Sarah got more coffee. She thought of the book of lists. The Perfect Mother, the Perfect Husband. She'd never written one called the Perfect Me. Maybe there wasn't enough paper to list all the things she expected of herself. She returned her seat. Elbows on the table, she propped her chin and looked bleary-eyed at Rose.

"I'm sorry."

"I understand you more than you give me credit for, Sarah." Rose stroked the cat. "You carry around this feeling that you've failed somehow. You failed at being pretty, you failed at winning Matthew. I don't see how you could possibly have thought you failed at being the smartest kid in the class, mostly because you worked so damn hard to make it happen."

Sarah smiled faintly. "Actually, I failed at that, too. Matthew was smarter, although I'd never tell him that."

"And now you've failed to charm his daughter. Lost out to her, just like you did to Elizabeth. Made a big fiasco of this Debbi Kennedy case. Chalk that up as another failure."

"Jeez, remind me not to call you if I ever feel suicidal," Sarah said, although she was quite aware of what Rose was doing.

"Well, you're forty-two, for God's sake, Sarah, and what do you have to show for your life? Do you have a husband? Kids? Property? Money in the bank—other than what your father left you? Your father, who wasn't a failure, I might add."

"Okay, you made your point. So what do I do about it?"

Rose smirked. "Quite honestly, I don't know. I've always been better at pointing out your faults than your attributes. No doubt why I'm listed in your book."

"I apologized," Sarah said. "Burn the damn book."

"No way," Rose said. "I find it charming. Hopelessly naive but charming, nonetheless." She set the cat down on the floor, opened a can of cat food and emptied it into a dish. "Here's my advice, for what it's worth."

Sarah waited.

"Just be yourself and quit worrying about not being perfect. Nothing is perfect. You're not perfect and you never will be no matter how hard you try. This—" she grabbed the newspaper from the table "—isn't perfect. There is news that hasn't been reported. There are probably typos. Pictures out of focus. Does that mean you shouldn't read it? Of course not. That's the point. Just because something is not perfect, it can still be very effective and useful."

"That's it?"

"Yep."

CHAPTER TWENTY-TWO

EVERY LIGHT IN THE HOUSE was blazing as Matthew pulled into Elizabeth's driveway. The living room was empty, but the television was on and a newscaster was yammering about the latest developments in the Alli Kennedy kidnapping.

"...which raises the question of how adequate hospital security..."

Matthew snapped it off and followed the sound of Lucy's voice up the stairs to her bedroom where she was lying on the bed reading a magazine and Elizabeth, seated at Lucy's dresser, was polishing her nails. The carpet, pale pink, was littered with magazines, socks and dirty glasses. They both looked up as he came in.

"Any reason why the TV is on when there's no one down there watching it?" he asked. "Or why the house is lit up like a beacon?"

Elizabeth gave him a puzzled look as though seriously considering an answer. "What's up with you?"

"Hey, Dad." Lucy tapped the magazine. "Check out this snowboard."

"Lucy," Elizabeth warned, obviously sensing something from his expression. "Let's go downstairs. I haven't started dinner yet."

"Let's go to Bella's," Lucy said.

Elizabeth had already started down the stairs. He followed her, Lucy behind him, and they all trooped into the kitchen.

"How about pasta?" Elizabeth opened the refrigerator. "I've got some cooked chicken and…asparagus."

"Do that later." Matthew pulled out a chair and sat down. Lucy had pulled herself up on the counter, and Elizabeth was still inventorying the fridge. "Okay, there's no easy way to say this, so I'm just going to plunge right in. I made a major decision today. Two ,actually. The first is I'm no longer with Compassionate Medical Systems."

Elizabeth's jaw dropped. She leaned against the counter. In the pin-dropping silence, her glance moved briefly to Lucy then fixed on him. "My God, Matt. You resigned?"

"I was going to. They beat me to it and fired me." He waited a moment for that to sink in. "Obviously, this is going to necessitate a lot of changes and some of them won't be easy. To start with we're going to have to sell this house."

"Da-ad." Eyes wide, Lucy stared at him. "Can't you just get another job?"

"I plan to," Matthew said. "But I'm probably going to bring in less money than I did even before CMS."

Elizabeth met his eyes. "You're going to go into practice with Sarah, aren't you?"

"I haven't discussed it with her yet, but that's my intention."

"I think you should," Elizabeth said.

Overwhelming relief mingled with his surprise. "You do?"

She laughed. "Matt, come on. You've always acted like I don't have a serious thought in my head and all I care about is shopping, but—"

"*You* come on," he said. "I've never thought that about you."

"Here, Elizabeth," she said in a gruff voice, meant to be his, "here's a hundred dollars. Go buy a dress or something."

"And I thought I was being a good provider."

"You were, Matt. Are. But it was like you never really saw me, or knew who I was."

Lucy sighed dramatically. "So do I have to go to a different school?"

"No," Matthew and Elizabeth said together.

"Lulu, your life won't be that different," Matthew explained. "But look at the size of this house. I know we can find something you'll like that makes more sense all around." Head bowed, Lucy silently picked at her fingernails, her hair falling like a curtain around her shoulders. His heart ached for her because her life was about to change and it would be more than just moving to a smaller house. Lucy was also at a crossroads, somewhere between the safety of childhood and the exhilaration of young adulthood with all its bumps and turns and unexpected obstacles. And his decision would make the going that much rougher for her.

"Are you going to marry Sarah?" she finally asked. And then she raised her head to look at him. Defensive, her back stiff, she braced for the answer. "Just tell me, okay?"

HOW DO YOU EXPLAIN why you've decided to end things with a man you've loved for as long as you can remember? Sarah had no idea. For the past ten minutes she and Matthew had sat silently on one of the benches that ran along the Olympic Discovery Trail, looking out at the water.

The third bench, she'd counted. He'd asked her to marry him and, when she hadn't replied instantly, had offered to get down on one knee. She'd laughed, although she hadn't felt like laughing. She'd refused the offer.

The wind from the straits was cool on her face, drying the tears on her cheeks. Wind blew her hair around her head, blew ripples across the water. Tossed the yellow dandelions that studded the grass, a brilliant green in the fading light. The receding tide had left dark green seawood on the rocks. A couple of gulls screeched.

"Big fight in gull land," Sarah broke the silence to say as she watched them duke it out midair for a dangling worm.

Matthew put his arm around her shoulder. "Why?"

"Because they both want the same worm." And then she started laughing, on the edge of hysteria. Matthew didn't join in. "Sorry," she said, growing sober again.

"If it's Lucy…"

"No. I mean, Lucy doesn't make things easy, but she isn't the reason I know this wouldn't work."

"You don't *know,* Sarah. You think. And sometimes you think too much."

"I don't need to be rescued, Matthew." He'd told her his plan. He would lead the exodus of physicians and other medical staff from CMS and they would join forces to purchase the old Port Arthur hospital. For just a moment, she'd entertained the idea. "You wouldn't have been suggesting this if it hadn't been for me."

"So what? You were the necessary catalyst. What's wrong with that?"

"Everything. This whole hideous kidnapping thing. I am so embarrassed by all that happened. Okay, maybe it wasn't strictly my fault, but I think—"

"There you go again."

"Please. There's something in me that…I don't know, leads to chaos."

Matthew laughed. "I'm sorry," he said after a moment, "but I think it was you who told me that Lucy's problem was that she thought the world revolved around her. Listening to you, I can't help thinking the same thing. It's not selfish with you, the way it is with Lucy, but, for God's sake, Sarah. Some things would happen regardless of whether or not you were involved."

Her teeth were chattering now and she hunched her shoulders, clasped her hands between her thighs for warmth. It didn't matter. On a deeper level, one that Matthew didn't fully understand, she knew her self-assessment was right. It was like a reverse Midas touch.

She drew in a breath. "You've asked me several times about Ted and I've never wanted to talk about him. The night before he died, we had this horrible, horrible fight. He told me he was unhappy, that he still loved me but…"

Matthew's arm tightened around her shoulder.

"He said I'd eroded his self-esteem. That I was destroying him." She started crying. "He felt he could never live up to my expectations. I tried to argue with him, tell him that what he was saying was ridiculous… and then I realized that was exactly the problem. The thing is, I didn't know how to be any other way. Rose told me to be myself. But myself isn't a good thing to be. After there was nothing more to say, he left. Went skiing."

"The only answer I have to that," Matthew said after a few moments, "is that I'm not Ted."

"But I've still messed up your life."

"Sarah, if I believed you'd messed up my life, why would I want to marry you? Or are you suggesting that only you have the ability to know that you've messed up my life?"

"I don't want to talk about it anymore."

MATTHEW DROPPED Sarah off at her apartment. Experience had taught him that once she'd set her mind on something, changing it was all but impossible. He drove into town, pulled up outside Brown's Outdoor and spent more than he wanted to think about on several pieces of luggage and a backpack that could carry everything but the kitchen sink. Then, as planned, he picked Lucy up from her mother's.

"What are all those for?" she asked when she saw the luggage in the backseat.

"Remember I told you I was going to join Sarah's practice?"

She slumped in her seat. "Yeah. So now you're going to marry her and go off on a trip."

"No. She turned me down." He pulled up outside the ice cream place. "I'm feeling kind of bad about it. A double dip of blackberry might help."

"Why doesn't she want you?" Lucy asked when they were sitting at their favorite table in the window alcove.

"No idea. Maybe she doesn't think I'm good enough."

"That's crazy," Lucy said.

"Thank you, Lulu."

She nibbled at the cone, licked some ice cream off her hand. "So are you going back to CMS?"

"They won't have me." He stretched his legs out. "They won't have me, Sarah won't have me. It's kind of hard not to take it personally."

"But you shouldn't, Daddy. Everybody knows you're a good doctor." She got up from the table to give him a quick hug. "And a good dad."

He managed a gloomy smile. "Well, I'm glad you think so, Lulu. That means more than you know. At least I'll have some good memories to take with me." Waiting a moment for the words to sink in, he drew a deep breath. "I'm going to Central America, Lucy. Sarah had told me so much about it that I'm thinking of applying to the clinic where she worked." He shot her a quick glance, just long enough to check the effect of what he'd said. Bingo. Stunned into gape-jawed silence. "Six months, maybe," he elaborated. "Maybe a year."

She kept staring at him. "You're joking, right?"

"No, I'm perfectly serious. It sounded interesting, the work she was doing. I like the idea of really helping people who need help."

"People here need help, too," Lucy said.

"True, but Sarah's got that covered. I don't want to encroach on her territory."

He stole another glance at his daughter, who was twirling a lock of hair around her finger, a sure sign she was deep in thought.

"I don't understand why she won't let you work with her."

Matthew shrugged. "Who knows?"

"But Daddy, when she came over…when we had that fight, she said she loves you."

"I guess she changed her mind."

ELIZABETH WAS SOAKING in the tub went Lucy burst into the bathroom, pink-faced, eyes blazing and a smear of what looked like ice cream on her chin.

"Dad's going to Central America for a year because Sarah won't let him join her practice. *A year.* And he's all bummed out because first Compassionate Medical Systems doesn't want him and now Sarah's acting hateful and he bought all this luggage. I saw it. And…" She burst into tears. "I don't understand what's going on."

Elizabeth, despite Lucy's tearful agitation, fought to keep a straight face. It didn't take a brain surgeon to realize that Matthew, after tolerating his daughter's manipulative tactics for some time now had decided that turnabout was fair play. Whether Sarah would see through the ruse, she wasn't sure. Maybe not. Sarah could be dense when it came to emotional stuff. But Sarah and Matthew belonged together—whether Sarah knew it or not. If Elizabeth had to lock them in a room together to duke it out, she'd do it.

"Mom, I don't want Dad to go to Central America," Lucy said. "Can't *you* say something to him?"

"Well, sweetie, let's think this through. If he doesn't go, he'll end up seeing Sarah again, probably marrying her, and you know how you feel about that."

"He might not marry her," Lucy said. "You don't know."

"Honey, I knew Sarah and your dad long before you came along. They were like…two magnets. Some people really are meant for each other."

"Why doesn't Sarah think so?"

"Because Sarah is very stubborn. She might be a doctor and really smart, but in some ways, she's like a kid and you just want to shake some sense into her."

Lucy frowned. "Is it because of me?"

"Well, I don't think you made it easy for either of them. I know Sarah felt bad because she thought you didn't like her."

"She doesn't like me."

"You *think* she doesn't like you. See, that's what

happens sometimes. I'm not saying it's just you, we all do it. We walk around acting a certain way—snobby, or friendly, whatever—and other people act the same way in response. I bet if you'd acted happy and friendly around Sarah, you wouldn't be sitting here thinking she doesn't like you."

Lucy was twirling her hair. "Do you think Dad would still go to Central America if I was nice to Sarah?"

"I don't know, honey. Might be worth a try though."

CHAPTER TWENTY-THREE

SARAH STOOD before the bathroom mirror, a pair of kitchen shears in her right hand. The reflection before her had red eyes, a swollen red nose and chapped lips. She caught the end of her braid with her left hand and held it out horizontally. She imagined the feel of the scissors cutting through the thickness of the braid. Her neck would feel bare. Empty.

Bereft? No, she was not bereft. And, regardless of what Matthew had said, it had to be this way. Coming back to Port Hamilton, expecting to just pick up the threads of her old life, had been naive. But she could put all of this behind her. Just as she'd done with Ted. She would call the agency, tell them she was ready for another assignment. Reinvent herself.

She held the braid between the scissors blade. One quick cut and it would be done, a symbolic way to end this chapter of her life and to begin another one.

Okay. She brought the scissors down on the hair. The braid was surprisingly tough to cut. She opened the scissors, closed them again, but after the first small cut, they wouldn't close down on the entire braid. She put them down in the sink and checked the braid. The scissors had cut about a fourth of the way through, but not in the clean, incisive way she'd imagined. Rather, it was as though it had been chewed by a dog.

In the kitchen, she found the butcher's knife and, without even looking in the mirror, applied it to the braid. Still, it wasn't exactly doing the job. She considered unbraiding her hair, then taking the scissors to it, although it didn't promise quite the dramatic satisfaction she'd had in mind—of watching the braid drop to the floor.

She kept hacking away.

The doorbell rang.

She froze. Matthew. God, he couldn't see her like this. She glanced around the kitchen, eyed the window as a possible escape route.

But wait! Maybe this was exactly how he should see her. Crazed, a butcher's knife in one hand. An image that would burn in his brain, drive home the knowledge that he should thank his lucky stars he hadn't thrown in his lot with her.

Brandishing the knife, she threw open the door.

Lucy screamed.

"Oh, my God," Sarah said. "I thought it was your dad."

Lucy's eyes widened. She looked ready to bolt.

"This isn't quite the way it looks," Sarah said. "I was just cutting my hair—"

"With a knife?"

"Well, I started to use scissors, but they wouldn't

work." She looked at Lucy, still wide-eyed but slightly less apprehensive, and wondered why it suddenly seemed important to reassure the girl. "You want to come in?"

"Oh, that's okay." Lucy shifted her weight. "I kind of wanted to talk to you about my dad. He's going to Central America and—"

"Your dad's going to Central America?"

Lucy scuffed her foot against the doorstep. "Yeah."

In the months since Sarah had met Matthew's daughter, she'd never felt an inclination toward physical demonstrations of affection, but looking at Lucy now, head bowed, Sarah put her arm around the girl's shoulders and led her inside. Leaving the door open just in case Lucy still harbored fears for her safety.

She sat next to Lucy on the futon. "You want to tell me about it?"

"Dad said he wanted to work with you but you didn't want him and CMS doesn't want him so now he's going to Central America." She sniffed. "And I really, really don't want him to go."

Sarah realized she was still holding the butcher's knife. The braid, still half attached, hung down over one shoulder. Her brain was buzzing with questions, the foremost being whether Matthew had set this up. If he had, it was diabolically clever of him, she had to give him that. As she mulled this, she realized Lucy was watching her.

"I cut my mom's hair for her sometimes," Lucy said.

"You do?"

"Yeah." Lucy eyed Sarah's hatchet job. "Yours might be a little harder to do, but I could try to work on it, if you want."

Sarah smiled. "You know, that might be a really good idea."

"Okay." Lucy bit her lip, her gaze still directed at Sarah's braid. "I'm sorry I was mean to you."

MATTHEW HAD RUN the length of Lopez Hook and was headed back into town thinking about getting some breakfast when he ran into a woman in a green track suit jogging in the opposite direction.

Head down, short auburn hair gleaming in the sunlight, she snarled something about idiots who didn't look where they were going and started to pass him when he realized who it was. In one quick move, he grabbed her by the arm, yanked her around to face him and saw Sarah's familiar triumphant grin.

"Ha-ha, fooled you," she said.

He smiled. "Well, obviously you didn't."

"Too clever by half, Cameron." She smiled right back at him. "Sending your daughter to plead your case."

"Had I known about the butcher's knife," he said, "I might have thought twice before enlisting her."

"You know, it's funny, I've always had this problem knowing what to say to people who cut my hair, but Lucy and I got along famously. Had a great talk, cleared up a lot of things."

"It looks very nice," he said.

"Really?" She ruffled it with her hand. "I feel naked, but it's also very liberating. There must be some scientific explanation. Hair absorbs negative energies, all the old emotional baggage. Cut it off and you effectively rid yourself of all that junk."

Matthew hadn't stopped smiling since they collided. "I would suggest conducting more research before submitting that to the *New England Journal*."

"But would it work for you, Matthew? If I told you that all the neurotic garbage I spouted was eliminated with my haircut?"

"I've bought more preposterous ideas from you in the past," he said. "Like the time you convinced me that the ferry pilings were actually planted there as saplings."

"So?"

"So what?"

"Damn it, Matthew, don't make me grovel. So, will you ask me again? To marry you?"

"How do I know the crazy ideas won't come back as your hair grows?"

Sarah glanced at her watch. "You have two minutes. You want to marry me, or not?"

"I was thinking you could ask me this time," he said. "Just to even things up."

Sarah narrowed her eyes. "Down on one knee?"

"Come here, you." He held her face between his hands, kissed her eyes, her mouth. It had taken so long to come to this, such a circuitous route, but here they were, back in the place they both knew so well, ready to start a new adventure together. "I love you, I've always loved you and I want to spend the rest of my life with you."

ON THE SMALL BEACH, where they had played together as kids, on a sunny July day with gulls floating like toy ducks in the water and the waves lapping behind them, Sarah looked into Matthew's eyes as she slipped the ring on his finger. In that very moment, she realized perfection was, in fact, possible.

* * * * *

Silhouette® Romantic Suspense
keeps getting hotter!
Turn the page for a sneak preview
of Wendy Rosnau's latest SPY GAMES *title*
SLEEPING WITH DANGER.

Available November 2007.

Silhouette® Romantic Suspense—
Sparked by Danger, Fueled by Passion!

Melita had been expecting a chaste quick kiss of the generic variety. But this kiss with Sully was the kind that sparked a dying flame to life. The kind of kiss you can't plan for. The kind of kiss memories are built on.

The memory of her murdered lover, Nemo, came to her then and she made a starved little noise in the back of her throat. She raised her arms and threaded her fingers through Sully's hair, pulled him closer. Felt his body settle, then melt into her.

In that instant her hunger for him grew, and his for her. She pressed herself to him with more urgency, and he responded in kind.

Melita came out of her kiss-induced memory of Nemo with a start. "Wait a minute." She pushed Sully away from her. "You bastard!"

She spit two nasty words at him in Greek, then wiped his kiss from her lips.

"I thought you deserved some solid proof that I'm still in one piece." He started for the door. "The clock's ticking, honey. Come on, let's get out of here."

"That's it? You sucker me into kissing you, and that's all you have to say?"

"I'm sorry. How's that?"

He didn't sound sorry in the least. "You're—"

"Getting out of this godforsaken prison cell. Stop whining and let's go."

"Not if I was being shot at sunrise. Go. You deserve whatever you get if you walk out that door."

He turned back. "Freedom is what I'm going to get."

"A second of freedom before the guards in the hall shoot you." She jammed her hands on her hips. "And to think I was worried about you."

"If you're staying behind, it's no skin off my ass."

"Wait! What about our deal?"

"You just said you're not coming. Make up your mind."

"Have you forgotten we need a boat?"

"How could I? You keep harping on it."

"I'm not going without a boat. And those guards out there aren't going to just let you walk out of here. You need me and we need a plan."

"I already have a plan. I'm getting out of here. That's the plan."

"I should have realized that you never intended to take me with you from the very beginning. You're a liar and a coward."

Of everything she had read, there was nothing in Sully Paxton's file that hinted he was a coward, but it was the one word that seemed to register in that one-track mind of his. The look he nailed her with a second later was pure venom.

He came at her so quickly she didn't have time to get out of his way. "You know I'm not a coward."

"Prove it. Give me until dawn. I need one more night to put everything in place before we leave the island."

"You're asking me to stay in this cell one more night...and trust you?"

"Yes."

He snorted. "Yesterday you knew they were planning to harm me, but instead of doing something about it you went to bed and never gave me a second thought. Suppose tonight you do the same. By tomorrow I might damn well be in my grave."

"Okay, I screwed up. I won't do it again." Melita sucked in a ragged breath. "I can't leave this minute. Dawn, Sully. Wait until dawn." When he looked as if he was about to say no, she pleaded, "Please wait for me."

"You're asking a lot. The door's open now. I would be a fool to hang around here and trust that you'll be back."

"What you can trust is that I want off this island as badly as you do, and you're my only hope."

"I must be crazy."

"Is that a yes?"

"Dammit!" He turned his back on her. Swore twice more.

"You won't be sorry."

He turned around. "I already am. How about we seal this new deal?"

He was staring at her lips. Suddenly Melita knew what he expected. "We already sealed it."

"One more. You enjoyed it. Admit it."

"I enjoyed it because I was kissing someone else."

He laughed. "That's a good one."

"It's true. It might have been your lips, but it wasn't you I was kissing."

"If that's your excuse for wanting to kiss me, then—"

"I was kissing Nemo."

"What's a nemo?"

Melita gave Sully a look that clearly told him that he was trespassing on sacred ground. She was about to enforce it with a warning when a voice in the hall jerked them both to attention.

She bolted away from the wall. "Get back in bed. Hurry. I'll be here before dawn."

She didn't reach the door before he snagged her arm, pulled her up against him and planted a kiss on her lips that took her completely by surprise.

When he released her, he said, "If you're confused about who just kissed you, the name's Sully. I'll be here waiting at dawn. Don't be late."

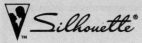

Romantic
SUSPENSE

Sparked by Danger, Fueled by Passion.

Onyxx agent Sully Paxton's only chance of survival lies in the hands of his enemy's daughter Melita Krizova. He doesn't know he's a pawn in the beautiful island girl's own plan for escape. Can they survive their ruses and their fiery attraction?

*Look for the next installment in the
Spy Games miniseries,*

Sleeping with Danger

by Wendy Rosnau

Available November 2007 wherever you buy books.

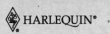
Charlie fell in love with Rose Kaufman
before he even met her, through stories her
husband, Joe, used to tell. When Joe is killed
in the trenches, Charlie helps Rose through
her grief and they make a new life together.
But for Charlie, a question remains—can
love be as true the second time around?
Only one woman can answer that....

Look for

The Soldier and
the Rose

by

Linda Barrett

Available November wherever you buy books.

REQUEST YOUR FREE BOOKS!

2 FREE NOVELS PLUS 2 FREE GIFTS!

HARLEQUIN®

Super Romance®

Exciting, emotional, unexpected!

YES! Please send me 2 FREE Harlequin Superromance® novels and my 2 FREE gifts. After receiving them, if I don't wish to receive any more books, I can return the shipping statement marked "cancel." If I don't cancel, I will receive 6 brand-new novels every month and be billed just $4.69 per book in the U.S., or $5.24 per book in Canada, plus 25¢ shipping and handling per book and applicable taxes, if any*. That's a savings of close to 15% off the cover price! I understand that accepting the 2 free books and gifts places me under no obligation to buy anything. I can always return a shipment and cancel at any time. Even if I never buy another book from Harlequin, the two free books and gifts are mine to keep forever.

135 HDN EEX7   336 HDN EEYK

Name	(PLEASE PRINT)
Address	Apt.
City	State/Prov.	Zip/Postal Code

Signature (if under 18, a parent or guardian must sign)

Mail to the **Harlequin Reader Service®**:
IN U.S.A.: P.O. Box 1867, Buffalo, NY 14240-1867
IN CANADA: P.O. Box 609, Fort Erie, Ontario L2A 5X3

Not valid to current Harlequin Superromance subscribers.

Want to try two free books from another line?

Call 1-800-873-8635 or visit www.morefreebooks.com.

* Terms and prices subject to change without notice. NY residents add applicable sales tax. Canadian residents will be charged applicable provincial taxes and GST. This offer is limited to one order per household. All orders subject to approval. Credit or debit balances in a customer's account(s) may be offset by any other outstanding balance owed by or to the customer. Please allow 4 to 6 weeks for delivery.

Your Privacy: Harlequin is committed to protecting your privacy. Our Privacy Policy is available online at www.eHarlequin.com or upon request from the Reader Service. From time to time we make our lists of customers available to reputable firms who may have a product or service of interest to you. If you would prefer we not share your name and address, please check here. ☐

HSR07

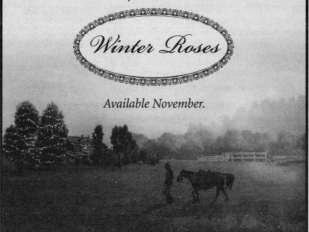

COMING NEXT MONTH